To Mrs [illegible]

Hope you enjoy

Philip

24/1/25

The Aegean Enigma

Alex Kalfas Thriller #3

By

Philip M Cooper

Dedications

To all my family and friends who supported me during the long two years it took to draft this book. The many friends who undertook editing and proofing duties but particularly Chris H, who used his magic proofing to give the book its final polish. Finally, to my understanding and beautiful partner, Pauline who put up with my long absences in the study. Without all these lovely people. I could never have finished this book.

Special Dedication

To my dearest friend, Chris Horsman.

Your keen eye and unwavering support were the guiding lights that brought this book to life. Your laughter echoed in the margins, your wisdom shaped its words, and your friendship brightened every page.

Though your journey on this earth ended on January 30th, 2024, your spirit lives on within these pages, a testament to the extraordinary person you were.

About the Author

Philip was born and educated in the United Kingdom and is half-Greek on his mother's side. He is an ex-investment banker who has worked in such diverse places as Greece, Lebanon, Germany, Italy, the USA, Canada, and of course, London. After leaving banking, Philip set up a financial training company in New York, and later after returning to the UK, worked for the Ministry of Defence as a training consultant.

He began his writing career in 2012 and to date, he has written a poetry anthology - **If I Could Paint Your Picture, Rape of the Aegean,** the first book in the Alex Kalfas series. **Smokescreen**, the second book in the Alex Kalfas series, and he is due to release the third book in the Alex Kalfas series – **The Aegean Enigma**, in late 2024. He recently had two successful non-fiction financial books, **Competing in the Financial Markets** and **Mastering Options**, published by Business Expert Press in New York.

Table of Contents

Prologue

An agitated Aristeidis mopped the gathering sweat from his brow. It was hot, he was hot, and so were his goats. They were agitated too, he was having difficulty in controlling them today. Even his faithful helper Alexi, a shepherd dog, seemed troubled.

Aristeidis gazed down towards the valley below, to where olive trees stretched in parade ground lines as far as the eye could see. Also, dotted around were signs of mining. The island of Milos with its deposits of marble, copper, silver, and lead had become one of the major centres of mining and metallurgy in ancient Greece in the eighth century BC.

The sky had been clear of any clouds since early morning but now Aristeidis noticed a strange cloud gathering on the horizon. He watched in curiosity as the cloud grew, moving steadily towards the mountain where he was tending his goats.

As the mysterious cloud approached, Aristeidis felt a surge of unease ripple through his body. The once serene atmosphere was now charged with an eerie expectation. His goats, usually docile and obedient, became increasingly restless, their bleats growing louder and more frantic. Even Alexi, usually calm and composed, looked on edge.

Aristeidis squinted, trying to discern the nature of the approaching cloud. It was not like any he had ever seen before. Its shape was irregular, almost formless, and it seemed to shimmer with an unearthly glow. The air around him grew colder as if an invisible hand had reached out to snatch away the warmth of the sun.

An inexplicable anxiety gripped Aristeidis as the cloud loomed closer. He could now see that it wasn't just a cloud but a swirling mass of darkness tinged with flashes of bright light. It reminded him of some ancient myth he had heard long ago; a tale of gods and monsters.

As the cloud drew nearer, its ominous presence cast a shadow over the entire mountainside. The goats, sensing an impending danger, began to panic, their hooves clattering against the rocky terrain. Aristeidis knew he had to act quickly to secure their safety.

"Alexi," he shouted, his voice drowned out by the cacophony of bleats echoing through the valley. With a sense of urgency, he untangled himself from the twisted ropes that had held the goats in place and rushed towards them.

The swirling mass of darkness continued its haunting approach, growing larger and more menacing with each passing moment. Aristeidis could feel its power pulsating through the air. It didn't feel malevolent, yet he was puzzled that he had shivers down his spine.

He and Alexi worked together to calm the agitated animals. But it was a futile effort; the goats were possessed by a primal fear that no amount of coaxing could quell. Their eyes darted frantically, their bodies trembled uncontrollably. Aristeidis knew that time was running out.

With the goats still in a state of panic, Aristeidis made a quick decision. He directed Alexi to lead the herd towards a nearby cave, a place they often sought refuge during storms. It was their only hope against the approaching darkness.

The two of them hurriedly guided the goats towards the cave, Aristeidis's heart was pounding in his chest with anxiety and anticipation. The ominous cloud grew closer, its ethereal glow casting an eerie light upon the mountainside.

Just as the first drops of rain began to fall, he managed to usher the last of the goats into the safety of the cave. The animals huddled together, seeking comfort and protection from the impending storm.

As Aristeidis closed the entrance to the cave, he turned his gaze back towards the approaching darkness. It had now enveloped the entire mountainside, swallowing everything in its path. Lightning crackled within its depths, illuminating glimpses of what looked like a strange-looking craft, the likes of which had never been seen on Greek Terra-Ferma before.

On the idyllic island of Milos, nestled amidst the azure Aegean Sea, life unfolded at its own unhurried pace. Fishermen mended their nets, tavern owners prepared their savoury dishes, and lovers strolled hand-in-hand along the sun-drenched beaches. However, fate had a surprise in store for this tranquil paradise. As the golden rays of dawn painted the sky in hues of orange and pink, a spectacle destined to alter the course of history was about to unfold.

A colossal spacecraft, its sleek black obsidian exterior shimmering like a thousand stars, descended from the heavens with a breathtaking grace that belied its immense size. With a gentle hum, it touched down in the heart of the village square, its arrival announced by a whirlwind of dust and hushed awe that descended upon the islanders. This otherworldly vessel, a testament to advanced technology beyond their wildest dreams, captured the attention and curiosity of everyone present. Among the awestruck onlookers was Aristeidis, who had just descended from the mountain. His heart pounded with a mixture of fear and excitement as he led his flock towards the village, his eyes fixed on the mesmerizing sight before him.

The air thrummed with anticipation as the crowd in the square held their collective breath. Moments later, a low rumble emanated from the spacecraft's bow, followed by a pneumatic hiss as a massive panel slid open, revealing a sight that would forever be etched in the annals of history. A delegation of beings emerged, their otherworldly presence radiating an aura of tranquillity and profound intellect. Despite their unfamiliar physiology, they bore a resemblance to humans, possessing four limbs, two elongated legs, and two slender arms, all seemingly disproportionate to their torsos. Their heads, too, were larger than those of humans, with strikingly high foreheads, enormous, luminous eyes that seemed to hold the wisdom of the cosmos, and delicate, pointed ears that twitched subtly as they surveyed their surroundings.

Aristeidis was the first person to react when the beings emerged. He sensed that their mission was peaceful cooperation, so he stepped forward to greet them. "Καλώς ήρθατε στη γη," said Aristeidis welcoming the beings to planet Earth. The five beings stood for a few moments staring at him, and then they smiled. Their smiles lit up the area around them and they held out their arms to show they were friendly. As they did this, Aristeidis heard a voice in his head that said, *"We have come to Earth with a mission – a mission to uplift humanity and share our advanced knowledge for the betterment of all on Earth."*

Word of the celestial visitors spread through the sun-kissed villages and bustling cities of Greece like a wildfire fuelled by a zephyr wind. From weathered fishermen casting their nets at dawn to philosophers contemplating the mysteries of the universe under a canopy of stars, people from all walks of life converged upon the village square, their hearts aflutter with a potent blend of trepidation and exhilaration. The aliens, with their wise eyes and gentle demeanour, embraced this influx of humanity with open arms. Linguistic barriers dissolved effortlessly as if by some unseen magic, replaced by an unspoken understanding that transcended the limitations of language.

A profound sense of unity blossomed, bridging the gap between two disparate worlds. In a gesture of profound respect, the extra-terrestrial emissaries explained that they had chosen Greece as their landing site due to its illustrious history, vibrant culture, and invaluable contributions to the tapestry of human civilization. They saw in Greece a glimmering beacon of human potential, a cradle of ingenuity and artistic expression, and sought to collaborate with its people in a harmonious symphony of progress, propelling humanity towards a brighter future.

Over time, the aliens shared invaluable scientific knowledge, technological advancements, and innovative ideas that revolutionized various aspects of Greek society. They introduced new energy sources that fuelled cities like Knossos in Crete. They showed the Greeks how to build temples like Delphi, Sounion, the temple of Aphaia on Aegina island, and the Acropolis in Athens. They showed them how to mine for metals and minerals more efficiently, both on dry land and also under the seabed.

In their quest to uplift humanity, the extra-terrestrial visitors sought out the brightest minds and most influential figures within Greek society. They established a profound connection with luminaries such as Socrates, the gadfly of Athens whose relentless questioning challenged conventional wisdom; Plato, the visionary philosopher who sought to unveil the eternal truths hidden beneath the surface of appearances; Aristotle, the polymath whose encyclopaedic knowledge encompassed everything from biology to politics; Pythagoras, the mathematician and mystic who saw the universe as a harmonious symphony of numbers; and Hippocrates, the father of medicine whose ethical principles continue to guide physicians to this day.

In a series of intimate gatherings, the aliens shared not only their vast scientific and technological knowledge but also the accumulated wisdom of countless generations on their home planet. They delved into profound philosophical teachings that emphasized the interconnectedness of all beings, the importance of cultivating empathy and compassion, and the urgent need for peaceful coexistence in a world often marred by conflict and strife.

The days turned into weeks, and the weeks into months, until the seasons themselves had danced their cyclical ballet across the Attica sky. The time had come for the celestial visitors to conclude their mission on Earth. With hearts overflowing with gratitude for the warmth and hospitality they had received, they bid a poignant farewell to the land that had embraced them as kindred spirits.

Their departure was not a final goodbye, but a promise whispered on the wind - a promise to return one day when humanity was ready to take its next giant leap towards the stars. As a testament to their enduring bond with Greece, they left behind ten enigmatic robots, silent sentinels who would carry out their masters' will in their absence. With a final, wistful glance at the shimmering Aegean Sea, the aliens ascended into the heavens, leaving behind a nation forever transformed. Greece emerged from this extraordinary encounter united in purpose, empowered by knowledge, and forever imprinted with the indelible mark of an extra-terrestrial friendship.

Aristeidis, the goatherd whose life was forever intertwined with the extra-terrestrial visitors, meticulously documented every detail of their extraordinary presence on Earth. His diary, filled with vivid descriptions and heartfelt reflections, became a testament to the transformative power of their encounter. The tale of the benevolent aliens, landing not only in Milos but in other corners of Greece as well, evolved into a legend whispered across generations, passed down through the ages like a precious heirloom.

Aristides's writings served as a beacon of hope, reminding all who encountered them that when humanity dared to embrace the unknown with open hearts and minds, the extraordinary could become reality. Bridges could be built between worlds, progress could be catalysed, and the limitless potential within every one of us could be unlocked.

Yet, fate had a cruel twist in store for Aristides's chronicle. Upon his passing, the diary vanished into the mists of time, its whereabouts became a mystery that would forever haunt those who yearned to uncover its secrets. The pages, filled with wisdom and wonder, were lost to the world, leaving behind an aching void in the collective memory of humankind.

Chapter 1

The room was almost in darkness, the only light coming from a small square of glass that had gathered years of grease and which now obscured the foliage of a ten-year-old rhododendron bush, growing strongly in the warm sunlight.

The subterranean chamber was cloaked in suffocating darkness, the only illumination provided by a flickering, naked bulb that dangled precariously from a wire above. Its feeble light danced across the walls, casting grotesque shadows that writhed and twisted like tormented spirits. The air hung heavy with the stench of sweat, blood, and despair. The room's sole furnishing, a rust-eaten metal chair, stood as a chilling monument to suffering. Upon it slumped a figure, stripped bare of clothing and dignity. Their head lolled forward, a grotesque parody of surrender.

Closer inspection revealed the horrifying extent of the figure's torment. Their flesh was a mottled canvas of bruises, lacerations, and burns, each mark a testament to the relentless cruelty inflicted upon them. Blood seeped from open wounds, staining the cold concrete floor beneath the chair. Their eyes, hollow and vacant, stared into the abyss, their spirit seemingly broken by the ceaseless agony. Time had lost all meaning within this subterranean hell, stretching into an eternity of pain. The figure had long since relinquished any hope of escape, their existence reduced to a symphony of suffering, echoing endlessly through the dimly lit chamber.

His captors took pleasure in his suffering, relishing in the power they held over their victim. The tortured person was named Petros, and he knew that he was being broken, piece by piece, his will to resist slowly diminishing with each passing moment.

But despite the pain and the fear, he refused to give in. He held on to a glimmer of hope, knowing that one day, somehow, he would find a way out of this hellhole. He just had to hold on a little longer.

Petros had always been drawn to the thrill of espionage. Petros had a successful career with the Central Intelligence Agency (CIA), a US government agency responsible for gathering, analysing, and disseminating intelligence to support national security. He joined the CIA after completing his studies in international relations and politics at the University of Athens in Greece. He was recruited for his fluency in several languages, including English and Arabic, and his expertise in Middle Eastern politics.

Throughout his career, Petros had held various positions within the agency, including as an analyst, a field agent, and a team leader. He had worked on a range of high-profile cases, including counterterrorism and espionage operations, and had been recognised for his contributions to the agency's mission. He was now assigned to a top-secret mission as an undercover agent in Greece. His brief was to infiltrate the organization of the notorious drug lord named Kappa - nicknamed "*the butcher,*" and gather intel on their illegal activities.

For years, Petros played the role of a loyal member of the organisation, rising through the ranks and earning the trust of the drug barons and his inner circle. It was a dangerous game, and Petros had to constantly stay on guard, never letting his true identity slip.

But the stakes were high, and Petros was determined to see the mission through to the end. He knew that his work would help bring down one of the most powerful criminal networks in Greece and Europe. It would save countless lives. It was a risky job, but he was up to the challenge.

Petros was a proud Greek, born and raised in the picturesque town of Parga. He had a close-knit family, consisting of his wife Maria and their three children. Petros and Maria had been married for over 20 years, and their love for each other only seemed to grow stronger with each passing day.

Their children were almost grown ups now, but Petros still remembered the joy and excitement of raising them. He had always been a hands-on father, taking an active role in their upbringing and education. He was grateful to have such a loving and supportive family by his side, and he knew that they were the foundation of his happiness as well as his reason for living. He drew on his intense love for his family to give him the strength to get him through his ordeal.

Petros knew that he was in for a rough night when his captors dragged him into the underground room. He had been caught when he took one too many risks. Perhaps because he had become too confident in his abilities, or he made a small mistake which alerted someone in the organisation. He was now being held by the drug baron's organisation, one that had no qualms about using torture to extract information.

Initially, the pain was a dull ache, bearable, almost ignorable. Petros gritted his teeth and weathered the first few blows, the mild sting of the electric shocks was a mere annoyance. But as the hours crawled by, the torture escalated, each moment a new circle of hell. The blows grew in intensity, each strike landing with bone-jarring force. The electric shocks, once a mere tingle, now surged through his body, a white-hot agony that made his muscles convulse and his vision blur. The air grew thick with the coppery tang of blood as wounds, both old and new, seeped crimson onto the cold concrete. Petros's body, a vessel of suffering, quivered under the relentless assault, his screams a hoarse testament to his torment.

Despite the pain, Petros tried to hold on to his resolve. He knew that he couldn't give in, that he had to protect the information that he had been entrusted with. But as the hours ticked by, the pain became almost unbearable. Petros's body was battered and broken, his energy all but spent.

And then, just when he thought he couldn't take any more, his captors brought out the pliers. Petros watched in horror as they approached, knowing full well what was coming next. He tried to struggle, tried to resist, but it was no use. The pliers clamped down on his fingers, one by one until he had lost several of them.

Petros's screams echoed through the underground room as he lost consciousness, the pain and the loss of blood finally overwhelmed him. When he woke up, he was alone, his body was a bloody mess, and his spirit was broken. He knew that he had failed, that he had let down his country and his family. All he could do now was pray for a miracle.

Petros knew he had to escape from the locked room and the chair he was tied to. Despite the pain and weakness he was feeling, he summoned all his strength and determination. He began by trying to wriggle free from the ropes binding him to the chair, but they were too tight. He then looked around the room for any objects he could use to cut the ropes, but he couldn't find anything. Just as he was about to give up hope, he spied a long nail in the corner of the room.

He used all his energy to rock the chair little by little towards the nail. Reaching the nail, he tipped the chair on its side, disregarding the searing pain emanating from his broken fingers he reached for the nail until finally it was in his hand. He carefully began sawing at the ropes, ignoring the scorching pain in his wrists and ankles. It took all his concentration and effort, but eventually, he managed to cut through the ropes and break free from the chair. He then made his way to the door and tried to pick the lock using the nail, but it was too big.

He knew he had to think of something else. He remembered the window in the room and decided to try and escape through it. He stumbled over to the window and used the nail to pry it open.

It was a tight fit, but he managed to wriggle through the opening and escape to freedom.

Petros had been held captive for what felt like an eternity, subjected to endless interrogations and torture by his captors. But he had never broken, never given them the information they wanted. He knew that it was only a matter of time before they killed him, so when the opportunity presented itself, he took it gratefully.

As he stumbled through the dense woods away from his prison, he tried to get his bearings and figure out a plan. He had no weapons, no supplies, and no idea where he was. He was exhausted, hungry, and dehydrated, but he kept pushing forward, driven by a fierce determination to survive.

After what felt like hours of walking, but was only a couple at the most, Petros finally emerged from the woods onto a dirt road. He had no idea where it would lead him, but he knew he had to follow it. As he walked, he started to recognise some of the landmarks around him. He had been in this part of the world before, on holiday with his family, perhaps. To his surprise, he was on the island of Milos, a small island in the Cyclades chain less than two hours by ferry from Piraeus. The strange thing was he could not remember travelling from the mainland, and as far as he could recall he had not been knocked unconscious. How he was on Milos was a complete mystery.

As he made his way down the hill towards the sea, that shimmered under a moonlit sky, he saw a village in the distance.

He was wary, not knowing who he could trust, but he knew he needed help. He approached the village cautiously, trying to blend in with the locals as much as possible. Eventually, his legs and strength gave out, and he collapsed to the ground in front of a baker's shop. Petros's final sense before he lost consciousness was the smell of fresh bread.

The door of the baker's shop opened and a young woman in her thirties stepped into the street. She wore a grey apron over her grubby shorts and a white stained T-shirt. The shorts and T-shirt were not suited to the outside air temperature but to the suffocating heat from the bakery's huge baking oven. Even though it was just four-thirty in the morning, the day's baking was almost complete. Just a few more loaves to take out and some special bread used by the local people to have the priest bless their family and relatives.

She had been baking since two-thirty this morning, and now as the first embers of sunlight began creeping across the eastern sky, she was almost finished.

The woman looked up and down the street, and then when she was sure no one could see her, she grabbed the prone man's collar. Pulling him through the open door, into the display area of the bakery, where she left him on the floor in an ugly heap. She quickly closed the door, then once again pulled Petros along like a sack of potatoes, into a small parlour, where she managed to dump him in a chair, tied him to it, gagged him, then picked up her mobile phone, and hit a speed dial number.

"Yes?" Answered a gruff-sounding voice, in a tone that conveyed an 'I don't care who you are attitude.'

"It's Phobia," said the woman. On hearing her voice and name, the man crossed himself and shivered as if a cold aura had enveloped him. He said, "How can I help you?" This time his tone was fearful.

"Tell Kappa that I have the escapee," she whispered in a menacing voice.

Chapter 2

Alex Kalfas rolled over in the king-size bed until he was facing his wife Gitta. To him, she was still as beautiful as the first time he saw her, twelve or so years ago in the offices of Dominik Vogel, the then economics minister of Germany. She was sleeping peacefully now, her naked chest rising and falling in a steady rhythm. Gitta never wore anything in bed, unlike Alex who always wore a T-shirt and shorts no matter how hot it was. Again, Alex's thoughts returned to the first time he met Gitta. It was the beginning of the operation, which once it was over, the Americans had named *Gladio*. Perhaps, a name was needed for the multitude of dossiers and files which accumulated over the life of the operation. It was this operation that propelled Alex from an obscure justice minister to the Prime Minister of Greece.

Alex detected a slight change in the rhythm of Gitta's breathing, he watched as her magnificent green eyes opened, a huge smile breaking out as their eyes met.

"Good morning, darling," purred Gitta taking hold of his hand, pulling it to her lips to kiss it.

"Good morning, sweetheart," said Alex. "Coffee?" He asked.

"Lovely," Gitta replied.

Alex left their bed dragging his short dressing gown with him. It was late spring in Athens and although most northern

Europeans would class the weather as mild, for Greeks the temperature was bordering on cold, at 16 degrees Celsius. He put the small "bricky," as it was called, onto the gas heater. It was filled to the brim with water, with two large spoonfuls of Greek coffee, plus two spoonfuls of sugar. As he waited for it to boil, his mind once again turned back to his earlier years with Gitta.

They had been together since two thousand and ten, twelve years ago. She was still working for the CIA as a live operative, as she was when they had first met. Alex too, was a type of CIA operative, courtesy of his stepfather and stepmother who were both CIA agents. Although he enjoyed the occasional immersion into an operation, he was careful to not let such actions jeopardise his premiership.

Besides, he had Gitta who was a skilled and dedicated CIA operative and a good mentor to Alex. She had spent years working undercover on various assignments around the world. She had a particular affinity for Greece and had been given several covert operations in the country over the last few years. Working out of the Athens Station under the guidance of CIA Chief Chris Horsman, Gitta used her extensive training and natural aptitude for deception to infiltrate various extremist groups and gather valuable intelligence for the CIA and Alex.

She was always careful to maintain her cover, building complex networks of fake identities and tirelessly working to keep her true purpose hidden. Despite the inherent danger of her job, Gitta was driven by a sense of duty to her country and a desire to make a difference in Greece. She was a true patriot and an invaluable asset to Greece and the Greek government.

Alex returned to the bedroom after he had poured two Greek coffees, snatching a couple of croissants on the way.

"You know, I was thinking yesterday that things in Greece are fairly quiet and have been that way for a while now. The call from Chris might change all that, but I'm sure you know more about that than you are making out," said Alex as he winked at Gitta. He was forever teasing her about that side of their relationship.

Alex and Gitta had been married for eight years, but their careers often put a strain on their relationship. They loved their jobs, but they often clashed when it came to their work. Alex wanted to report the truth, no matter what, but Gitta's job required her to be cautious with the information she shared.

They couldn't discuss their work with each other in detail because they were both bound by confidentiality agreements of their offices – she being a CIA operative and he being a Prime Minister. The lack of transparency and understanding between them caused a lot of friction. They constantly had to walk on eggshells to avoid any professional mishaps. Despite their love for each other, the constant career-related tension did take a toll on their marriage.

Gitta looked at Alex, pulled her knees up to her chest, and then gave him one of her loving smiles. She took his hand and said, "I can't go into any detail as you know but the drug operation which Chris has been asked to head up has hit problems. I believe that is what Chris wants to talk with you about. Your wish for something to break the flatness may be about to come true," she blew him a kiss, hoping that would calm his impatience for information.

Alex knew that she was trying to divert him from the subject, but instead of being annoyed, he was once again thinking what an amazing, beautiful woman she was with deep green eyes that seemed to sparkle in the sunlight. He loved to run his fingers down her long, golden blond hair that flowed down her back like a cascading river of sunshine. She was tall and slender, slightly taller than Alex, with long, gorgeous legs that seemed to go on forever. He loved that she was confident and strong, but also had a warm and gentle nature. She was intelligent and driven, with a keen sense of purpose in her career and her personal life.

Despite the challenges she faced, Gitta remained optimistic and always had a smile on her face. She was the kind of woman who could light up a room just by walking into it, and she had a unique way of making everyone around her feel loved and appreciated.

She was also a strong and courageous woman. She had faced many challenges in her life and had always come out on top. She was determined and fiercely independent, never backing down from a test or a tricky situation. She had a powerful sense of self and knew what she wanted in life. She was confident in her abilities and was not afraid to take risks or stand up for what she believed in. Despite her many successes, Gitta remained humble and always looked for ways to help others. She was a true leader and an inspiration to those around her.

As she had hoped, Alex melted and instead of questioning her further, he pulled her to him and kissed her passionately on her lips.

An hour later, Alex was downstairs in his office in the Mega Maximo, awaiting Chris's arrival. He was drinking his favourite coffee, a sweet Greek double coffee, which Maria, his personal assistant, always had ready for him with uncanny foresight, whenever he arrived at his office. He sat and contemplated what Chris wanted to tell him.

Greece has had a short but worrying history of drug trafficking and drug-related violence. In the early 1980s" s, marijuana and opium were the main drugs being smuggled into Europe and North Africa from Greece. However, in the 1990s, the drug trade shifted to focus on cocaine and, more recently, methamphetamine and fentanyl.

The Greek government, with support and assistance from the United States, had been engaged in a long-standing battle against Middle Eastern drug cartels. This led to increased violence and corruption, as well as human rights abuses by security forces. Despite these efforts, drug trafficking continued to be a major problem in Greece, but thankfully, the country still had one of the lowest murder rates in the world.

Recently, Greece saw an increase in drug addiction, particularly among young rich people. This led to a growing problem with drug-related crime and an overburdened treatment system. The government was criticized for not doing enough to address the issue, and for failing to provide sufficient funding for prevention and treatment programs.

A knock on the door broke into Alex's revere. The door opened and Maria ushered Chris into his office.

"Come in, Chris," said Alex as he went across the room to greet him. After their customary two-cheeks' kiss, Alex motioned to Chris to sit down on the settee. "Coffee?" He asked.

"Maria's already asked me. She's bringing one in."

"Okay good. So, what was the urgency of your visit, Chris? Not that I don't enjoy your company whatever the situation."

Chris said, "We've discussed many times about the drug problems in Greece. It's getting worse by the day."

"Yeah, I know. The drug cartels are becoming more powerful and violent. It's scary," said Alex.

"It's not just the cartels though, more and more young people are getting hooked on drugs. And we're not doing enough to help them," added Chris.

Alex sipped his coffee while he gathered his thoughts. "I know, it's sad. There aren't enough treatment centres and the ones that do exist are overcrowded and underfunded and I feel responsible for that."

"Exactly," said Chris. "And it's not just the people who are addicted that are affected. Drug-related crime is on the rise, and it's putting everyone in danger."

"I know, it's like we're stuck in a vicious cycle," Alex said. "We need to do more to address the root causes of drug addiction, like poverty and unemployment, and the cartels who take advantage of, not only the underprivileged in society but also the nouveau riche. Tell me, are we any nearer to shutting down the drugs entering Greece from the Middle East? Don't you have an inside man?"

Chris laughed and raised his eyebrows. "As always you get straight to the point, don't you, Alex? We did have an insider until a few days ago, but I'm afraid he has dropped out of sight completely."

"I'm sorry," said Alex, with a look of genuine surprise on his face. "Wasn't he your best man?"

"Yes, he was, and hopefully he still is. But it's worrying that he's missed three consecutive pre-planned contact drops," said Chris with a touch of sadness in his voice.

"What are you going to do now?" Asked Alex.

Chris furrowed his brow as he gathered his thoughts. "We think Petros was about to find out how the cartel gets those damn drugs over our borders, whether by sea, land, or air. Perhaps he got too close, maybe he made a mistake, and they became suspicious of him. We don't know. However, we do have a clue which Petros left in a drop a couple of weeks ago."

"What was it?" Alex interrupted impatiently.

Chris laughed. "Not so fast Alex, are you going to solve the clue?"

Now it was Alex's turn to laugh. "Sorry Chris, it's just that it's the best news we have had so far."

"Yes, on the one hand, good news but on the other hand, we haven't an idea as to what the clue means. Petros left a piece of paper with the words 'golden triangle.'"

Alex furrowed his brow, which was a sign that he was concentrating. He was trying to recall where he had heard that phrase before. And then he had it, 'Of course,' he thought, 'Drugs, this was all about drugs as well.'

"The golden triangle is in south-east Asia," blurted out Alex. "Myanmar, Laos, and Thailand, isn't it?"

Chris smiled, "And you don't think the combined brains of the CIA hadn't thought of that Alex?"

Alex laughed, "I'm Taking the Fifth on that Chris. Seriously though, has no one come up with an answer yet?"

"No, we are stumped and without Petros we might never know what he meant. The problem we have is that Greece has never been a centre for drug smuggling, so we are learning as we go along. Unfortunately, we are not learning fast enough. All we know is that somehow the raw heroin comes into Greece and somewhere it's refined, then leaves Greece by an unknown route with a street value of $100 per gram. About a third of the price of a gram in the United States, but more than any other country in Europe," explained Chris.

"I heard from Langley this morning; they said the National Security Agency was breathing down their necks for some results. Langley doesn't want them poking their noses into our operations here. But one bit of bad news is that some of the drugs leaving Greece are finding their way into the States. That's got to be bad news."

He sipped his coffee giving Alex time to take in what he had said. Then he said, "But, we do have a small breakthrough, an opportunity that we must not let slip through our fingers. We will have to move fast and smart."

"What has happened?" Asked Alex.

"We got lucky when one of our low-level snitches overheard one end of a telephone conversation where the discussion was centred around the potential hiring of a female runner," said Chris, with a neutral expression on his face.

"What would this woman have to do? What is a runner?" Asked Alex, a puzzled look on his face.

"Runners are people who carry something, could be money, drugs, or even important papers, from one neighbourhood, or district, into another area," said Chris.

"So, have you someone to put into play?"

"Not yet, but we have identified a candidate."

"CIA?"

"Yes, very."

"In Greece?"

"Yes."

Alex stared at Chris. "You don't mean Gitta, do you?"

"Why would you say that?"

"It is Gitta, isn't it?"

"If it was, would you mind?"

"Of course, I'd bloody mind," said Alex in a raised voice.

Chris retorted, "Alex, your wife is the perfect person to infiltrate the cartel. She has the training and the skills to gather intelligence, and she could blend in with the cartel members without raising any suspicion."

"I don't know, Chris. It sounds dangerous. I don't want to put my wife's life at risk."

"I understand your concerns but think about it. Gitta is highly trained and experienced in this kind of operation. She's exactly the kind of person the CIA needs for this mission."

"I still have reservations," said Alex ruefully. "What if she gets caught? What if something goes wrong?"

"Look, Alex, I'm not going to sugar-coat it. This is a dangerous mission. But if we want to take down this cartel and end the harm they're causing in Greece and Europe, we need to take risks. And your wife is the best person for the job."

"Okay, I see your point. Let me talk to her about it and see what she thinks."

"Thanks, Alex," said Chris. "You know that I could have simply ordered her into the field, don't you? But out of respect for you as my friend, I prefer to discuss it with you. I'm sure she'll see the value of this mission. Let's hope she agrees to take it on."

"I appreciate that, Chris. I'll talk to her later today."

As Chris left Alex's office, he felt confident that Gitta would agree to join the operation, but he also felt sorry for his friend for putting him into such an awkward position, a choice between country and wife, an unenviable position to be in. At least Alex hadn't realised just how dangerous Gitta's mission would be.

Chapter 3

Soula looked around her in awe. It was the first time in her short twenty-one-year-old life that she had visited the ancient site of Delphi. From where she stood on the Sacred Way, she could see all around standing proud in its magnificence Mount Parnassus, still snow-capped even though it was late spring. The sacred way she was on, led to the Tholos, one of the most distinctive and important monuments in Delphi.

She did a three-sixty-degree turn taking in the Sanctuary of Apollo, which was at the far end of the Sacred Way. Then the ancient theatre which was built into the hillside, and which still boasted an incredible acoustic sound as well as seat five thousand people. It was still used for musical and theatrical events during festivals. Behind her was the stadium which, in ancient times was used for the Pythian games held once every four years. It too held five thousand people easily.

Soula continued towards the Temple of Apollo. As she got nearer, she saw that the sanctuary had been reconstructed to resemble how it was in the eighth century BC. It had been a huge project as the original stone was used for the restoration. The project had been shrouded in mystery as the funds to recreate the site had been donated by a company registered in the Middle East. The company had done other such ventures around the world but none as big as the Temple of Apollo. The Greek government welcomed the huge donation, and the help to physically reconstruct the building, which was veiled in secrecy, and done by the donating company's construction workers.

Soula knew from her history lessons at school that in ancient times, Delphi was considered the centre of the world and was one of the most significant religious and cultural centres of ancient Greece. It was now a popular tourist destination and a UNESCO World Heritage Site.

She continued toward the temple trying to imagine how it was over eight hundred years ago. It had been built up against an escarpment of Mt Parnassus, and she imagined there would have been queues of people from all corners of the world waiting to see the Oracle. Now there was only a family and a couple making their way up the stone stairs towards the entrance which stood proud between the Doric marble columns.

Soula followed them through the great wooden door into the outer chamber where in ancient times the supplicants would offer sacrifices to the god Apollo before they were led into the inner chamber called the Adyton. The Adyton was a small, dark chamber, accessible only by a narrow passageway. The room was filled with the scent of burning incense, and the walls were adorned with precious offerings from those who in ancient times sought the Oracle's wisdom. Actually, burning incense was a nice touch, thought Soula, as she looked around the chamber.

She noticed that at the far end of the chamber was the door that led into an inner chamber where the Oracle would immerse herself in the waters of a sacred spring while she performed her divinations. She recalled from her history lessons that the Oracle herself was a priestess, chosen from among the local women of Delphi. She was chosen for her purity and piety and underwent rigorous training to prepare for her role as the Oracle.

She would fast for several days before performing her divinations and would immerse herself in the waters of a sacred spring. When a supplicant arrived at the Temple, they would first offer a sacrifice to the god Apollo. They would then be led to the Adyton by a priest, who would take their question to the Oracle. The supplicant would wait in the chamber as the Oracle performed her divinations.

Soula entered the inner chamber and immediately she was surprised to see that there was indeed water bubbling up through the floor which flowed into a shallow pool, its surface covered in white lilies. Above the pool was a replica of the bronze triangle on which the Oracle would sit to deliver her prophecies.

Beyond the pool was a wall that was adorned with hundreds of butterflies, fluttering their wings in the soft light coming from oil lamps placed around the pool. Soula smiled to herself, the reconstruction was perfect. Whoever did this had kept faith in the ancient texts which had described the Sanctuary of Apollo, including the amazing butterflies. Feeling a little dizzy, a feeling she put down to the strong incense, the calming ripple of the spring water and the low lighting, Soula sat down on the floor at the wall where the butterflies were.

She looked up at the butterflies. “Wait a minute,” she said in a low voice. She stood up on unsteady feet and peered closely at the nearest butterfly. She reached out and touched it. It felt like nothing she had felt before. It wasn’t made of metal, wood, material, or plastic as far as Soula could tell, but she could tell it was made of a strong but light material which enabled its movements to mimic those of a real butterfly. What power drove these butterflies to move, she wondered. Perhaps, there was a small battery in their flimsy bodies, she concluded.

As she scanned the wall, she noticed that not all the butterflies moved, and the ones that didn’t move were slightly bigger and fatter. Soula reached up to one that was just within her reach. As her fingers closed around it, a wave of nausea caught her by surprise and she plucked it off the wall. It slipped from her fingers and fell to the floor, breaking in several places. Soula sat down with a thud on the marble floor, closed her eyes and waited as her nausea subsided.

When she opened her eyes, she saw that the family and the couple who had entered the chamber before her had left. So, they hadn’t heard the noise that the broken butterfly made when it hit the floor. Grateful, she now turned her attention to the butterfly. She gasped; the broken butterfly was covered in a white powder. She tentatively stretched out her arm, letting her forefinger gather some of the powder on its tip. “Cocaine,” she said breathlessly, the words barely audible.

She had tried cocaine several times during her university years, and now she had only one year to go. She was a bright and curious student who was always eager to explore new experiences. Unfortunately, she also had some exposure to cocaine because of her peers, and she had tried it a few times herself. While she did not use it frequently, Soula was aware that this kind of behaviour could have serious consequences and was not something to be taken lightly. She knew that she needed to be careful and mindful of her choices moving forward, and she was determined to make responsible decisions that would not jeopardize her health or her future.

Another wave of nausea washed over her causing her to feel hot. The smell of incense was more pungent and spicier to her now and she was feeling decidedly more uncomfortable. She noticed that her big toe was bleeding over the strap of her sandals. Shit! She thought, 'I must have done that when I fell.' No damage to her jeans or t-shirt though and she hadn't broken any bones. She looked at the white powder again. 'Should I collect it up?' She asked herself. That amount would certainly be worth a lot of money on the streets.

She knew from her dabbling at university that a gram of cocaine cost thirty-five dollars and there must be at least one hundred grams in the butterfly. Soula did a swift calculation and decided that the street value of one of these butterflies full of cocaine was easily three thousand five hundred dollars, maybe more.

Soula stood up gingerly using the butterfly wall as a support. She waited a few moments for the nausea waves to subside, then looked up and started to count the static butterflies. She counted forty-five before the nausea struck again and she had to look down, taking support from the wall until she felt better. She moved away from the wall and looked at her watch. Five minutes past five - she needed to run as she knew that Delphi closed at five-thirty. Taking a last look at the butterfly wall, she whispered to it, "I bet you don't know that you are worth more than two hundred thousand dollars, do you?"

As she said it, she turned and started to slowly make her way out of the Adyton. Behind her, the butterfly wall quietly started to revolve until it was at ninety degrees to its original position. Two men emerged from the space opened up by the change in position of the wall. Unknown to Soula, they had been watching her since she accidentally dislodged the butterfly, an act which triggered an alarm in their office behind the wall, where they were keeping an eye on the security camera feeds from inside the Temple of Apollo. They converged on Soula before she even knew they were there. At the last moment, she felt rather than heard their presence, but it was too late, she felt the cloth over her mouth and smelled the chloroform moments before she passed out.

With Soula's limp form cradled in their arms, the men retreated through the threshold, swallowed by the yawning darkness of the hidden chamber. The intricate wall, as if guided by an unseen hand, continued its graceful pirouette, sealing the passage with a gentle thud as ancient locks clicked into place.

A new facade emerged - a mosaic of vibrant butterflies shimmering against the cool stone. Unlike the hidden wall now facing the chamber's depths, this surface bore dozens of empty recesses, each a silent invitation for a future butterfly to be placed there, completing the ever-shifting puzzle that guarded the secrets of the Adyton.

Chapter 4

Yannis, the head of EKAM, the Greek anti-terrorist squad, and his lover, Kaliope, the Home Secretary arrived at the scene of the crime, an area of volcanic rock between two villages on the Greek island of Milos – a volcanic island in the Aegean Sea, just north of the Sea of Crete.

They had been called to the island by the local police. The body had been discovered by a local fisherman who was walking his dog as dawn was breaking. They stared at the body of a man lying in the middle of a circle of scorched earth. Yannis knelt and examined the body. The man was naked and had been burned beyond recognition. Kaliope looked on in horror.

Now she wished she hadn't come. She had no urgent business this morning, so when Yannis had suggested she accompany him to the crime scene, she had agreed.

"What happened here?" Kaliope asked.

"I don't know," Yannis said. "But it looks like he was burned alive."

Kaliope turned away, unable to look at the body any longer. "This is terrible," she said. "What could have happened?"

Yannis shook his head. "I don't know," he said. "But we're going to find out."

Yannis stood up and walked around the circle of scorched earth. He looked for any clues that might explain what had happened. But there was nothing. The ground was scorched and blackened, but there were no footprints or other signs of a struggle.

Kaliope looked at Yannis. "Do you think this might be a suicide?" She said.

Yannis shook his head. "I don't believe so," he said. "This man was murdered. But we'll have to wait for the autopsy to be sure."

The Yannis and Kaliope stood in silence for a moment, looking at the body.

"I'm going to call for a team to come and take the body away," Kaliope said. "Then we'll start our investigation."

Yannis nodded. "I'll take some men and visit the nearest villages and start making some house calls," he said. "And see if I can find out anything about this man."

"Okay," said Kaliope. "Also, I should tell Alex what we have found. I'll come to your office when I've finished up here." Yannis nodded, and then she turned and walked away, leaving the unknown body in the circle of fire with Yannis.

Before she had gone no more than a few hundred metres, she heard a shout behind her. She turned around to see one of Yannis's men standing over an object she couldn't make out, gesticulating to Yannis. She hurried over to where the man stood. Looking down, she saw what had excited him, half buried under a large stone was what looked like a small pile of clothes and a pair of sandals.

After putting on a pair of thin surgical gloves, Kaliope crouched and gingerly pulled out the clothes and sandals into plain sight.

"That T-shirt has blood on it, a lot in fact," said Kaliope as she scrutinised the clothes. She stood up with the T-shirt in her hands. "Bag this please," she said, handing the item to the man who had spotted the pile of clothes. There was a faint smell to the T-shirt that she vaguely recognised but couldn't put a finger on its source.

Yannis had already donned his surgical gloves and picked up a pair of loose-fitting trousers, the sort that surgeons wear in the operating theatre.

"So, what do you think? Suicide or murder?" Asked Kaliope.

Yannis replied, "I'm not sure yet. There are some things that point to suicide, but there are also some things that point to murder."

"Like what?"

"Well, for one thing, the body was found in a field. That's not a very common place to commit suicide. Most people who commit suicide do it in their homes, or in a secluded area where they won't be found," said Yannis.

"True. But maybe the victim wanted to be found. Maybe they wanted their death to be a public statement."

Yannis furrowed his brow and gazed off into the distance. "That's possible," he said. "But then again, maybe they didn't want to be found at all. Maybe they wanted their death to be a mystery.

"I see your point," Kaliope conceded.

"And then there's the way the body was burned. It was almost completely incinerated. That's not the way most people commit suicide. When people commit suicide, they usually just use a gun or a knife. They don't go to the trouble of burning their own bodies."

"That's true," admitted Kaliope, "But maybe the victim wanted to make sure they were dead. Maybe they wanted to be sure there was no chance of revival."

Yannis nodded his head. "That's possible. But then again, maybe they didn't want to die. Maybe they were trying to escape from someone. So, as you can see, there are a lot of things that point to both suicide and murder. It's going to take some more investigation to figure out what really happened."

"I agree. We'll start by finding out who the man was and then interview the victim's family and friends. Maybe they can shed some light on what happened," Kaliope said.

"Good idea," agreed Yannis. "In the meantime, we should get the body and the clothes to the pathologist in Athens for a post-mortem. The quicker we start by running some tests on the body, the quicker we'll get some answers. Maybe we can find some evidence that will help us figure out what happened."

"Great. Let's head for the village."

"Παμε, let's go," said Yannis taking her hand.

Yannis instructed one of his men to arrange for the body to be taken to Athens together with the clothes and sandals, and the other four to follow him. The two colleagues and lovers walked away from the body, each lost in their thoughts. Kaliope was leaning towards the suicide theory. She thought the victim might have been struggling with depression or some other mental illness. Yannis, on the other hand, was leaning towards the murder theory. He thought the victim might have been killed by someone who wanted to silence them.

When they reached the village, they decided to split up. It was unusual for a Home Secretary to conduct operational interviews, but Yannis seemed okay with her doing it and Kaliope wanted to practise her interview skills anyway, so it was a win/win all around.

Kaliope took two of Yannis's EKAM officers and half of the police contingent of the island, which amounted to only two sergeants. Yannis also took two of his men and the other half of the island's police force. Although this was not strictly true as the desk sergeant was, as he did every day, sitting in the local caffenion drinking coffee and playing backgammon with whoever would give him a game. Kaliope chose to knock on doors on the main street where most of the shops were, and Yannis took his men away from the main street to knock on the doors of houses.

The small Greek village of Trypiti is perched on the edge of a cliff overlooking the Aegean Sea. The whitewashed houses with their blue-tiled roofs are built in a labyrinthine pattern that winds its way up the hillside. The narrow streets are lined with shops selling souvenirs, traditional clothing, and fresh produce. About two thousand people live in the village and they provide the daily bread of the several tavernas where authentic Greek cuisine is served. Kaliope had been here before on vacation and loved the village and its people.

She entered through the door of her fourth shop, a bakery. She had been going door to door in the village, asking if anyone had seen a stranger in the village or if any male was missing.

A woman with a kind face peered out from behind the counter. "Can I help you?" She asked. Behind her were the ovens that had been used earlier in the small hours of the morning and were now quiet and no longer stifling hot. The shelves which earlier that day had been full of fresh bread of all shapes and sizes were now almost empty. However, the smell of fresh bread, an aroma that Kaliope adored, lingered on, even though it was now almost midday. It also triggered something else in her memory bank. It was frustrating as she couldn't put her finger on it.

Kaliope introduced herself. "Kalimera madame, my name is Kaliope. You probably recognise me, I'm the Home Secretary. I'd like to ask you a few questions if I may."

The woman behind the counter nodded. "Am I in trouble?" She asked.

"Not at all. Don't worry. We want to find out if a man who was found dead near the next village came from here. As far as you know has anyone reported a missing person?"

"No, I haven't heard anything, sorry."

"How about a stranger hanging about the village the last few days," asked Kaliope.

The woman shook her head. "No, sorry."

"Thank you," said Kaliope. "If you remember anything please call this number," she said, handing the woman a card.

"Thank you, I will. But you should speak to the owner of the bakery, she'll be back in a few minutes. Why don't you wait in the little parlour back there," she said, pointing to a door at the back of the shop.

Kaliope thanked her and headed for the parlour after first instructing one of Yannis's men to wait for her outside the shop.

In the parlour, the smell of fresh bread was almost overwhelming. Kaliope looked around. The parlour was very small and had little furniture, just a wooden chair in the middle of the room, and a dresser under the window. A curtain, the size of a doorway, swayed in an alcove in the farthest corner of the room. Kaliope moved the curtain aside so she could see what was behind it. A bedroom and a couple of gas-fired rings for cooking on a trestle table.

"What the hell are you doing?" Said a menacing voice behind Kaliope. She turned around and scanned the woman's face carefully.

"Can you state your name for the record?" Kaliope asked, her voice cool and professional.

There was no denying that she was beautiful, but there was something off about her too. The way she moved, the way she spoke - everything about her seemed calculated and cold.

The woman smiled, a little too sweetly. "My name is Phobia. I own this bakery."

Kaliope nodded. "Yes, we're aware of that. I wanted to ask you some questions about the events of last night. Did you notice anything unusual or suspicious around the bakery?"

Phobia's smile faltered slightly. "No, I didn't see or hear anything out of the ordinary."

Kaliope raised an eyebrow. "Really? Because we have a reason to believe that one of your customers may have been murdered inside the shop." Kaliope moved to the wooden chair and sat down. There it was again the smell of fresh bread. The dead man was in this very parlour whilst the bread was being made.

Phobia's eyes widened, but Kaliope couldn't read the emotion behind them. "That's terrible. I had no idea, Home Secretary."

Kaliope leaned forward. "Are you sure about that, Phobia? Because we have a reason to believe that you might have been involved. The man might not have been killed here but we are one hundred percent certain he was in here last night."

Phobia's smile disappeared completely now, and her eyes turned icy. "I'm not involved in anything, I swear.

Kaliope studied her for a moment, then spoke again. "Tell me, Phobia. Do you have any enemies? Anyone who might want to harm you or your business?"

Phobia hesitated for a moment, then shook her head. "No, I don't think so. I try to keep to myself and focus on my work."

Kaliope leaned back in her chair, studying Phobia for a long moment. "Well, we'll be conducting a thorough investigation into this matter. I advise you to cooperate fully with us, or things could get very difficult for you."

Phobia stood straight, her voice raised, and her eyes blazing. "I have nothing to hide, Home Secretary. Do what you need to do, but don't accuse me of something I didn't do."

Kaliope watched as she stalked out of the room, her blue eyes almost alive with malevolent thoughts. Something about her didn't sit right with Kaliope, and she made a mental note to keep a close eye on the beautiful owner of the bakery.

As Kaliope walked away from the bakery, she could smell the fresh bread. It was a comforting smell, but it was also a reminder of the danger that Phobia posed. Kaliope knew that she had to be careful, but she was determined to get to the bottom of it, no matter what it took.

Kaliope called Homeland Security and instructed them to see if any reconnaissance satellites had passed over the island in the last 24 hours. It was a long shot, but they could get lucky. She then ordered a surveillance drone to the island, to patrol Milos for a couple of days. Perhaps, it would show up something.

Her last call was to her boss, Alex Kalfas. She relayed the events as far as she and Yannis had managed to work out and told Alex about her suspicions concerning Phobia, the owner of the bakery.

"Have we identified the body yet?" Asked Alex.

"No, not yet. The body is in Athens at the main crime autopsy unit."

"When will the results of the autopsy be ready, do you know?" Asked Alex.

"No, but as soon as I have the report, I'll send it to you."

"Thank you, Kaliope. I have a nagging feeling that the dead man could be someone who Chris Horsman is looking for. I hope not. Keep me updated," said Alex, closing the call.

Kaliope's phone pinged. It was the autopsy report being transmitted to her phone. She opened the document and scanned it.

Autopsy Report

Name: Unknown

Approx Age: 35 to 40

Sex: Male

Date of Death: April 28, 2023

Cause of Death: Burns and blunt force trauma.

Manner of Death: Homicide

External Examination:

The body of a well-developed, well-nourished, Caucasian male was received at the morgue. The body was badly burned, with the skin charred and peeling off in large strips. There were also numerous bruises and abrasions on the body, consistent with blunt force trauma.

The head was severely burned, with the hair and scalp destroyed. The eyes were closed, and the mouth was open. The teeth were intact.

The neck was not injured.

The chest was severely burned, with the ribs exposed. The heart and lungs were intact.

The abdomen was severely burned, with the intestines exposed. The stomach was empty.

The pelvis was not injured.

The legs were severely burned, with the muscles and tendons exposed. The feet were intact.

Internal Examination

The brain was severely burned and could not be examined.

The heart was enlarged and congested. The coronary arteries were atherosclerotic.

The lungs were severely burned and oedematous.

The liver was enlarged and congested.

The spleen was enlarged and congested.

The kidneys were enlarged and congested.

The stomach was empty.

The intestines were severely burned.

The bladder was empty.

Toxicology

The blood alcohol level was 0.00%.

There were no drugs or poisons in the body.

Conclusion

The cause of death was burns and blunt force trauma. The manner of death was suspected homicide.

The evidence of torture on the body suggests that the victim was subjected to a prolonged and brutal attack before being burned alive. The injuries to the head suggest that the victim was struck repeatedly with a blunt object. The injuries to the chest and abdomen suggest that the victim was stabbed or slashed with a sharp object. The injuries to the legs suggest that the victim was kicked or stomped.

The victim's body was found in a field. There were no witnesses to the crime and no suspects have been identified. The investigation is ongoing.

Identification of the body was attempted through dental records, however, although a match was found the files were classified as "top secret."

****

Kaliope scanned the file a couple more times as she tried to make sense of the events of that morning. She forwarded the autopsy report to Yannis and then called him.

"None of this makes sense," she said. "What do you make of it?"

"I agree," said Yannis. "We have an unidentified John Doe murdered on Milos in a mafia-style death and a woman suspect who owns a bakery. Question, why would a bakery owner be involved in a mafia-style gangland murder? Question, why Milos Island, a tourist island which has no history of hard drugs or gun running? Question, why would someone who was working for or with the Secret Service or a similar agency be working on a small Greek island?"

"Too many unanswered questions, Yannis. We need to get some answers quickly. But where to start?" Questioned Kaliope.

"Perhaps, with Chris Horsman," replied Yannis. "He has just messaged me requesting a meeting with you and Alex at three o'clock this afternoon at the Mega Maximo."

Kaliope looked at her watch. "It's going to be tight; I'll call the helicopter to pick us up near where the body was found. Let's go!

Chapter 5

Four people sat on the two sofas facing Alex's desk, in his office in the Mega Maximo, the official residence of the Greek Prime Minister. Behind Alex was the huge bulletproof window that looked out onto the magnificent gardens which had held many official garden parties in the past. The view from Alex's office looked out onto the manicured circular lawn with a water fountain as its central feature. Sitting in front of Alex were Gitta, Chris, Yannis, and Kaliope.

Alex opened the meeting, "Okay, everyone, let's discuss the plan to insert Gitta into the drug warlord's organisation. We need to ensure her safety and provide her with effective ways to gather valuable information. Any suggestions?"

Chris said, "I think the first step should be creating a solid backstory for Gitta. We need to establish her credibility and make sure she blends in seamlessly. Perhaps, we can portray her as someone with a troubled past, seeking refuge or protection within the criminal world as a backstory to why she wants to join their organisation."

"Agreed," concurred Kaliope. "It's crucial that we provide her with appropriate support to maintain her cover. Perhaps, we should also consider her appearance and personality traits to align with the gang's culture and expectations."

"Absolutely, we must ensure Gitta can defend herself and gain respect within the gang," said Alex, concern showing on his face. He felt that he was in a conflicting position, and it was uncomfortable for him. On the one hand, his love for Gitta made it painful for him to hear how dangerous the mission was, yet on the other hand, he had a responsibility to his people and the country to stop the flow of drugs through Greece.

"Yes," agreed Yannis. "Once Gitta is embedded within the gang, we should set up communication channels to retrieve the information she gathers. One option could be a concealed, in plain sight, communication device, such as a piece of jewellery, which would allow her to relay information discreetly."

"But we must also be cautious not to compromise Gitta's identity or safety," Alex said with an anxious look on his face.

Gitta looked at her husband smiling; she poked out her tongue at him. "Don't worry, darling, I can take care of myself. You know that, don't you?"

"Alongside the direct contacts, we should consider utilising encrypted messaging apps to exchange sensitive information. This way, she can communicate securely with us and her handlers without arousing suspicion," said Yannis, forever the technocrat amongst them. "We should dedicate a drone to be our eye in the sky, so Gitta has an umbrella over her."

Chris chipped in, "I like that. We should devise a contingency plan in case her cover is compromised. It's essential to provide her with escape routes, safe houses, and emergency protocols to ensure her safety in case of an unforeseen event."

"Agreed," concurred Alex. "We need to ensure a reliable extraction plan. Once she has gathered enough evidence and achieved her objectives, we must be prepared to extract her swiftly and discreetly to prevent any harm coming to her."

"Absolutely. We should have a dedicated team ready for extraction, equipped with the necessary resources and backup to guarantee her safe return. Alright, we seem to have a solid plan in place. Let's refine these strategies, document everything, and prepare the necessary resources. We'll need to coordinate closely and stay vigilant throughout the entire operation. The safety and success of this operation depends on it," said Chris. Turning to face Alex he continued, "We'll not bother you with the fine details, Alex, so Yannis, Gitta, and I will retire to another room to iron out the details if that's alright with you?"

"Go ahead," said Alex waving them away.

As the three of them left the room Chris's phone rang. He listened intently to what was being said at the other end of the line, his brow furrowed as he concentrated on what was being said. His eyes flashed firstly with anger and then a sadness came over them. He thanked the other party and closed his mobile. Everyone looked at him waiting.

Kaliope was the first to break the silence. "The body has been identified," she said. It was more of a statement than a question.

"Yes," said Chris. "It's our man on the inside." He sat down heavily in his chair. "Poor, poor man, dying the way he did. I'll get the bastards who did that to him!"

"What on earth was he doing on Milos?" Said Yannis, to no one in particular.

"If that weird bakery owner, what's her name - Phobia, did have something to do with the death of your inside man, then surely she is involved with the drug lords in some way," said Kaliope.

"Why keep referring to him as the inside man?" Questioned Gitta. "Does that mean I shall be the inside woman?" She said laughingly as she tried to lighten the tension in the room. "His name was Petros, was it not?"

"Yes," said Chris. "Sorry, if we made you feel like you were an appendage to this operation."

"No worries, you are forgiven," Gitta said smiling. "Now let's get the show on the road, shall we retire to another room to brief me on my cover and how you are going to insert me into their operation?"

Once again, Chris, Yannis, and Gitta headed for the door of Alex's office. This time there was no phone call to interrupt them.

As the three formulated the plans for Gitta's insertion, protection, and extraction, a young couple was wandering amidst the picturesque landscapes and ancient ruins of the enigmatic site of Delphi.

Its rich history had beguiled them during their studies at John Hopkins University in New York City, where they had met and subsequently married. Now, as they recalled the whispered tales of divine oracles and sacred prophecies, which had drawn travellers from far and wide to Delphi, they marvelled at the ambience of the tranquillity at one with nature. But amidst the allure of its past, a sinister secret had remained hidden for centuries. A secret that only the drug lords knew of, as did the ancients over two and a half thousand years ago, a secret that Soula had stumbled upon a couple of days ago.

As the couple walked hand in hand through a small copse of trees near the ancient theatre, the couple spotted a flash of colour behind a bush to the right of the pathway they were on. Full of trepidation, they approached the bush, and as they drew nearer, they realised that they were looking at a female form lying on the ground. The young man, whose name was Christos, crouched down beside the prone body of a young girl.

"She's still alive," he said to his wife, Vivi.

"Thank god," Vivi replied making the sign of the cross on her chest, starting from her left shoulder in the tradition of the Greek Orthodox religion. "Is she unconscious?"

"Yes, and she has traces of white powder around her mouth."

“What do you think happened?” Vivi asked, her voice shaking.

“I’m not sure,” Christos said. “But it could be an overdose, as it looks like the white powder around her mouth is cocaine. We should call 112.”

They quickly called for help, and then they stayed with the woman until the paramedics, police, and also the head of security for the Delphi site arrived. While the paramedics worked on the girl, the police officer took statements from the couple. The officer, who had searched through the girl’s handbag and found out that her name was Soula, asked the couple if they knew her. They, of course, had never seen her in their lives, but it gave Christos who was no mug, the opportunity to ask them something which was bothering him about the scene.

“Just out of interest, was there any trace of cocaine in the girl's bag?” asked Christos.

“Not that we can see,” answered one of the officers. “Why do you ask?”

“It seems strange that someone would choose to take a drug overdose in the middle of a thicket in the centre of Delphi. Also, I can’t see any of those small Ziploc bags which hold ten grams of cocaine. For her to overdose, she would need many more Ziploc bags and there is no sign of them.”

“You have a keen eye,” said the officer. “How come?”

"I've studied forensics at John Hopkins in New York. I'm a forensic scientist as is my wife."

"Ah! No wonder you are interested in the incident. Tell you what, while we wait for our forensic people, why don't you take a look at the scene and give me your observations, without contaminating any evidence, of course," said the officer.

"No worries, I know the drill," Christos said as he moved towards the area where the woman had been lying. She was now on a stretcher and being wheeled to the back of the ambulance which was parked on the dirt track fifty metres away.

The first thing Christos noticed was that the area around where the woman had lain, didn't show any signs of someone rolling around on the ground, as they would have done if they had taken an overdose. No broken or trampled grass fronds or broken branches of small bushes. Christos crouched down spotting two pairs of shoe prints, almost two metres apart and heavily indented into the earth. 'They were carrying a heavy weight,' said Christos to himself, and the weight was probably Soula.

He joined the police officer who was chatting to Vivi and told him of his findings.

"So, it's a crime scene then?" Asked the officer.

"I'm afraid so, that's what it looks like," confirmed Christos.

"That's interesting, she is the third person to die of an overdose of cocaine in the past month in Delphi. Now, I'm worried that we messed up and they too were deaths by foul play and not accidental," said the officer, a worried frown lining his forehead.

"Sorry," said Christos. "Did you say she is the third to die?"

"Yes," said the officer. "This young woman passed away while the paramedics were treating her. They couldn't save her. The previous two, and they were both women, were found inside the Temple of Apollo, sitting on the floor, again with traces of cocaine around their mouths and no apparent foul play. So, I guess we are going to have to reopen those two cases."

"Yes," agreed Christos. "I think you need to. You'll need a tip-top forensic team going over every inch of that temple. I don't mean to be disrespectful, but the team should be from Athens not the surrounding villages or small towns. Athens is where the most experienced forensic people are. In fact, my uncle, Yannis Spanos, who is head of the Greek counter-terrorist squad and who I know is involved in trying to flush out the drug lords who are exporting cocaine into Europe and onto the USA. He has an excellent team of forensic scientists."

The officer thought for a moment, then agreed with Christos that an Athens team would be the best option. He authorised Christos to contact his uncle and request a forensics team to investigate the apparent overdoses. Christos was pleased because now he saw that he had the opportunity to lead a forensics team far sooner than he ever dreamed of. He would call his uncle immediately.

The call for Yannis came through just as his meeting with Chris and Gitta was breaking up. He listened intently to what his nephew had to say, then suggested that they meet over a coffee later that afternoon to discuss the matter further. 'This just might be the breakthrough we have been waiting for,' Yannis thought to himself after closing the call. It was tenuous he knew, but at least it was something to finally get their teeth into.

Chapter 6

In the dimly lit room, a foreboding presence looms over those who gather there, casting a shadow of dread upon all who dared cross his path. Kappa "the milkman" Galatas, the drug lord who by his late forties, was head of the biggest, most feared, and most successful drug ring in Greece. A figure whose physicality exuded an aura of terror and commanded fear from even the boldest souls.

Standing at a commanding height, Kappa's broad frame was a testament to his power and dominance. His shoulders, wide and imposing, hinted at the strength and brutality beneath his tailored suit. Every movement he made was deliberate, each step resonating with an eerie confidence that left no room for doubt.

The contours of his face told a story of years spent in the depths of darkness. Deep-set, piercing eyes, like smouldering coals, seemed to hold the secrets of countless atrocities committed under his command. They flickered with a blend of cunning intelligence and unyielding cruelty, capable of reducing a man to trembling submission with a single glance.

Kappa's weathered skin bore the marks of a life lived on the edge. Like battle scars, lines etched across his face betrayed a ruthless existence. The subtle creases around his eyes spoke of countless sleepless nights, spent orchestrating his criminal empire, while the hardened jawline served as a testament to his unwavering resolve.

A cascade of raven-black hair slicked back with precision, framed his face like a sinister crown. It was an immaculate facade that concealed a malevolence too great to fathom. There was an almost serpentine quality to his appearance as if his very presence was a slithering reminder of the venomous nature that lay within.

When Kappa spoke, his voice carried a weight that sent shivers down the spines of those unfortunate enough to hear it. Each syllable dripped with a lethal blend of authority and menace, leaving no room for dissent or negotiation. It was a voice that reverberated with the echoes of untold horrors and commanded unwavering obedience from his subordinates.

As his dark gaze fell upon you, one couldn't help but feel a primal instinct to flee, to escape the clutches of this malicious force. Kappa "the milkman" Galatas, a predator among predators, stood as a chilling testament to the horrors lurking in the darkest corners of the human psyche. To encounter him, was to glimpse the abyss and understand the true meaning of fear.

Beside him, as he leaned forward over his desk were his trademark throwing knives, six of them, ornate silver handles protruding from black leather sheaths. He never carried a gun; he didn't need to. He could throw a knife with unerring accuracy at ten metres before his enemy could get off a shot.

Kappa stepped back from his large oak desk, picked up his knife belt and strapped it around his waist. He surveyed the dimly lit, smoke-filled luxurious room, which had twenty of his most trusted lieutenants, including his trusted assistant, Takis Penza and Phobia. She perhaps was the one person whom Kappa felt very uncomfortable around.

Someone had committed a foolish but serious mistake that has endangered Kappa's empire. The tension in the room was palpable as Kappa prepared to address the situation and deliver the appropriate punishment.

Kappa's eyes burned with anger as he scanned the room, his gaze eventually settling on a young and nervous-looking lieutenant. The lieutenant, stood frozen, aware of the grave consequences that awaited him.

Kappa's voice boomed through the room, commanding the attention of everyone present.

"Step forward!" Kappa's voice reverberated with a mix of fury and disappointment.

With trembling steps, the young man inched closer to the table. Sweat dripped down his forehead, in evidence of his fear.

"Explain to me, how your foolish mistake has endangered our operations," Kappa demanded, his voice sharp and cold.

The young man stammered, struggling to articulate his words. "Boss, I... I didn't realize... I-I underestimated the tenacity of the forensic scientists... They caught us off guard... I'm sorry, Boss!"

Kappa's face turned a deep shade of crimson, his anger bubbling to the surface. He slammed his fist down on the table, causing the room to tremble.

"Sorry, won't cut it, you fool!" Kappa's voice thundered through the room. "You've put us all at risk! Punishment must be dealt!"

The young man's knees buckled, and he collapsed to the floor, begging for mercy. His pleas filled the air, desperate and futile.

Kappa's gaze shifted, his eyes now fixed on his trusted assistant. In his late forties, Takis Penza exuded an aura of commanding presence that captivated those who dared to meet his gaze. Standing tall and imposing, he carried himself with an air of confidence that demanded respect. Every feature on his face seemed to be etched with the marks of a life led on the edge, his rugged countenance told tales of triumph and hardship.

"Takis, bring forth the punishment," Kappa commanded, his voice laced with authority.

Takis stepped forward, his every movement exuding an intimidating presence. He placed a cold, steel gun on the table, its mere presence sending shivers down the spines of those present.

The young man's tears flowed freely as he realised the gravity of his mistake. He pleaded one last time, his voice trembling with desperation. "Please, Boss! I promise I'll make it right! Give me another chance!"

Kappa's eyes narrowed; his thoughts concealed behind a facade of impenetrable rage. He nodded to Takis. His right-hand mind stepped forward and stood in front of the young man.

"Your life hangs by a thread," Takis whispered, his words dripping with venom. "Your next mistake will be your last."

With a deliberate step backwards, Kappa returned to his seat, his piercing gaze fixated on the trembling young man. The room fell into a suffocating silence, the air heavy with impending judgment.

"Who decided on how to dispose of the bodies of the three females who died in Delphi?" Takis asked in a soft voice accompanied by a disarming smile which completely surprised but also caused the young man to feel relieved, as he had been expecting at the very least a bullet in his head.

"It was a joint decision by my Delphi team."

"Why did you deviate from our standard protocol for disposing of bodies?" Asked Takis.

"I.. we thought if it looked like a drug overdose the local police wouldn't get involved. And it worked with the first two but not the third because we were unlucky that a forensic scientist stumbled upon the body," said the young man, his voice sounding more confident as he saw the spectre of death diminishing.

"Look, the protocol is so simple and almost fool-proof. A quick death, preferably a bullet or even a knife, and then put them ten feet under. Completely emotionless, less risk involved and clean," Takis emphasised the word *clean* to stress its importance.

The young man was getting fidgety now as he realised where Takis was taking the conversation.

"There is something more to this, isn't there, Kostas?" Addressing the young man by his name for the first time. "Who could blame you, spending month after month in Delphi, filling ceramic butterflies with cocaine? No women stuck behind that wall. No play time here on the island of Aegina. I can imagine that the sight of drugged women not knowing what they were doing, was too tempting, perhaps. You raped them, didn't you, and somehow in doing that you made a connection and couldn't bear to let them be lost forever to their families."

The tension that had been dissipating in the room returned once again. Kostas stared widely at Takis and then at Kappa. His thoughts were racing around his mind. Should he bluff it out, they couldn't possibly know for sure, or should he admit it and hope the punishment was an embarrassment in front of the other Lieutenants in the room?

"Sorry," stammered Kostas. "Yes, we raped them," Kostas's voice tailed off into a whimper.

Takis turned to look at Kappa, a smile playing around his lips. Kappa stood up slowly, fury on his face, and exhaled deeply. He nodded to Takis to step to one side.

"Stand up!" Kappa shouted at Kostas.

With his legs feeling like appendages of jelly, Kostas struggled to stand up. He glanced at the gun that was still on the table, waiting for either Kappa or Takis to pick it up and use it.

He registered the flash of metal hurtling towards him in the milliseconds it took the knife to traverse the few metres between Kappa and Kostas. The thud, as it buried itself up to the hilt in his chest, was heard throughout the room. Kostas looked down, a surprised look on his face. Then slowly sat back down into the chair he had just vacated. Now, his eyes instead of showing surprise were completely blank as his life was snuffed out.

Amidst all the tension, Phobia, a woman shrouded in mystery and darkness, remained silent, her presence seemingly untouched by fear. Her eyes glimmered with an otherworldly power, a force that even Kappa hesitated to challenge.

Kappa's gaze eventually shifted toward Phobia, a mixture of caution and reverence in his eyes. "Phobia, my dear, it seems you've made an error as well. But your fate will be different. What possessed you to burn alive the undercover agent, in full view of the authorities?"

Phobia maintained her composure, a slight smirk dancing across her lips. "Boss, I admit my mistake. But you know my unique abilities. I admit I was possessed but I shall deal with that home office minister my way. You know what I am capable of and the powers I possess."

Kappa felt the tension and anger draining from his body as Phobia spoke, it was almost as if she was hypnotising him, controlling his mind. "Mind you, do it," he told Phobia trying to assert himself over her.

Kappa turned to the room. "Will someone get rid of the body? Takis, could you find a replacement for Kostas and get them in post before the day is out."

"Yes Boss, I'm on it," said Takis as he handed Kappa the blood-stained knife he had pulled from Kostas's chest.

Chapter 7

Gitta stood in front of the mirror, nervously adjusting her attire. Her reflection gazed back at her, a captivating woman with piercing green eyes, flowing blonde locks, and an allure that could ensnare even the most guarded of hearts. She possessed a rare combination of extraordinary beauty, undeniable sex appeal, and sharp intellect. But beneath her stunning facade, she concealed the resolve of a trained undercover agent.

Tonight, was the night she would meet her new employer for the first time—a man known as Takis Penza, the trusted assistant of the notorious Kappa, the drug cartel boss. Takis was infamous for his womanizing ways, but it was his reputation for ruthlessness that truly sent shivers down her spine. Gitta had heard stories of his violent tendencies, his swift retribution for the smallest of transgressions, and the autonomous power he wielded over the cartel's operations. As she prepared to step into this treacherous world, Gitta's anxiety grew with each passing second.

The meeting had been arranged in the vicinity of Omonia Square in downtown Athens. The square was a tourist area, surrounded by four- and five-star hotels, but behind this façade of opulence, the surrounding streets were the haunts of drug traffickers, prostitutes, undocumented immigrants and the homeless. Gitta's meeting was on Athinon Avenue at a large five-story building of neoclassical style, of the late 19th century.

Gitta rapped three times on the imposing oak door using the heavy brass knocker. The door was opened by a young woman who looked the worse for wear, her drug-affected eyes, bloodshot and almost vacant, confirmation of her addiction to the white stuff. She beckoned Gitta to come inside and pointed to a room on the left-hand side of the hallway. The door was ajar.

As she walked into the dimly lit room, the atmosphere crackled with an air of danger. The scent of cigarettes hung in the air, mingling with the musky odour of fear. Gitta's heart raced, her nerves threatening to betray her as she scanned the room for Takis. Finally, her eyes met his, and she felt a chill run down her spine.

His eyes, like two piercing orbs of obsidian, held a chilling intensity that penetrated deep into Gitta's soul. They possessed a hypnotic power, capable of captivating and commanding attention with just a mere glance. Cold and calculating, they revealed the depths of his ruthlessness, harbouring secrets that only the most daring would dare to unravel. Gitta shivered involuntarily, hoping that Takis Penza would not have noticed.

She noticed his strong jawline, expertly shadowed by a hint of a five o'clock shadow, which added to his rugged allure. The carefully trimmed salt-and-pepper beard framed his mouth, which was set in a thin, enigmatic smile. A smile that could effortlessly shift from charming to menacing, leaving others unsure of his intentions and wary of crossing him.

Takis Penza sat at the head of a long mahogany table. His dark eyes bore into her, seemingly seeing through her every facade. Gitta knew that her cover as a drug runner had to be impeccable if she wanted to survive in this perilous game.

Summoning all her courage, she approached Takis with a confidence that belied her inner turmoil. The dangerous glint in his eyes told her that he saw right through her charade of confidence. She reminded herself that she was playing a role—a seductive, cunning woman who had come to earn Takis's trust.

As Gitta engaged Takis in conversation, her mind calculated every move, every word spoken. She flirted, teased, and enticed, skilfully using her extraordinary beauty and charm to manipulate him. Beneath her alluring facade, she remained vigilant, ready to adapt and seize any opportunity that presented itself.

Minutes turned into hours as Gitta danced on the thin line between danger and survival. Takis's gaze never wavered, his piercing eyes searching for any signs of deceit. She could feel the weight of the cartel's expectations pressing down on her, the immense responsibility she carried on her shoulders.

As evening approached, Gitta continued to play her part flawlessly, her intelligence and wit matching Takis's every move. She was glad she hadn't worn anything too revealing - a tight pair of jeans, high heels and a shirt tied at the front showing a few inches of her midriff was the right statement, not too dressy but also not too flirty. She maintained the dance of deception, leaving no room for doubt or suspicion. But deep inside, she longed for the moment when her mission would be over; when she could shed the persona she had crafted, and return to her true self.

As the evening drew to a close, Takis leaned in, his voice a whisper that sent shivers down Gitta's spine. He spoke words that made her stomach churn and her heart race, reminding her of the dangerous game she had willingly entered.

"Remember, Gitta," he said, his voice laced with equal parts menace and intrigue, "Loyalty is rewarded, but betrayal is met with a fate far worse than death."

Gitta nodded; her expression a careful blend of submission and resilience. She knew that her journey had just begun, and the road ahead would be treacherous. She would have to navigate the murky waters of deceit and danger, relying on her intelligence and resourcefulness to survive.

"Don't worry, Takis, no one is more loyal than I am. I won't cause any trouble. By the way, when do I make my first run?" Said Gitta, hoping that it would be very soon. She was tired of the banter, if Takis had not made up his mind yet he never would.

Takis jutted out his jaw, his eyes piercing into hers as if to say, I ask the questions, not you. There was a lengthy silence as he contemplated what she had said. Slowly, he extracted a cigarette from the silver cigarette box on his desk, just as slowly he brought his lighter up, flipped the cover, thumbed the flywheel and lit the cigarette. Gitta was feeling more and more uncomfortable as she worried that she had said the wrong thing. Finally, Takis smiled, showing his even teeth.

"You are keen, aren't you? I like that. You can start this evening, or you can start after breakfast," he said with a smirk on his face. "But first I must check that you are not carrying a wire. I'd hate our conversation this afternoon to be transmitted over the ether."

Gitta realised that what Takis had said was pure bullshit. If he had been concerned about a wire, he would have searched her as soon as she had entered the room. He just wanted to show her that he had power over her, he was the boss and could lay his hands on her without seeking permission. She braced herself for what lay ahead, glad that she had not activated the transmitter behind the green stone in her necklace, and Alex would not hear what was to come.

"Stand up," instructed Takis as he rounded his desk and walked towards her. He stood facing her, their noses almost touching. Gitta was trying hard not to feel or even show him that she was intimidated. His eyes were dark orbs penetrating her own like black lasers seeking to burn through to her thoughts. Pulling Gitta to his body, he wrapped his arms around her feeling for a wire down her back.

Gitta shivered involuntarily, as his hands crawled down her back like a venomous snake stalking its prey. Not so much because she loathed him at that moment, but because to her surprise, she was succumbing to his animal magnetism. There was something primaeval and hypnotic about his presence in her space. Takis's hand reached her buttocks, his fingers taking their time as he pretended to search for that elusive wire.

"Your jeans are so tight, there is no room for a wire," mumbled Takis as he put his hands to her sides, making sure he touched her breasts. "Undo your shirt!" Demanded Takis.

"My shirt has no buttons, but if you move away, I'll pull my shirt up and give you a twirl so you can see I'm not wearing a wire," Gitta said in a strong voice, pushing away her feelings of having some attraction for this offensive man.

Takis moved away, a smirk still on his face. "I could help you with the shirt," he said without any conviction, realising that she had slapped him down. Luckily for Gitta, he was amused rather than angry, even though Gitta had been the first woman to have ever turned him away.

Gitta pulled up a shirt, giving a quick turn just long enough that Takis could see she wasn't wearing any wire. "Satisfied!" She said. "No wire. Now can we get down to some serious business? I want to start tonight not in the morning. So, are you going to tell me where I'm picking up the package?"

Without answering her, Takis stabbed the intercom button on the phone on his desk. "Dimitris, come out here and meet our new recruit. Bring the car keys, the cash, and one of our transit bags," Takis released the button, then turning to face Gitta, he said, "As this is your first run for us, you'll bring the package back here. It'll probably be a five-hour trip for you."

Dimitris talked Gitta through what she had to do. He explained that she was to drive to Delphi, where she would show the card that she had just been given to the night guard at the entrance. The guard was in the pay of the cartel, and she should hand him the envelope containing cash that Dimitri handed to her. Once inside, the Delphi site she should make her way to the Temple of Apollo, unlock the entrance with the key the guard would give her, and make her way to the inner chamber. Once there, she was to go to the wall covered in butterflies where she would find, amongst those that moved, twenty that were fixed. She was to remove those, place them carefully in the bag, and bring them here.

"I take it that the butterflies have cocaine in them," said Gitta.

"Yes, each butterfly has one hundred grams of cocaine."

"What's the street value?"

"Around three to four thousand dollars per butterfly. So, don't lose them," said Dimitris laughingly.

An hour later, Gitta was driving northwards out of Athens towards the imposing shadow of Mount Parnassus which guarded the western side of the great city and was the skiing playground of the rich and famous during the winter months. Even though it was late spring, there were still patches of snow on the peaks.

She felt anxious because she could see the flashes of lightning flickering along the peaks of the mountain. A storm was coming. She wondered if the reconnaissance drone, which was using the transmitter signal hidden in her necklace to follow her almost four thousand feet overhead, would be able to ride out a storm. It was a comfort to her that it was up there but although she wanted to ask the drone pilot that question, she couldn't because the Audi Quattro GT she was driving was probably bugged.

The road began a long sequence of twists and turns as it began its climb towards the summit of the mountain. There, Gitta planned to stop at the casino and retrieve a micro earpiece from the heel of her right shoe to hear whoever was sitting with the drone pilot. She hoped it would be Yannis or Chris.

As the Audi Quattro roared up the mountain, its sleek, red exterior glistening under the dark, ominous clouds, Gitta tightened her grip on the leather-wrapped steering wheel. She knew she was in for a treacherous journey up the mountain road, winding through nature's fury.

The rain poured relentlessly, drenching the road and reducing visibility to a mere few meters. Thunder roared above, and lightning streaked across the turbulent sky, illuminating the twisted path ahead. The Audi's powerful headlights cut through the darkness, piercing the veil of raindrops as Gitta cautiously pressed the accelerator.

The mountain road, already notorious for its sharp bends and precipitous drops, had become an even more daunting challenge. The Quattro's all-wheel-drive system provided confidence in the face of adversity, enabling optimal traction on the slick surface. The car's tyres gripped the wet asphalt, struggling against the torrential downpour.

With each twist and turn, Gitta wrestled with the steering wheel, her skills tested to the limit. The Audi Quattro's advanced suspension system absorbed the undulations of the road, offering stability and control amidst the chaos.

As the elevation increased, the wind intensified, whipping against the Audi's streamlined body. Gusts threatened to push the car off course, but the Quattro's aerodynamic design and advanced stability control system countered the forces, keeping it firmly planted on the road.

Suddenly, a flash flood cascaded down the mountainside, partially submerging the road ahead. Gitta had to make a split-second decision. Braving the perilous current, she accelerated, pushing the Audi through the rushing water with determination and courage. The Quattro's elevated ground clearance ensured it stayed above the rising flood, surging forward undeterred.

The storm raged on, unleashing its full fury upon the mountain road. But the Audi Quattro, with its intelligent drivetrain and engineering excellence, proved to be an indomitable force. The car navigated the treacherous bends and steep inclines with a balance of power and control, a testament to its legendary handling capabilities.

Finally, as the storm began to subside and the road straightened out, Gitta let out a breath of relief. She had conquered nature's wrath, emerging victorious from the tumultuous journey up the mountain. She was safe and filled with a sense of exhilaration. She continued along the now less twisty road, ready to face the next adventure that awaited her a thousand feet below in Delphi itself. But first the casino stop, and a mug of coffee.

Chapter 8

Three hours and ten minutes after leaving Athens, Gitta guided the Quattro into a parking space outside the Parnassus Casino near the peak of the mountain. As the engine roared to a halt, she swiftly emerged from her car, her heart pounding with a mix of urgency and fear. Ignoring the curious glances of passers-by, she sprinted towards the towering entrance of the bustling Regency Casino.

Unlike the casino in Monte Carlo which was renowned for its luxurious and sophisticated ambience, exuding an elegant and refined atmosphere, attracting a more upscale clientele, the Regency offered a vibrant and energetic atmosphere, with an ambience which was lively, bustling, and filled with excitement, designed to create an immersive and entertaining experience for visitors. Bright lights, loud music, and flashy displays contributed to the energetic atmosphere that catered to a more diverse range of visitors.

Its interior design didn't display the classic and opulent interior design of Monte Carlo, with its architecture and decor features in intricate details, presenting grand chandeliers, plush carpets, and rich colours, in a style of timeless elegance and refinement, understated, with an emphasis on quality and artisanry.

Her high heels clicked against the pavement as she weaved through the crowd, her determined gaze fixed on her destination: the coffee bar. Pushing open the glass doors, she entered the aromatic haven and exhaled a sigh of relief.

Taking a moment to compose herself, she approached the counter.

"ἐναν ελληνικὀ καφἐ παρακαλὠ," she said placing an order for a Greek coffee, her voice betraying a hint of unease. "Triple and in a mug," she added as an afterthought.

As the barista skilfully prepared her drink, she discreetly scanned her surroundings, several men were eying her up and down, that was until their spouses angrily said something. Slowly, she slid her hand into the depths of her shoe, feeling the concealed compartment hidden within the heel. With a delicate touch, she retrieved an inconspicuous earpiece, obscured from prying eyes.

Securing the earpiece in her ear, she activated the hidden microphone nestled within her necklace. The barista placed her Greek coffee on the counter.

"Thank you," said Gitta, handing over some cash. "Keep the change." Hurriedly, Gitta picked her coffee up and headed for a quiet corner of the café. The less she said the less likely that anyone would remember her - one of the tricks of her trade - mind you giving the barista too much tip was not a good idea either, he probably would remember her now. She realised that in her anxious state, it was a silly mistake.

"Hello." Her voice quivered slightly as she activated the transmitter on her necklace. "Who is listening?"

"It's Chris, how are you getting on? Where are you?" Asked Chris in a tone that conveyed his anxiousness.

"Hello Chris, are you the only person listening in?"

"At the moment, yes," answered Chris. "But both Yannis and Alex can listen in whenever they want to. Do you want me to get them patched in?

"No!" Gitta almost shouted. She looked around the casino afraid that someone might have overheard. "Sorry, Chris, but I'm very nervous at the moment, and I really don't want Alex to hear what I have to say. He worries far too much. I don't mind if Yannis gets patched in though."

"You sound as though you've had a really rough day. Has it been tough?"

"I'm scared, Chris," admitted Gitta. "Today, I met the second in command of the cartel. Takis Penza. He is both the most mesmerising man I have ever met but also the most menacing in every move and every glance he makes."

"Do you want to give up? You can, you know. I can get another agent, but they won't be half as good as you are." Chris knew that she wouldn't back out now. She was stubborn and even if it meant that she might not make it out alive, she would stick with it.

"No, Chris I'm still in the game. It's just that I feel dirty, not soiled and I can't read this man. He is an expert manipulator."

"You have to stay focussed, Gitta, it's the only way you are going to help take down the cartel."

"I know, Chris, but this is going to be my last gig whatever the outcome. Whether I come out alive or dead it'll definitely be my final operation," said Gitta emphatically.

"You can do what you like once this is over, Gitta, and what's more, Alex would be so happy if you retired from the CIA. Now tell me, where you are and where you are going."

Gitta proceeded to relate the events of the day. She told Chris about her meeting with Takis Penza and the instructions she had been given about what to do when she arrived in Delphi. While she related her journey up the mountain, she heard several sharp intakes of breath from Chris.

"I don't blame you for taking a rest at the casino," Chris said. "That drive sounded horrendous. Should be okay for the drive down to Delphi through, no heavy downpours, just the occasional shower. How long do you think it'll take to the gates of Delphi?"

"My sat-nav says forty-five minutes, should get there just after one-thirty this morning," said Gitta as she finished off her coffee and contemplated ordering a second one. She decided against it even though she was tired, and the caffeine would have been welcome, it was too risky to engage the barista a second time.

"So," said Chris. "We haven't much time to get some things in motion. I'm going to ask my people to get hold of Yannis and tell him to get some EKAM agents up there, as well as techies to try and hack into the security cameras in the Delphi complex."

"They'll have to be careful. We don't want them to do anything that might make the cartel suspicious, do we?"

"No, of course not but that means that you will have more responsibility in trying to find out how the cocaine gets into the butterflies," warned Chris. "The cartel must have some sort of surveillance system inside the Temple of Apollo."

"And they have to control it tightly," said Gitta. "Someone must put the cocaine into each false butterfly, and then place them on the wall of butterflies."

Chris nodded his head as one of his assistants slid a piece of paper onto his desk.

"I doubt whether they fill the butterflies inside the temple, they'd never have enough time. Unless of course, it is all done overnight when the tourists have left the Delphi complex," he said.

"And we don't know how many of the night or day staff are in the cartel's pay," said Gitta."

"No, we don't," agreed Chris. "Looks like we're in luck. One of my people has just tracked Yannis down. He is in the town of Delphi with his nephew who apparently discovered that three deaths attributed to suicides, were, in fact, murders. All three were tourists, two died in the Temple of Apollo and the third died within one hundred metres of the temple."

"The work of the cartel?"

"Probably, as all three seemed to have overdosed on cocaine."

"If that's the case they must have seen something which they shouldn't have. Reinforce your premise that the cartel has more than one person on their books in the complex." Gitta was not happy. This operation was getting more dangerous by the minute.

Chris sensed her discomfort, as her case officer, it was his responsibility to boost her up a little otherwise, she'd make a mistake. She was a brilliant agent with an eye for detail and was usually ice-cold in her approach to her tradecraft.

"Gitta we've got your back twenty-four-seven, you'll have a drone overhead to allow us to keep an eye out for you. Yannis and a squad of men will be as close as possible without being detected, ready to pull you out if something goes wrong. The only time you will be blind to us is when you collect the cocaine from the Temple of Apollo. In there, maintain a high level of concentration and vigilance and you'll be fine."

Gitta smiled to herself as Chris spoke. She could sense that he needed her to succeed however risky the mission was, but he was torn by his friendship with Alex and his guilty conscious because he had promised Alex that she would come safely home. Alex must be having kittens, she thought, but she knew he would immerse himself in his work and try not to think about her.

"I won't let you down, don't worry," reassured Gitta. "Now I need to get going, Chris, can't keep my date waiting." She giggled softly into her microphone.

Chris allowed himself a nervous laugh, "Good luck, Gitta."

Gitta picked up her bag and then strode purposely towards the entrance of the casino. Once outside, she headed for her car, got in, switched on, gunned the engine, and reversed out of the parking space. She turned the car towards the road down to Delphi and floored the accelerator.

Behind her, a black Mercedes glided out of its parking bay and followed her towards Delphi. Its driver listened to the instructions being given to him over his car phone – instructions that Gitta would not have wanted to hear.

Chapter 9

Ten minutes after leaving the Regency car park, Gitta noticed that a car was behind her. If it hadn't been pitch-black but daylight, she would never have noticed it because the road down the mountain had almost as many curves as the road up to the casino. But, at night, the headlights could be seen several bends behind.

Seeing the headlights had disturbed the thoughts she was having about her son. She missed him almost as much as she missed his father. 'What if something happened to her, would Alex be able to cope with looking after him?' When her son was born, she named him Alex in memory of the man she had an affair with during the Gladio Protocol operation, thinking she would never see him again.

But, now that she and Alex were married, she found it too American to have a son with the same name as his father. Even Alex had Americanised his name from Alexandros, which was what his relatives called him, to Alex. She made a note to talk to him as soon as this operation was over about changing their son's name from Alex Junior to Alexander, the English equivalent of Alexandros.

The flash of headlights in her rear-view mirror alerted her to the fact that a car was following her.

"Chris! Are you still there?"

"Yes, I'm here. We saw from the drone that a car followed you out of the car park at the casino. We said nothing in case it was a false alarm, but the car has been gaining on you little by little. We are dealing with a skilled driver."

"Is the car a danger to me?" Asked Gitta.

"I'm afraid so," confirmed Chris. "Even before you had pulled out of your parking space the barista had followed you out and gone to the black Mercedes which was following you."

"Too much change and he probably noticed I was talking to the ether. They took my phone away, so he knew I was not talking on a phone. Sorry Chris, I don't normally make those elementary mistakes. What do you want me to do?"

"I want you to concentrate on the mission and cut out these out-of-character mistakes, you can't afford any mistakes from now on. We'll deal with the black car and make it look like an accident. One of Yannis's EKAM snipers is on his way up from Delphi on a motorbike. At his and your closing speed, you'll pass his firing position in ten minutes. The plan is to shoot out two tyres causing the Mercedes to crash into the retaining barriers and fall into the ravine below that point in the road."

"Should I maintain current speed?"

"Yes, we don't want the driver of the Mercedes getting suspicious at all," explained Chris. "Now please remember what we said, one hundred per cent concentration, no more slips." Although he didn't show it, Chris was angry with Gitta. She had made not one but two elementary errors, and if they had not had a drone up, she would probably not have made it to the gates of Delphi.

Chris was also angry with himself because he should have warned Gitta that there was a danger that as it was her first run for the cartel, they would have someone keeping a close eye on her. Still, that didn't really excuse her as she was a very experienced agent. He feared however that being married and having a young son had softened her. He prayed he would be proven wrong.

He knew that the driver had not made a phone call because the drone didn't pick up a signal emanating from the car. The same could be said for the barista also unless he had used a landline. However, Chris was fairly confident that neither of them had called to report any suspicions they might have on Gitta. That was good. Hopefully, if the sniper were successful, the crash would be reported as an accident. On his monitor, the feed from the drone showed that the black car was closer to Gitta, as it continued its strategy of closing the gap at a steady pace. He sat back and watched as the scenario played out in front of him.

Almost a kilometre behind Gitta on a dark deserted stretch of winding road, the stage was set. In the black of night with just twin beams of brilliant light cutting through the darkness, the black car prowled like a predator, stealthily gaining ground on the white car up ahead.

Gitta felt a tingling sensation at the back of her neck, an inexplicable feeling that she was being watched. Her instincts heightened, and she checked the rear-view mirror, only to see the silhouette of the approaching black car growing more distinct as it crept closer.

The black car seemed to move with calculated precision, mirroring Gitta's every turn and speed adjustment. As if playing a cat-and-mouse game, it seemed to momentarily slow down whenever Gitta glanced in her rear-view mirror, only to pick up the pace again as she returned her attention to the road ahead. This peculiar dance between the two vehicles set an eerie atmosphere, evoking images of a relentless predator stalking its prey.

In the darkness, the black car seemed to grow larger, its presence dominating Gitta's rear-view mirror; and her imagination began to play tricks on her, as she began to see the black car's grille as sharp teeth ready to pounce.

With no other vehicles in sight and no safe places to seek refuge, Gitta had to trust that Chris and his sniper would do their job. A shiver ran down her spine, as she approached the area where the sniper would be waiting. She looked in her rear-view mirror, the headlights were much nearer now.

Suddenly, the twin headlights started to fishtail along the road as the first of the sniper's bullets struck the off-side rear tyre. *Sniper* said Gitta to herself. Then, the headlights shone vertically upwards seconds after the second bullet struck the front near-side tyre causing the front of the car to hit the barrier. For a moment, the car seemed to fly horizontally, its twin beams lighting up the mountainside on the opposite side of the ravine, then slowly inexorably gravity took over and the car's bonnet started to tip down before plunging to the bottom of the ravine five hundred metres below.

Gitta heaved a sigh of relief. "Thank you, Chris."

"Perfect," uttered Chris. "Thank you, sniper. Okay, Gitta you've got a worry-free journey now to the gates of Delphi. I know they have taken your phone so one of Yannis's men is going to leave a bodycam under the bush to the right of the entrance to the temple. If you can retrieve it safely, do it. If not, it's not a problem."

"Okay, Chris. Don't worry I'll be fine from now on and please don't mention any of this to Alex."

"I won't, good luck."

Up at the casino Regency, the barista was frantically trying to get hold of the driver of the black Mercedes. He had started to feel that it was a mistake to have involved their respective bosses in the cartel. He wanted to tell the driver that he was going to call his boss, but the phone was dead, with no ring tone and no voicemail. Either, the phone had been turned off, but then there would have been voicemail, or the unthinkable had happened – there had been an accident and the phone had been damaged. If that were the case, he would not call his boss because he would be blamed and who knew, maybe punished. No, best to keep quiet.

That decision played into Gitta's hands because now the cartel would not learn of the accident, and nor would they hear about her secretive conversation in the ether at the casino. Of course, neither Gitta nor Chris knew of the barista's decision so they both were still slightly anxious, but it was out of their hands now and they had to carry through their plans.

Back at drone headquarters, Chris was studying the video feed from the drone which was showing the wreckage of a burning car at the bottom of the ravine. Satisfied that any evidence of the tyres being shot out would be obliterated by the flames, Chris asked the drone pilot to continue following Gitta's car. Two minutes later, Chris's monitor showed the car rounding the final bend before Delphi and Gitta brought it to a stop at the gates.

"Game on," said Chris to no one in particular.

Chapter 10

With the rain now long gone, carried on the wind by the dark clouds that had trapped Gitta in their embrace on her journey up the mountain, the clear skies revealed the moonlight casting an ethereal glow over the ancient site of Delphi.

Gitta approached the mystical gates in her Audi Quattro. The engine's soft purr seemed to harmonize with the whispers of history that surrounded her. She had done her best to ingratiate herself with the cartel, earning their trust, and now, the time had come to take the next perilous step.

The imposing guard, a man with a friendly countenance but steely blue eyes, stepped forward to inspect her approach. Gitta's heart raced, but her composure remained unwavering. She handed over the cartel's emblematic card, her badge of entry into their inner sanctum. The guard's eyes flickered over the emblem, and a glimmer of recognition danced across his face. Satisfied, he motioned for her to proceed, his movements deliberate, betraying the secretive dealings he was a part of.

With her entry granted, Gitta was led further into the darkness, away from the prying eyes of any casual observer driving passed the site. The cobbled path beneath her feet seemed to vibrate with history, each step echoing the footsteps of those who had gone before her. The scent of ancient stones and sacred incense enveloped her, evoking a sense of reverence and trepidation.

As they approached the Temple of Apollo, the grandeur of the structure took Gitta's breath away. She had read that the temple had been renovated but she was not expecting to see a building replicating the original. Moonbeams danced across the marble columns, creating an otherworldly spectacle. The guard produced a large padlock key from his pocket, it was rather plain for a key that used to open such a magnificent building. Without a word, he handed it to her, and Gitta accepted it with a nod, hiding her anxiousness behind a stoic facade.

She was not alone in this clandestine affair. In the shadows, Yannis and some of his elite EKAM team observed every move she made, their well-honed instincts attuned to any potential threat. They had become her silent guardians, ready to intervene if the situation turned dangerous. She knew the drone was above her somewhere, another silent guardian, ready to protect her if need be.

The guard was walking away returning to his guard post at the entrance to the site. She waited a few seconds until he was out of sight in the darkness, and then she quickly walked to the bush where the bodycam was hidden. It was there as promised, tucked behind a large stem. She slipped it into her bag before heading to the main door of the temple.

Yannis's eyes narrowed as she did this, his gaze unwavering as he followed her every step, a mix of admiration and concern for her braveness.

With the key clutched firmly in her hand, Gitta again approached the ancient door. The centuries-old wood seemed to breathe, bearing witness to countless secrets and ceremonies. As she inserted the key and turned it, the mechanism creaked to life, and the door opened, revealing the outer chamber lit by the soft glow of candles around the walls.

Without hesitation, she stepped inside, her heart pounding with anticipation. This was her moment; the mission hinged on her every move. She was on her own now, but she knew that in the darkness, she had unseen allies watching her back. But could they protect her in the shadows which embraced her as she looked around?

Gitta shut the door behind her, then looked around to see if any security cameras were in the room. She spotted four, but there were no red lights on them to indicate they were working. She sat down on one of the benches that were available for tired visitors, leaned down, and fiddled with one of her shoes. She could talk now without the cameras noticing.

"Are you still there, Chris?" Gitta whispered hoping that Chris would hear her.

"Yes, what is it?"

"There are four cameras in this outer chamber as far as I can see, and none of them has a red indicator light visible, so I don't know if they are working or not."

"We are about to hack into them as we speak. Hold on for a moment."

Gitta sat back relieved. She had been worried that the communications wouldn't work in the temple and anxious about not being able to wear the body cam.

"We're in!" exclaimed Chris. "We're going to start running a loop of you sitting where you are now. That will give you enough time to strap on your body cam and give us a tour of the outer chamber. I'll tell you when the loop is ready. So, sit back and close your eyes as if you are napping, and don't talk till I give you the go-ahead."

Gitta sat back and closed her eyes. She could have fallen asleep right there, the soft lighting, and the tinkle of falling water coming from the inner chamber, were all designed to give a feeling of peace and contentment. Instead, Gitta's thoughts returned to her son. He was now nine years old and like her had blonde hair and green eyes. His nose was Alex's, a little too big but cute. She felt proud that she and Alex had brought him up to be a nice boy, clever too, and very competitive, just like his mother. Her musings were disturbed by Chris's voice.

"Okay, Gitta, the feeds from the cameras are in a loop. You have ten minutes to give us the body-cam tour. Any more than that might cause whoever is monitoring the camera to become suspicious."

Behind the revolving wall of butterflies in the inner chamber, two of the cartel's gang members were monitoring the cameras from both the inner and outer chambers. Unusually, the two were siblings, each one meaner than the other. They had been with the cartel for ten years but were only keepers of the secrets of the Golden Triangle for the last two years. Such were their responsibilities, they reported directly to Kappa, the cartel's boss.

The brother, called Raul (knuckles) Konstantinos, wore a perpetual scowl that etched deep lines across his rugged face, hinting at a life marked by violence. His closely cropped black hair, peppered with hints of grey, framed a forehead bearing a few faint scars from past encounters. His pale blue eyes, though often bloodshot from long nights of questionable activities, held a cold intensity that sent shivers down spines.

Raul's attire reflected his street-hardened persona. He favoured dark, worn-out jeans that cling to his powerful thighs, a testament to his brawny build. His arms, perpetually inked with an assortment of tattoos representing his allegiance to the cartel, peeked out from beneath the sleeves of a sleeveless black leather jacket. Fingerless gloves revealed knuckles that bore the marks of countless brawls. A gold chain dangled around his neck, punctuating his attire with a hint of ostentation.

His demeanour is one of controlled aggression. His walk was deliberate, almost a predatory swagger, exuding an aura that warned others to keep their distance. Raul's speech was laced with street slang, his voice had a low growl that rarely rose above a menacing whisper. Though he rarely smiled, his lips curled into a cruel grin when intimidation was called for. Standing at a solid five-foot ten inches, his compact frame brimming with muscle and menace was perfect for the role he performed in the organisation.

Raul's sister was equally as menacing as her brother. Standing at a slightly shorter five-foot-seven inches, her lithe frame belying the lethal force she embodied. She had an exotic allure, with a caramel complexion that hinted at her mixed heritage. Her piercing emerald eyes held a feral intensity, often set beneath a raised eyebrow that gave her an air of perpetual challenge. Her long, raven-black hair which cascaded down her back, was occasionally pulled back into a fierce ponytail for practicality.

Her wardrobe was an eclectic mix of street chic and practicality. She favoured form-fitting black leather pants that allowed for ease of movement, while a sleeveless black tank top highlighted the intricate tattoos that wound around her arms, bearing symbols of her loyalty to the gang. A collection of silver piercings glinted from her ears and nose, lending her an air of rebellious nonconformity.

Her body language exuded a blend of confidence and unpredictability. She moved with an almost feline grace, a coiled spring ready to pounce at a moment's notice. Mia's speech was sharp and deliberate, her voice holding an underlying hint of danger. A mischievous smirk often graced her lips, hinting at a penchant for sadistic pleasure in the chaos she created.

"What the hell is she doing?" said Raul, his perpetual scowl etching deep lines across his rugged face. "First, she falls asleep and now she is just sitting staring at the wall in front of her."

"How the fuck would I know?" answered Mia. "And what does it matter as long as she collects that white powder from the other side of this wall," she said fingering the silver piercings on her nose.

Meanwhile, unseen by Raul and Mia, Gitta had donned her body cam and was giving Chris a tour of the outer chamber. The room was filled with the smell of burning incense coming from several gold incense bowls dotted around the chamber. The walls held several murals depicting hunters in ancient times, and between the murals were plinths with statues of men, women and children making offerings to the gods. The walls were also adorned with inscriptions and dedications in the form of smaller sculptures, plaques, and painted depictions of significant events or personal stories. Gitta felt that she had stepped back in time almost three thousand years, such was its authenticity.

However, as far as Chris and Gitta could tell there was nothing in this chamber with any connection to the cartel whatsoever.

"Right, Gitta, sit down again on the same bench and stare straight ahead. My guys will take the cameras out of their loops back to real-time; then once it's in real-time you can go into the inner chamber. It will be too suspicious to have you sitting still again, immediately after you enter the chamber, we will hack into the cameras and view the room through the live feed for a while. Not as detailed as your bodycam, but at least we will have you in sight. When you are packing your bag with the white stuff, sit on the floor, back to the wall, and we'll freeze the feed into a loop."

Gitta sat down on the bench she had used before. She tried to get as near as possible to the position she was in when the camera started looping. In the room behind the revolving wall, both Raul and Mia noticed a slight judder on their monitors as the feed switched from loop to real-time. So slight they thought nothing of it.

"Hey, she's woken up, bro," exclaimed Mia.

"About bloody time, I hope she hurries up and we can get some kip. Mind you, she's a looker, isn't she, Mia?"

"Mm, not bad," agreed Mia, who wasn't averse to dating women occasionally.

Gitta stepped into the inner chamber. What she saw took her breath away and she almost spoke to Chris in her amazement. What she saw was that instead of the fissure, with the bronze tripod, on which the priestess Pythia, the Oracle, would have sat and delivered prophecies, there was a spring with water bubbling up into a small pool covered in lilies. A replica of the bronze tripod was astride the spring and Gitta mused that they must have covered the original fissure for safety reasons. The aroma of incense assailed her nostrils which together with the low lighting curated to inspire a sense of awe and reverence. Then she spied the wall of butterflies at the far end of the inner chamber.

She walked over and stood below them. Yes, she could see it now, not all the butterflies were using their wings, and there were fifty-plus static ones. She reached up to the one nearest to her, took it down and studied it. She was impatient to get the bodycam out of her bag and show Chris the butterfly wall in detail. But she knew she couldn't, not without whoever was monitoring the cameras, detecting what she was doing.

Gitta noticed that the butterfly she had picked from the wall was made of porcelain and had a ridge the length of its body. On further examination, she found a small catch which, when released, allowed the top part of the body to be separated from the bottom half. The inside of the lower half was filled with white powder. My god, thought Gitta, this must have a street value of over three thousand dollars. So, the wall had a street value of approximately one hundred and fifty thousand dollars, she figured.

Heeding Chris's instructions, Gitta picked fifty porcelain butterflies off the wall and sat on the floor with her back to the wall, ready to place each one into the bag the cartel had given her.

"Good," said Chris. "We are going to take the cameras out of real-time and into a loop. We'll only do it for a couple of minutes to avoid suspicion. Keep still for a moment."

Gitta sat where she was and closed her eyes. Ten seconds later, she heard Chris. "Okay put your bodycam on and show us that wall."

With her bodycam on, Gitta walked slowly across the length of the wall and back again, trying to make sure that she captured all the butterflies as well as the entire wall. Like Chris, she was studying the wall very carefully.

"Chris, the operation of collecting cocaine from this wall doesn't strike me as being efficient at all. Someone must put those butterflies up on the wall. Doesn't make sense, why bring them into this building? Why not just bypass the building altogether?"

"I agree," concurred Chris. "It doesn't make sense at all. Time to sit down again. We need to get the cameras back to real-time."

Behind the wall, both Mia and Raul were staring intently at their monitors.

"Damn it! She's fallen asleep again," complained Raul. "I want to get back to Aegina before morning, at this rate, it will be light by the time she has finished."

"She looks so beautiful sitting there against the wall," murmured Mia. "I think I'm falling in love, bro."

"Shut up sis! Concentrate on the business at hand."

"She's moving!" exclaimed Mia.

"Did you notice that?" said Raul.

"What?"

"The video jumped again," said Raul exasperatedly. "Look she is in a slightly different position."

"Well, I'll be damned," exclaimed Mia as she played a recording of the previous few minutes of camera feed. "What the hell!"

Now, the real-time feeds showed Gitta collecting the cocaine-filled butterflies and placing them carefully in the bag. She was eager now to get on the road back to Athens with her contraband. Even though she kept telling herself that she was on the right side of the law, she was still nervous about being stopped by the police.

With a sigh of relief, Gitta carefully put the last of the fifty butterflies into her bag. She stood up took one last look around then headed for the outer chamber and the exit door to the temple.

Chris watched on the hacked feed coming into his monitor, as Gitta walked with an easy manner towards the door to the outer chamber. Suddenly, he saw Gitta stop and then turn around.

"Switch cameras!" he shouted into his mic. A worried frown creased his forehead.

His monitor now revealed the shocking spectacle that Gitta was staring at. The wall of butterflies had totally disappeared and in its place was a black space two metres high and ten metres long. Standing in front of this space were Raul and Mia both with their handguns pointing at Gitta.

Chapter 11

The phone by Alex's bed vibrated loudly as it danced its way across his bedside table. Struggling to wake up, Alex looked at the clock dial projected on his ceiling. Gitta was into her tech gadgets.

"Saves rolling over with blurry eyes to look at a clock with a tiny face," she told Alex one morning.

The time was six in the morning. Now Alex was starting to feel a little anxious. He reached for the dancing phone. On the phone's display was the name Chris. Alex hit the green button.

"Hello Chris, is there anything wrong?" Each of Alex's words tumbled out of his mouth in rapid succession.

"Don't panic, Alex!" Chris commanded. "Now calm down and listen."

Okay, okay, I'm calm now. Go ahead."

"I've just conferenced Kaliope and Yannis into our call, Alex."

Once pleasantries had been exchanged and the moaning about the lateness of the hour, Chris proceeded.

Gitta met with the cartel's number two in a house in Athens. She was given instructions to collect an amount of cocaine from of all places Delphi."

"Delphi!" exclaimed Alex. "Village or ancient site?"

"Site, the ancient Temple of Apollo to be precise."

"And did she manage to get the cocaine back?"

"Well, no, there is a problem," conceded Chris.

Chris then related to them the events of the previous evening. He reminded them that everything had been put in place to protect Gitta. The drone, their eye in the sky, Yannis and his men hidden in the trees near the temple itself. He told them about the hacking of the cameras inside the temple and the trick they used to allow Gitta to use the bodycam. Chris admitted that it was the switch from the static view back to the real-time view wasn't as seamless as they had hoped and that had caused the two cartel members to become suspicious.

"So, the last thing you saw on the camera inside the inner chamber was an empty space where the butterfly wall had been and a man and a woman aiming their pistols at Gitta," said Kaliope.

"That's when me and my men went in," explained Yannis, joining the conversation. "We, ourselves, were baffled but soon realized that there was none. We pondered various possibilities - could Gitta have vanished through a hidden passageway? Or perhaps, she was held captive within these hallowed walls by the two cartel members?"

"What about a revolving wall?" Chris suggested. "The last we saw through the camera was an empty space where the butterfly wall had been. I recall reading about similar mechanisms used to conceal secret areas. Maybe Gitta was taken through this hidden doorway."

Intrigued by Chris's suggestion, Kaliope countered with an alternative theory - an underground tunnel. She remembered myths passed down through generations, and whispered about hidden passages beneath ancient temples. These tunnels were said to connect sacred sites, carrying a mysterious energy between them.

"There is a myth intertwining with our present situation," revealed Kaliope. She shared her newfound insight with Chris and Alex, "It's the legend of the Golden Triangle of Energy. According to myth, Delphi, Milos, and Aegina were known as the three corners of this mystical triangle. The temple Yannis stands within is situated at one corner - Delphi – apparently, harbouring unimaginable powers fuelled by their convergence."

With this newfound knowledge hanging in the air like a whisper from ages past, Chris, Alex, and Yannis were speechless for a moment before realizing that their quest for answers might lie beyond conventional explanations. But, of the three, Chris was the doubtful one. His knowledge of Greek mythology was weak.

"Are you trying to tell me that there is something mystical about the Temple of Apollo which had the power to transport Gitta to god knows where?" said Chris, his voice sounding exasperated and at the same time frustrated. "Come on, people, we're in the twenty-first century, aren't we?"

"Aegina and Milos," said Kaliope.

"Say again," said Chris.

"Not anywhere, but to either Aegina or Milos," stated Kaliope.

"Come on, are you serious?" irritation clear in Chris's voice. "You are talking about ancient myths instead of modern detection methodology."

"Except," chimed in Yannis. "My men have scoured the area around the temple and also checked every inch of the exterior of the building. No entryway in or out was detected. Gitta must still be inside."

Alex who had been quiet up to that point decided to join the debate. "Yannis, have you kept men on guard inside the temple?"

"Yes, Alex, so they could not have taken Gitta out through the front entrance while we were distracted outside."

"Then we should break through the butterfly wall. She must be held hostage in whatever space lies behind that wall."

"And if she is not?" questioned Kaliope.

Chris answered, "There is no concrete scientific evidence supporting the existence of mystical powers in the so-called

Golden Triangle, which comprises ancient Delphi, Aegina Island, and Milos Island. My experience as a CIA field agent has taught me to rely on concrete evidence and logic, not on myths and legends. People have disappeared or met unfortunate fates in various places around the world, often due to natural or man-made causes. Gitta's disappearance should be treated as a missing persons case, and we should focus on practical investigation methods."

"I appreciate your scepticism, Chris, but history is filled with mysteries and unexplained phenomena. The Golden Triangle has long been associated with ancient Greek legends and myths, suggesting a hidden power," said Kaliope.

"Yes, I agree with Kaliope," said Alex. "The ancient Greeks believed that Delphi was the centre of the world and that the Oracle of Delphi could predict the future. It's possible that this triangle holds ancient secrets we've yet to discover. Perhaps Gitta's disappearance is connected to these mystical forces."

"I have to say that there is something eerie about your fascination with the Golden Triangle, darling," declared Yannis.

Both he and Kaliope often resorted to endearments in public and professional situations now that everyone knew of their relationship.

"She believes in its mystical powers and perhaps that belief together with her encounter with Phobia, the woman who owns the bakers' shop on the island of Milos, has drawn her to the possibility of some ancient mystery being harnessed by the drug cartel. Maybe there's some truth to it, something beyond our understanding. I ask you all to consider all possibilities, not just the logical ones."

Chris could not be deterred from his pragmatism refusing to believe that there was anything magical going on. He said, "I understand your concern, Kaliope, and I'm deeply sorry for Gitta's disappearance. However, our job as investigators is to follow the evidence, and until we have any concrete leads suggesting mystical involvement, we must treat this case like any other. The search for Gitta is our top priority, and we'll explore all avenues, including those related to the Golden Triangle. First, we must get through that butterfly wall. Yannis, could you get your demolition experts to assess how it can be done without bringing the whole building down?"

Yes, Chris, I'm ahead of you on that. They are already on their way; ETA is an hour from now."

"Good man," acknowledged Chris. "I presume you'll need to get permission to do this from your culture minister, Alex. Or at least brief her on what we are planning to do. What's her name?"

"Aliki Traka," answered Alex.

"Right," said Chris. "I remember now. Listen, I've got a job for you and Kaliope. The reconnaissance drone on Milos has spotted that dreadful woman who owns the bakery going down to Adamantas, where the entrance to the catacombs is. She was out of sight for several hours before reappearing, then tracked back to the bakery in the village. Could you both get over to Milos,

I'll send a helicopter over to the Mega Maximo's landing pad. All you need to do is watch the feed from the drone. Kaliope can you arrange for the feed to be patched to yours and Alex's phone, please?"

"Of course, but won't Alex be recognised? After all, he is the Prime Minister of this country," said Kaliope sounding worried for Alex.

"No, because Phobia only leaves the bakery in the early hours of the morning, so it will be dark and there's no need to get close because you will use the drone's feed to follow her," said Chris reassuringly.

"Thanks, Chris," said Alex. "A bit of safe action will take my mind off thoughts of Gitta and her whereabouts."

Chris was happy that something was happening; a plan was taking shape and he could rely on his friends. They were now all united by curiosity and armed with the new knowledge of the Golden Triangle, they all vowed to themselves, to delve deeper into the secrets hidden within the temple walls and the catacombs of Milos.

Could there also be a connection to all this on Aegina Island? mused Chris to himself. He hadn't mentioned to the others that the autopsy of poor Petros had revealed that he had vegetation spores in his clothes that were ingenious to Aegina alone. That was where he was heading. He didn't want to admit it, but could Kaliope be right, and the ancient myth of the Golden Triangle had somehow magically entwined itself into the present day? So undeterred by the mysterious disappearance of Gitta, they embark on a journey that would severely test their own beliefs and understanding of the world around them.

Little did they know that the endeavour they were embarking on would amplify their connection to the ancient energy flowing through them, unravelling truths they never thought possible and leading them closer to unveiling not only Gitta's fate but a realm where myths and reality intertwine with the disappearance of Gitta.

We gathered in the dimly lit inner chamber, surrounded by ancient artefacts and statues, pondering over the enigma that was before us. We meticulously searched the inside walls for any possible exit.

Chapter 12

In the peaceful town of Delphi, renowned archaeologist and historian, Vangelis Diamantis was with Yannis and his men inside the Temple of Apollo. They all found themselves puzzled by the baffling mystery. One minute, Gitta, a brilliant field agent and their colleague, was inside the sacred Temple of Apollo, and the next she had vanished without a trace. Perplexed by this enigma, Yannis and Vangelis set out on a journey to unravel the truth behind Gitta's sudden disappearance.

Examining the ancient temple's architecture meticulously, they grew increasingly convinced that there was no visible exit from within its walls. Their minds raced with possibilities: could Gitta have been held captive inside a secret chamber concealed by the revolving wall? Or perhaps there was an inconspicuous underground tunnel that nobody knew about?

Deep in their discussion about these options, Vangelis, a wise local historian as well as a renowned archaeologist, suddenly referred to an old myth - the fabled Golden Triangle of Energy. He confirmed what Kaliope had said. According to legend, Delphi, Milos, and Aegina represented the mystical corners of this triangle.

Vangelis recollected how Delphi was believed to possess extraordinary powers of transformation and enlightenment. Was it possible that Gitta had stumbled upon these hidden forces within the temple? Could she have unlocked some deeper connection to this legendary energy? The idea both intrigued and daunted Yannis and Vangelis as they contemplated the implications.

The demolition experts studied the butterfly wall very carefully, using instruments to determine how thick the stone wall was, and to assess that if it were destroyed, would it compromise the integrity of the whole structure. After careful consideration, they reluctantly had to inform Yannis that it was too dangerous to destroy the wall using explosives. It was three metres thick and would need a large charge to bring it down. But, during their examination of the wall they had detected a small box-shaped area, about head height, that was hollow. It was possible that this housed the controls that opened and shut the wall from the public area.

Yannis instructed one of his officers to try to discover how to access the box. It wasn't too long before the officer had detected a small depression in the stone that if depressed, sprung open a small door, revealing two square buttons, one green and one red. Yannis immediately ordered the twelve officers and men he had at his disposal to face the wall with guns at the ready.

The green button was pressed and the wall silently, like an ancient behemoth, swung on its centre axis, stopping when it was at a ninety-degree angle to its original position. Yannis's men raised their machine guns pointing them into the dark space beyond the wall. Yannis ordered them to step into the room, six passed on one side of the blank side of the wall and six passed on the now visible butterfly side of the wall. In unison, they crossed the threshold, and immediately the room beyond was flooded with light turned on by a motion detector triggered by their movement.

The square room was empty except for three computer monitors. One of them was displaying the room they were in, fed from a camera in the far corner of the room. The second monitor was displaying the inner chamber they had just come from. The third monitor displayed an office with a tall imposing man with raven hair standing behind a desk on which was a set of six throwing knives. The man spoke, his voice full of authority but at the same time a menace.

"Good morning, gentlemen, welcome to the last few days of your life."

"Kappa," said Yannis under his breath, a brief tremble of fear surged through his body before his training brought his emotions under control. He forced himself to breathe slowly, calming his body down.

"You're under arrest, Kappa," said Yannis with all the authority he could muster.

"Come and arrest me then," said Kappa laughing. "Look around you are shut in."

Yannis looked around, they were surrounded by four empty walls. The place they had just entered the room from was now a blank wall. Shit! thought Yannis, the damn wall has closed, and we never heard a thing.

Kappa was laughing at the sight of their surprised faces. "I'm leaving you for a few hours, I'm quite busy today. Don't go anywhere!" The monitor went dark, and Kappa was gone.

Then the room plunged into darkness.

On the island of Milos, with its sun-kissed shores and picturesque villages, which, for tourists and most residents held an air of tranquillity - for Kaliope and Alex that peacefulness masked the shadows of mystery lurking beneath the surface. Both Kaliope and Alex found themselves drawn to the mysteries that this enigmatic island held, but, of course, their motives weren't typical of sightseers. They had reluctantly embarked on a quest to uncover the truth behind a woman named Phobia, the mysterious owner of the local bakery.

Opposite the bakery belonging to Phobia was a small caffenion; Kaliope and Alex settled themselves down at an inside table, both drinking the popular cold coffee frappe, ideal for the hot weather. They had decided that they would wait until Phobia had left the bakery and then they would use the eyes of the drone high above to follow her at a very safe distance. It wouldn't take much to persuade the owner of the premises to allow them to stay through the night if needed. Like all Greeks, if the money were the right colour, they would comply with one's wishes. Kaliope did all the negotiating while Alex kept his head down fearful of being recognised. There was no need to worry as the owner only had eyes for Kaliope.

As the sun dipped below the horizon, casting long shadows across the cobbled streets, the two adventurers began to feel more nervous; the scent of freshly baked bread wafted through the air, a stark contrast to the unease that churned in their stomachs. They waited several hours in the darkness; they were alone in the café as the time was just before midnight. Suddenly, there was movement at the bakery. With bated breath, they observed as Phobia locked up the bakery, only to slip away into the darkness through a narrow alleyway.

Kaliope and Alex followed discreetly, their steps muffled by the sound of their racing hearts, but safe in the knowledge that they could not be detected because Kaliope was guiding them via the drone's eyes. The island's alleys twisted and turned like a labyrinth, leading them down from the village of Trypiti towards the small seaside tourist village of Adamantas.

They watched as Phobia turned into the entrance to the catacombs. They followed, more slowly now. The catacombs were a tourist attraction. They had been transformed by the Nazis during WWII, who used it for housing their communication systems, ammunition and the workers who were making gas masks. But since the war, it has been converted into a museum and become a magnet for tourists.

As they reached the entrance to the catacombs, they faltered. The yawning darkness seemed to swallow them whole, and for a moment, doubt gnawed at the edges of their determination. With a deep breath, they pressed on, the flickering flame of a lantern casting eerie shadows on the cold stone walls. The air was thick with a sense of foreboding as if the very walls held ancient secrets that had long yearned to be revealed. The catacombs stretched before them like a vast, underground maze, the winding passages a testament to the secrets they concealed.

Phobia's footsteps echoed faintly in the distance, guiding them like a haunting melody. But as they navigated the labyrinthine twists and turns, their lantern's glow casting an ever-shifting dance of light, the echoes grew fainter. Panic welled up within them as they realized they had lost her trail, left only with the oppressive silence of the catacombs.

Time seemed to lose all meaning as they continued their desperate search, their voices swallowed by the darkness. It was then that they stumbled upon an anomaly—a faint glimmer of light that emanated from a small, unassuming crevice in the wall. Hope surged within them, and they rushed toward the light, their hands brushing against the cold stone.

With a gasp, they found themselves before a concealed door, its intricate carvings hidden beneath layers of dust and time. The door seemed to pulse with otherworldly energy, and as Kaliope's fingers brushed against its surface, a shiver raced down her spine. It was a secret entrance, a threshold to the heart of the enigma that was Phobia.

Exchanging a determined glance, Kaliope and Alex pushed open the door, their lantern's light revealing a hidden chamber beyond. The air was heavy with the scent of ancient incense, and the walls were adorned with symbols and glyphs that seemed to dance in the flickering light. At the centre of the chamber stood Phobia, her back to them, her form silhouetted against a massive stone altar.

The scene was surreal as if they had stepped into a realm that existed on the fringes of reality. But before they could utter a word, Phobia turned, her eyes locking onto theirs with an intensity that sent a shiver down their spines. Her smile was knowing as if she had anticipated their arrival all along.

"Welcome, seekers of truth," she intoned, her voice echoing in the chamber. "You have ventured far to uncover the secrets that lie hidden within these catacombs. But do you possess the courage to face the revelations that await?"

Kaliope and Alex exchanged a glance, the weight of their journey settling upon their shoulders. The room seemed to hum with an electric energy, anticipation and apprehension intertwining in the air.

"We seek answers," Kaliope said, her voice steady despite the uncertainty that churned within her.

Phobia nodded; her gaze unwavering. "Then prepare yourselves, for the truth, is not always what it seems."

With a gesture, Phobia beckoned them to approach the stone altar. As they drew near, the intricacies of the carvings became clearer, revealing a tale of ancient gods and forgotten rituals. Phobia's hand traced the lines of the carvings, her touch imbuing them with a sense of life.

"Milos holds secrets that stretch back through the annals of time," Phobia began, her voice a melodic cadence that seemed to weave a spell around them. "Long ago, this island was a haven for a society that sought to harness the power of the elements. They believed that by channelling the energies of the earth, air, fire, and water, they could shape the world to their desires."

Kaliope and Alex listened in rapt attention, the pieces of the puzzle falling into place. Phobia was the guardian of this ancient knowledge, a keeper of a legacy that had been passed down through generations.

"But power comes at a price," Phobia continued, her gaze growing distant. "The society's hubris led to their downfall, and they vanished from the annals of history. Yet their teachings endured, hidden within these catacombs, waiting for those who were worthy to unravel their mysteries."

As the tale unfolded, the chamber seemed to come alive with spectral energy, the walls pulsating with a rhythm that seemed to resonate with the very heart of the island. Kaliope and Alex held hands, realizing that they stood on the precipice of a choice that could forever alter the course of their lives.

"The knowledge of the ancients is a double-edged sword," Phobia warned, her eyes holding a weight of sorrow. "It can empower or consume, depending on the intentions of those who seek it. Are you prepared to bear the burden of this truth?"

The tension in the chamber was palpable, the air charged with a sense of destiny. Kaliope and Alex shared a silent exchange, a wordless agreement passing between them. With a nod, they stepped closer to the altar, their hands reaching out to touch the symbols that adorned its surface.

At that moment, the catacombs seemed to come alive, a symphony of whispers and echoes filling the air. The ancient energies surged around them, intertwining with their very beings. They both began to sway, dancing to the rhythms of the forces that swirled in intricate patterns around them. Their ears attuned to the sounds of the voices of centuries past. Their bodies moved faster their legs seemingly detached from both head and torso. Quicker and quicker, they danced until suddenly overcome by the energy and forces surrounding them, they collapsed in a heap on the ground.

As Alex and Kaliope gradually stirred from their trance-like state, they found themselves in a surreal and unfamiliar setting. Their eyes blinked open to reveal the dimly lit interior of an ancient tunnel, carved in ancient times deep into the heart of the Aegean Sea, not that they knew that at the time. The tunnel's walls, rugged and unforgiving, loomed overhead like the stony jaws of some primaeval beast. Confusion washed over them as they realized they were seated side by side in an open carriage with plush fabrics on the bench seating. The wheels glided over the rails as the carriage moved forward at speed.

They exchanged bewildered glances, their minds struggling to piece together the bizarre puzzle of their surroundings. To their astonishment, in the low illumination from lights set into the walls of the tunnel every ten metres, a figure loomed over them – the inscrutable Phobia, who had been their guide through this bewildering journey into the unknown. Her presence only added to the surreal nature of their situation.

Their initial instinct was to leap from the carriage and escape this unsettling tunnel and the menacing Phobia, but a glance outside revealed the perilous truth; the wagon was hurtling forward at an alarming speed. The sheer velocity and the ominous darkness that lay ahead of the carriage made the prospect of jumping off seem far too dangerous. As they gripped the sides of the carriage, Alex and Kaliope exchanged worried glances, realizing that their fate now rested in the hands of their mysterious guide as they hurtled further into the depths of the ancient tunnel.

Suddenly, the carriage began to slow as ahead they could see not impenetrable darkness but a glow of light that grew bigger as they drew nearer to what they realised was an opening in the tunnel. A few seconds later, the carriage glided to a stop in what could only be described as a station. They looked at each other, understanding dawning on them. The ancient myth of the Golden Triangle was not a myth, it was a reality; the station according to the signage was Aegina Island.

Chapter 13

Gitta was unhappy. She had been captured by Raul and Mia and taken to the room behind the butterfly wall. The room was empty, except for three computer monitors, a stool in front of each monitor, and a single chair in the centre. Gitta was told to sit in the chair and her hands were loosely tied behind her. She looked around just in time to see the butterfly wall rotate until the butterfly tableau faced into the room. Raul who had taken her bag when she had been grabbed, immediately began putting the heroin filled butterflies back onto their placeholders on the wall.

Meanwhile, Mia stood in front of her, watching her like a hawk. Gitta studied Mia carefully, her CIA training kicking in as she looked for any weaknesses which Mia might reveal. There was no doubt she was fit, lean, and full of self-confidence, and her complexion gave her an exotic allure, which to her surprise, Gitta appeared to find attractive. She noticed that Mia seemed to be appraising her not as an enemy but as a potential catch. Gitta found this both disturbing but also quite alluring.

Mia's raven-black hair was pulled back into a business-like ponytail. A style she preferred whenever she found herself having to scrap and fight out of a situation. She kept fiddling with the band that was keeping her hair pulled up as if she were undecided whether she should leave it or let her hair down.

"Cut it out, sis!" shouted Raul noticing what Mia was doing. "She's our prisoner not a potential bit on the side for your pleasure."

"Oh, shut up," mumbled Mia. "I can do what I bloody well like!"

Gitta quickly realised that Mia possessed an intriguing duality. While she exhibited aggression towards men, her attraction towards women created an unexpected vulnerability within her. Gitta understood that this unique aspect of Mia's personality could potentially be her way out.

To take advantage of this revelation, Gitta decided to employ her charm and wit to gain Mia's trust. She would subtly use Mia's attraction towards women to manipulate her emotions and elicit sympathy. With luck with each passing hour, the bond between them should grow deeper, blurring the lines between captor and captive. But, at the same time, she had to look for ways to get back in touch with Chris and Alex who she missed terribly. She was worried that he was worrying too much about her.

She smiled at Mia, shifting her legs, crossing one over the other, wishing she was wearing a short skirt so that she could flirt a little. She decided that she needed to be patient and wait for an opportunity to escape. She needed to be careful and not do anything to make her captors angry. She also needed to stay strong and hopeful and believe that she would eventually find a way to escape and get back to her beloved, Alex.

She swivelled around in her chair watching Raul carefully as he worked on filling the vacant placeholders with heroin-filled butterflies. 'So, this is how it is done,' thought Gitta, 'A revolving wall.' When it was closed with the butterflies facing into this room, heroin filled butterflies were put on their placeholders on the wall between the animated butterflies. Then the wall revolved so the butterflies were facing the inner sanctuary. 'Then what happens?' Gitta asked herself. 'Of course, like me, a runner is instructed to pick the heroin-filled butterflies from the wall and transport them to where? A distribution centre, presumably.'

Gitta couldn't see the sense in that process, particularly as the heroin must come from somewhere. As far as she could see there was no way the heroin could enter the room except through the revolving wall. She nervously fiddled with her necklace, not knowing if anyone was listening or if it was still working. For all she knew, the walls were so thick that radio waves could not penetrate them. Her revere was rudely interrupted by Raul angrily shouting instructions to his sister.

"For fuck's sake, sis, haven't you searched the bitch yet?"

"Just going to do it now, sorry bro," said Mia sheepishly. At the same time, as she said this, she winked at Gitta. Moving closer but still a little wary and making sure she didn't get anywhere near her legs, Mia moved behind Gitta.

"Stand up!" she ordered.

Gitta stood up as Mia pulled the chair aside. Thoughts rushed through her head of ways in which she might overpower the two clowns who held her. She held her instincts in check and braced herself for the frisking she would endure from Mia. Now was not the time, she would wait for a much better opportunity, which she felt would surely present itself soon. Gitta stiffened slightly as she sensed rather than felt Mia's hands nearing her. She could feel her hot breath on her neck: pleasant, in fact, it was a nice sensation.

Mia slipped her hands inside Gitta's shirt, moving them slowly over her back, deftly she undid her bra. Gitta drew in a sharp breath.

"You could be hiding a transmitter inside your bra," whispered Mia as her hands moved round to Gitta's tummy, lingering a few seconds before moving up to her breasts. To Gitta's astonishment, her nipples began to harden, and she realised that Mia was pressing her body up against her arse and back. With a heavy breath, Mia caressed Gitta's breasts, realising that Gitta liked what she was doing, she lingered a few seconds, longing to rip Gitta's shirt off and suck her nipples. Suddenly, Raul appeared in front of Gitta, he obviously had finished playing with his butterflies. To Gitta's horror, he had a switchblade in his hand.

"Move back, sis!" Raul commanded as he stepped forward, the switchblade held intimidatingly pointing towards Gitta.

"Don't you hurt her, Raul," Mia shouted, "We'll only hurt her if she doesn't give us the information we want from her."

Raul smiled at his sister. "Don't worry, I won't spoil your fun, sis, but we have to take this bitch to Kappa soon and anyway the EKAM mob are still in the inner sanctum and might get lucky, and break in while we are still here." While he was talking, Raul stepped up until he was standing right in front of Gitta. He swiftly used his knife to slice open her shirt from top to bottom, revealing her breasts, he then sliced her jeans from her waist to her crotch, so that they fell down her legs, leaving Gitta standing in just her panties and nothing else.

"There," said Raul with a leery smile on his face. "Now it's easier to search her, sis. Mind you, I can't see she could hide anything in those flimsy panties. You might have to do a little probing to find that transmitter, ha-ha."

At that moment, Gitta realised that they must have suspected she was carrying a transmitter. Once they have exhausted every avenue on her body they would go for her necklace and in all probability smash it destroying both the transmitter and the necklace. Suddenly, Gitta stepped forward towards Raul, jumped into the air and drop-kicked Raul smack on the chin. Raul went down like a sack of potatoes. Gitta twisted around so she was facing Mia, but Mia wasn't rushing at her as she expected, she was simply standing by the side of the chair smiling.

"That was beautiful," she enthused. "Even though he is my brother I enjoyed watching that. Now come on. let's get out of here. I'll undo the bindings on your wrists. Then I'll take you somewhere we can get naked. Fuck the cartel!"

Gitta was astonished but at the same time relieved. She turned around so that Mia could cut her bindings. Too late, she felt a slight prick in the side of her neck. She managed to turn and face Mia, but Mia's face held no malice, just sorrow as she said, "I'm sorry," moments before Gitta blacked out and fell to the floor.

Gitta awoke in a dimly lit, windowless, one-door room, the tension hung heavy in the stale, cold air, mainly from Raul. The two menacing gang members known for their ruthless tactics, now had Gitta bound to a sturdy chair. She could see that she was in a different room, and she wondered if she was still in the Temple of Apollo or somewhere else. She was still groggy from whatever concoction had been in the hypodermic needle and she was still almost naked with only her panties and necklace to keep her company. They were probably going to interrogate her in this room thought Gitta. She wasn't afraid because she had seen that even though they both looked intimidating, they had proved themselves incompetent. Also, on the plus side, Mia was definitely attracted to her, however, on the minus side she found herself being attracted to Mia too. Gitta took solace in the fact that she was a seasoned CIA field agent, trained to withstand intense interrogations and maintain her composure under pressure.

Mia, whose piercing emerald eyes had a demeanour both as sharp as a knife, but also showing the passion that Gitta had awakened in her, took the lead in the interrogation. She paced around Gitta, who sat in the sturdy chair, her wrists tightly bound by coarse ropes. Raul, who wore his permanent scowl, stood leaning against the wall, his arms crossed, watching the proceedings with a menacing glare.

"Let's make this simple, sweetheart," Mia began, her voice dripping with malice, but not her eyes. "You tell us your name and who you work for, and we might let you leave this place with your pretty face intact."

Gitta, her jaw clenched, maintained a steely resolve. She knew the importance of her mission, and revealing her identity would jeopardize not only her life but others too. "You'll have to try harder than that," she retorted, her voice steady, her eyes locked on Mia's.

Raul cracked his knuckles, the sound echoing ominously in the cramped room. "We've broken stronger people than you, bitch," he sneered, his heavy accent adding a menacing edge to his words.

Mia circled Gitta like a predator closing in on its prey. "You see, we don't like secrets around here," she hissed, then winked at Gitta. "And secrets have a way of slipping out when you're in pain. Now, who do you work for?"

Gitta remained defiant for an hour or so as her captors fired questions at her. They kept repeating "What's your name, who do you work for, who sent you, do you have accomplices?" She held firm even after she had been slapped around the face viciously by Raul. All the time her mind raced with contingency plans and escape routes. She knew that if she gave in, her mission would be compromised, and lives would be at risk. "I can't help you with that," she replied calmly to every question.

Raul's patience wore thin. He reached into his pocket and pulled out his switchblade, flicking it open with a menacing click. The blade gleamed in the dim light as he brought it dangerously close to Gitta's cheek. "You're playing a dangerous game, bitch. You might lose more than just your secrets."

Gitta's heart raced, but she refused to show fear. She had been trained to withstand physical pain and psychological pressure. "I'm not afraid of you," she said, her voice unwavering.

Raul, frustrated by Gitta's resilience, approached her with a sinister grin, switchblade pointing at her nipple. "You know, there are many ways to make people talk," he muttered, placing the point of the switchblade against her left nipple.

As Raul bent closer, Gitta's mind raced. She needed a way out, a chance to turn the tables on her captors. With a quick, calculated move, she swung her bound legs, catching Raul off guard. He stumbled backwards, cursing loudly as he crashed into the wall, dropping his switchblade in the process.

Mia lunged at Gitta, but Gitta had anticipated the move, with a burst of adrenaline-fueled agility, using her bound hands, she grabbed Mia's wrist, twisting it with surprising strength. Mia yelped in pain as Gitta forced her to the ground. She grabbed the chair and brought it down on Mia's head, knocking her out. She quickly turned around as she heard Raul starting to get up from the floor. Another perfectly executed drop-kick made Raul crashing backwards hitting his head against the wall.

Gitta cut free from her restraints by using the switchblade which Raul had dropped. She undressed Mia and donned her black tank top and her leather jeans. Pocketing the switchblade, she made for the door. It was unlocked. Carefully opening it, she peered around the door. What she saw absolutely amazed her. Another piece of the puzzle slipped into place. Now she knew how the heroin arrived at the Temple of Apollo.

Chapter 14

Chris was beside himself, sitting in his CIA operations room in a southern suburb of Athens, looking out over a calm deep blue Mediterranean Sea. The CIA had converted a small block of apartments into their Athens Station offices, on the Athens riviera. Despite the technology and resources at his command, Chris had lost communication with Alex and Kaliope. After they had followed Phobia into the catacombs, Chris decided to keep the drone that was following them on station till they came out. Two hours later, there was still no sign of them, so Chris sent in the local police to comb the catacombs, but they found no trace of Alex or Kaliope. It was as if they had vanished into thin air. Now, Chris was really worried. He needed architectural plans for the catacombs and the Temple of Apollo. He had already tried sources in Athens to see if they could track them down, but they had come up empty. There was only one thing for it, he'd have to call Barry Lightford, head of the CIA's Balkans Overlook section at Langley.

"Hello, Chris. What's up?" said Barry recognising where the call was coming from. "Have you smashed that drug cartel yet?" Although not directly involved Barry had kept an eye on Chris's current operation. Since Chris had made a name for himself during the Gladio Protocol operation, Langley viewed Chris as a future section head in the CIA. Chris was often mentioned favourably at morning prayers, the seven o'clock operational review meeting held every morning by the heads of sections. Then Chris's reputation blossomed even further at the conclusion of the Arthur Eckersley operation in Macedonia. Barry knew that when the next section head post had a vacancy, Chris would be at the head of the line. But he also knew that Chris loved field work too much to be tempted back to Langley.

"Oh, you know Barry, one step forward and two steps back. I thought we were making headway a few days ago but we've had some setbacks."

"Well, I figured you wouldn't be calling me just to make small talk. What do you need help with?" asked Barry.

"I've lost the Greek Prime Minister," said Chris.

"Who Kalfas?" questioned Barry. "I knew that guy would get into trouble one day. He should make up his mind whether he is a civil servant or a spy, and not confuse the two," said Barry with a chuckle. "Isn't he married to that Gitta women?"

"Yes, he is."

"Wasn't she able to protect him?"

"Another setback, she was captured and we don't know where she is," said Chris in exasperation.

"Shit! Okay, Chris, how can I help you?"

"Two things," ventured Chris. "I need a drone or a satellite that has powerful infrared capabilities and can see deeply under the surface of the earth. Can you send me anything like that?

"I have a drone on station over Palestine which has been mapping out Hamas tunnels. I could spare that for a few days. Its pilot is sitting in a container not far from Athens, at the Greek air force base in Tatoi. I'll clue her in that you'll be running her for a few days."

"Great," interjected Chris. "Thank you. What about a satellite? I have two targets some distance apart to investigate." Chris didn't want to have to use a drone over Delphi for a few days and then after it had done its work, they had to send it over Milos Island. Time was of the essence.

"I can divert GEO034 from its current station to one of your targets. If you give me the coordinates, I can retarget the bird to be on station by midnight your time tonight."

"Perfect," enthused Chris. "Now, here is a tricky one. We cannot find any architectural plans or schematics for either target. However, there must be plans that are sitting on a server somewhere in the world. There is a rumour that a Middle Eastern company was responsible for the complete refurbishment of the Temple of Apollo in Delphi. The second site is the catacombs on the island of Milos. That is where Kalfas disappeared together with his Home Office Minister."

"And you've searched the catacombs?" asked Barry.

"Of course, we have," said Chris sounding a little peeved that Barry would ask such a basic question.

Barry detected in Chris's voice that he was not happy with the question. "Sorry, Chris, I didn't mean to doubt your expertise. It was rhetorical."

"Don't worry, I'm just a little sensitive about everything that is happening. I have no idea if there were any changes to the catacombs since WWII, but Alex must have gone somewhere, so there must be another entrance."

"I'll get Jim onto it immediately, Chris. I'll be in touch as soon as I can."

Chris let out a long sigh of relief. "Thanks, Barry, I owe you one."

While Chris was asking Langley for help, Alex and Kaliope were staring at a sign that said Aegina Island.

"Can't be," said Alex in disbelief. "Did we just travel from Milos Island to Aegina Island through a railway tunnel?"

"Looks that way," agreed Kaliope. "Didn't I tell you that the ancients believed that there was an invisible force between Milos, Aegina and Delphi, called the Golden Triangle?" With a triumphant smile on her face, Kaliope said, "I told you so."

Visibly irritated, Alex retorted. "Never mind that now. Who the hell are these people?"

He nodded towards two men dressed rather scruffily in jeans, sneakers and identical white t-shirts, who were walking purposely along the platform towards them. Nervously, they waited as the men approached, then stopped in front of them. They expected that the men would be rough with them, but to their astonishment, the taller of the two men politely asked them if they would both follow them.

To their surprise, the men led them through a labyrinth of narrow corridors lined with many doors. They heard sounds coming from behind many of the doors, sounds which they tried to decipher but to no avail, until they arrived at an inconspicuous door behind which was silence. With a click of a lock and a creaking sound, following the two men they found themselves stepping into a room that appeared frozen in time. The furniture exuded an antique Tudor style, transporting them to another era.

Alex and Kaliope were instantly transported back to the 16th century, captivated by the rich tapestries, ornately carved wooden panels, and period-specific décor that filled every corner.

The room breathed a majestic air, illuminated by the soft glow of candlelight that danced upon the polished oak floors. The walls were adorned with intricately woven tapestries depicting scenes from medieval history and vibrant floral motifs, their colours still as vibrant as they were centuries ago.

At the centre of the room stood a grand oak dining table, its massive legs intricately carved with scenes of knights and maidens engaged in chivalrous acts. Adorned with fine silverware and delicate porcelain plates with delicate floral patterns, it seemed ready to host a banquet for royalty.

Alongside the table were high-backed chairs covered in a luxurious velvet upholstery, providing both comfort and regal aesthetic. Each chair featured meticulous carvings that intertwined vines and flowers, adding an exquisite touch to their already grand presence.

Against one wall was a magnificent four-poster bed draped in heavy velvet curtains. Its headboard displayed masterful woodwork depicting mythical creatures and intertwined foliage. The bed was layered with sumptuous silk bedding that whispered tales of opulence and indulgence. A stone fireplace dominated another wall; a focal point for warmth and relaxation. Above it hung an imposing coat of arms displaying intricate designs symbolizing nobility and heritage. The crackling fire cast flickering shadows that enhanced the room's timeless ambience.

To complete this Tudor masterpiece, there were cabinets displaying delicate China figurines, gilded mirrors reflecting an image of pure sophistication, and shelves displaying leather-bound books containing knowledge from ages past. Both Alex and Kaliope looked around in awe and something akin to reverence for the skilled artisans who had brought this historical period to life. The room stood as a testament to the elegance and grandeur of the Tudor era, inviting them to step back in time and experience the opulence that once graced the lives of nobility.

As Alex and Kaliope tried to make sense of their surroundings, the door swung shut behind them. Standing before them was the formidable Kappa - head of the biggest drug cartel in Greece. His presence commanded respect and evoked fear in equal measure. Kappa's eyes bore into theirs as he spoke with an air of authority. He revealed that he had been keeping an eye on Alex's and Kaliope's adventures for some time now, admiring their courage and resourcefulness, but knowing that one day, he would have to deal with them. That day had come.

"Are you going to kill us?" asked Alex with as much authority in his voice as he could muster, even though it seemed as if everyone in the room could hear his beating heart.

"I don't need to, Alex. Can I call you Alex or would you prefer Prime Minister?" said Kappa with a rare twinkle in his eye. "Besides killing a Prime Minister, and his Home Secretary would provoke such a reaction from the authorities that my operations would be severely compromised."

"So, what's going to stop us from destroying your organisation then?" asked Kaliope.

Kappa grinned at Kaliope before saying, "My dear home secretary, where would you find us?"

Kappa's answer stumped both Kaliope and Alex. They looked at each other in astonishment. Alex was the first to speak. "We are on Aegina, a small island, you can't hide here."

"Hmm, I can hide anywhere. But, the main reason you won't be trying to find me or break up my organisation, is that I have your dear wife as my guest, all be it an unwilling one."

Both Alex and Kaliope paled on hearing Kappa's revelation. Of course, they had suspected that might be the case since the moment the news broke that she was missing. Kappa's booming voice broke through their thoughts.

"I can promise you that if you turn a blind eye to my organisation's operations in Greece, I will guarantee Gitta's safety. My reach is long, so if you renege on our agreement, her life would suffer a very painful death. I'll leave you alone now for a while to make your decision."

Caught between their desire to protect Gitta and their commitment to upholding justice, Alex and Kaliope were torn. They knew that by accepting Kappa's offer, they would be compromising their political integrity and aiding a criminal organisation responsible for countless lives ruined by drugs.

However, driven by their love for Gitta and desperate to keep her out of harm's way, they contemplated accepting the proposition. They grappled with inner turmoil as they weighed the consequences of their choices - betraying their values or risking Gitta's life.

But deep down inside them burned a desire for true justice. They couldn't bear the thought of enabling the cartel to continue its nefarious operations unchecked. With heavy hearts, they realised they had to refuse Kappa's offer. Alex, had tears in his eyes as he agreed with Kaliope that they should take the high ground. He would never see her again, his guilt for agreeing to let her work undercover for Chris, would be with him for the rest of his life.

While they waited for Kappa to return, they looked around their surroundings. The room only had one door, the one they had used to enter it. Then Kaliope, who had wandered over to the large picture window suddenly exclaimed. "Alex, come over here, look carefully outside."

Alex walked over, and then a look of astonishment came over his face. He reached out of the window that Kaliope had opened. His hand touched, not the fresh air that should be sustaining the olive trees that stretched out up the hill slopes into the distance, and whose branches were dancing to the tune of a slight breeze, but a solid object. He turned to look at Kaliope.

"Well, I'll be buggered," he said, as he stuck his head through the open window. "It's a bloody screen!"

"Yes," agreed Kaliope. "It's all smoke and mirrors. But why?"

At that moment, Kappa walked back into the room, with beautiful but menacing Phobia by his side.

Chapter 15

It was pitch black for a few seconds before Yannis pulled down his night vision goggles from the mount on his helmet and told the others to do the same. There was a collective murmur of appreciation from his men at what they were seeing. Gone was the sea of green which lacked contrast and proper depth, the new technology they were using enabled them to not only see what was all around them but also accurately discern what they were seeing. The images were white and had the added advantage of a thermal viewer to see through dust and smoke.

"What do you think, lads?" asked Yannis.

"Amazing, fantastic, brilliant," said a chorus of voices.

"Right, silencers on, and turn your comms on, I don't want to shout. We don't know what we'll be facing when we get out of here. I want every inch, every centimetre even, of this room searched for a way out other than that revolving wall. There must be another way out."

In the night googles-lit, eerily sterile room, Yannis and his unit of twelve elite EKAM officers found themselves in a dilemma like no other. It was a high-tech nightmare, devoid of doors or windows, with only three stools positioned in front of three computer monitors and one solitary chair in the centre. The very wall through which they had entered had seamlessly sealed shut, imprisoning them within its mysterious confines. With grim determination, they knew their only escape lay in discovering the concealed controls for the revolving wall, as well as unlocking the puzzle of another improbable exit method.

They began to meticulously search the room for any signs of concealed controls. It was during an intense examination of the floor in front of the butterfly wall that one of the soldiers, with a keen eye, discovered a subtle seam along the edge of the floor. Further inspection revealed a small, barely noticeable pressure slab embedded under a layer of synthetic tile. Upon pressing it, a flap of the floor opened, uncovering a recess in which four switches were labelled - wall open - wall shut - room down - room up, and a bank of light switches.

One of the officers flipped the wall open switch, the room's rough stone walls trembled, and the revolving wall started to emit a faint, mechanical hum before slowly turning on its mid-point axis. The unit then turned their attention back to the computer monitors fearful that somehow Kappa would know when the butterfly wall was in use. What they noticed was a holographic display materializing into a replica of the butterfly wall, indicating which of the porcelain butterflies contained cocaine, which didn't and which needed refilling.

"So," said Yannis to his men. "So, presumably, this switch which is labelled - floor down – is the alternative way out of this room. The room must be an elevator of some sort, a subterranean transportation device. Are we ready? We don't know what we will be facing, so keep your wits about you and let's cover each other's backs. Let's go."

As Yannis flipped the switch labelled room down, the room started its descent into the ground. The initial sensation was a gentle lurch as the room began to move downward. The men inside the room felt a slight sense of weightlessness or a subtle drop in their stomachs as the descent commenced. The journey downward was both intriguing and somewhat unsettling. As the room descended, their only illumination was their night vision goggles. They had decided that turning on the lights might alert Kappa. Mind you, he was probably alerted by the movement of the descending room.

Even though the walls of the room were made of stone and very thick, the sound of machinery, gears, and cables operating in the background was audible, creating a mechanical hum or vibration that added to the atmosphere. The men in the descending room were experiencing a mix of emotions. Some felt a sense of excitement and curiosity as they descended into the unknown, eager to discover what lay beneath the surface. Others were more apprehensive, feeling a touch of unease or uncertainty about their destination. The rhythmic motion and the changing sounds in the room contributed to a surreal and tense atmosphere, intensifying the range of emotions they were experiencing.

The descending room slowed its momentum before gliding to a stop. At first, they saw nothing different – the walls were the same stone – then it clicked.

"The room hasn't descended," stated Yannis. "It's only the floor that has moved downwards. Look there's a door where there wasn't one before. Come on, eyes wide and watch your six."

One of Yannis's men carefully opened the door, a door which was nothing special, no locks, no hi-tech, just a handle. The door opened onto a long corridor stretching at least five hundred metres in length, in a straight line. The walls were metal and reflected the soft light emanating from recesses between the walls and ceiling. There were doors on both sides of the corridor and no doubt there would be other corridors leading off the one they were in. Yannis noticed that there were cameras every twenty metres or so. He decided to reassure and warn his men at the same time. He keyed his mic.

"We are probably being tracked by several sources, cameras, audio sensors and maybe even pressure pads. You're an elite squad, well-trained and capable of thwarting anything that this lot in here could throw at you. Let's go exploring!"

Five minutes into their exploration of the underground facility, Yannis and his unit came across a delicate necklace, unmistakably belonging to Gitta, one of their own, and it appeared to have been ripped off in a struggle. A mixture of relief and concern washed over them, for finding the necklace suggested that Gitta might still be within the complex. Their feelings of relief were swiftly overshadowed by the gravity of the situation, as they realized that she might be in deadly peril.

They now faced a critical decision, one that would require them to weigh the urgency of finding Gitta against the unknown dangers lurking within the facility. Determined to uphold their unwavering loyalty to one another, they decided to split into two teams, one team continuing the search for an exit, while the other team embarked on a mission to locate and rescue Gitta. Any team that encountered heavy resistance would call for the other team to reinforce them.

Yannis's men crept through the dim, underground complex, their weapons trained forward. The two squads of soldiers moved slowly and carefully, checking each room before proceeding. The complex was vast and labyrinthine, with endless corridors and chambers. The soldiers knew that the cartel members could be anywhere, so they had to be on high alert. As they moved through the complex, the soldiers heard curious noises coming from the surrounding rooms – whispers, footsteps, and the occasional shout.

They knew that the cartel members were aware of their presence and that they were prepared to fight. The squad Yannis was leading came to a large set of double doors. They paused for a moment, listening for any sound from the other side. Hearing nothing, Yannis slowly opened the door and peered inside. What he saw made his jaw drop onto his chest.

"Take a look at this," he said. The six officers in his squad stepped through the door. They looked at each other in astonishment. They were standing in a railway station - a single track disappearing into the gaping mouth of a dark tunnel at the end of the platform they were standing on. Yannis sensing that a firefight might be imminent, immediately ordered the squad looking for Gitta, to join them at the station. The officer in charge of the second squad laughed in disbelief when Yannis ordered them to join them at the station. He wasn't laughing when he stepped through the double doors a couple of minutes later.

Halfway down the platform was what looked like a large waiting room. Yannis led his men there as he didn't think being exposed on an open platform was a good idea. When they got there, they found the waiting room empty, save for a few crates and barrels stacked in the corner. The soldiers cautiously entered the room, their weapons still raised.

From his gigantic office on Aegina, Kappa followed through his security monitors the journey of Yannis and his men from their exit from the descending floor to the station's waiting room. He was annoyed with himself because in retrospect he should have cut off the power to the room and then watched them die as their air ran out. But, he had been distracted by the bitch who was Alex's wife. When she had emerged into the station he knew that something bad had happened to Raul and Mia.

For a second or two, he had been fooled by Gitta wearing Mia's clothes. But as soon as he realised it was Gitta, he sent three of his best men to capture her. She put up a fight but three men were too much and they had her trussed up like a turkey in no time. She was now, tied up in a chair in Kappa's office, watching him issue orders to his men to take out Yannis's squad, no prisoners. Gitta's heart went into her mouth when she heard this.

Just at that moment Mia and Raul entered the office. Both were limping due to their fights with Gitta. They walked up to Gitta.

"Wait," demanded Kappa. "Let me say something before you start."

"Of course, boss," said Mia. Raul just stood next to Gitta looking sullen.

Kappa proceeded to explain to Gitta the conversation he had just had with Alex and Kaliope. "The upshot is I'm afraid, my dear, your husband and the Home Secretary have thrown you to the wolves."

Gitta knew at that moment that Alex and Kaliope had signed their death warrants. They were so naïve; how on earth could they think that Kappa wouldn't kill them? It would be easy for him to make their death look like an accident. They should have agreed to leave the cartel alone in exchange for Kappa not killing her. Alex should have put his trust in Chris. Now, he was messed up. Her thoughts were interrupted by Mia stepping in front and facing her.

Mia grabbed Gitta's chin, pulling her head up and forcing Gitta's lips to form a pucker, then she sat astride Gitta's lap and placed a kiss on her lips. Kappa laughed out loud. He had seen Mia work on women prisoners before. She was an expert in her craft. By the time, Mia had finished with her, Gitta would be her submissive acolyte, so much in love she would endure any amount of pain Mia inflicted on her.

Chapter 16

The phone on Chris Horsman's desk rang and before it had sounded two rings, an impatient Chris grabbed the handset.

"Yes, Horsman here," said Chris. It had only been two hours since his conversation with Barry about the drawings. Surely, he couldn't have found them already?

"Hello, Chris, it's Barry. Good news, we've tracked down, or rather hacked down," Barry allowed himself a little chuckle. "Both sets of drawings. You were right about a Middle Eastern entity being involved. We found the drawings for the Delphi complex on a server in Qatar. I'm transmitting them over by secure link."

"Fantastic, thanks, Barry. What entity are we talking about?"

"It's got a weird and wonderful name. "Bags of Cement" is the name. Registered as a Qatari company with a capital of twenty billion dollars. They mean business and the shareholders make interesting reading too."

"Anyone we know," asked Chris.

"A few known drug moguls from Pakistan, Cambodia, and China. However, the most interesting is from your neck of the woods, a Mr. Dimitri Karagianis, president of The Golden Dawn, an extreme right-wing party."

Chris's jaw dropped. That man has been a thorn in Alex's side for a decade or so now. "Wait until Alex hears about this," said Chris, forgetting that Alex was unreachable.

Barry chose to ignore Chris's comment and continued. "The second set of architectural drawings for the expansion of the catacombs on Milos island were on a private server in Karagianis's office. Very heavily encrypted but no match for Jim," chuckled Barry. "They are on their way to you as we speak."

"Thank you, Barry."

"No worries, Chris. I've also sent instructions to our drone pilots in Tatoi that they will be under your command for a week. I've sent you their direct lines, the password is Milos. You can deploy one over Delphi and one over Milos Island. Both are heat-seeking to a depth of twenty metres."

The chugging of a high-speed printer told Chris that the plans were being printed. "Thanks again Barry, speak soon." Chris grabbed the printed drawings and compared them with the original plans for Delphi and the Milos catacombs. Bingo, there was a massive structure under both sites. He began to study the drawings.

Chris could hardly believe his eyes. The structure was vastly complex, with countless rooms and corridors branching off in every direction. He traced a finger along the drawings, trying to make sense of the maze-like layout. It couldn't be a coincidence that the Milos catacombs and the Delphi site both covered a similar structure.

Then his eyes spied something strange. Two parallel lines were running through both structures. The lines under Milos were running towards the west and the lines under Delphi were running to the south-east. Kaliope's words came back to him. The Golden Triangle was what she had referred to.

Chris took the diagrams and overlaid them onto a large map of Greece and then extended the lines from where they left the complex under Delphi. The lines went directly towards Athens. He did the same with the lines under the catacombs. They went from the catacombs directly towards the north coast of the island.

'Nothing concrete there,' thought Chris, 'if they are railway lines, they could run in any direction after leaving the underground complex.' He could instruct the drone pilots to set the drones to follow the heat signatures of the passengers when a train was leaving the complex.

The phone on Chris's desk shrilled.

It couldn't be Barry; calling again already?

"Chris, it's not Barry," a sultry voice on the other end of the line purred. "My name is Phobia and I'm calling to schedule a private session with you."

Chris felt a jolt of surprise and excitement. He had never received a call like this at work before, and he couldn't help but feel intrigued by Phobia's proposal.

"Uh, I'm sorry, I don't think I understand," Chris stuttered. "What kind of private session are you referring to?"

Phobia laughed, a throaty sound that sent shivers down Chris's spine. "Oh, I think you know exactly what I mean, Chris. I've heard all about your reputation as a dominant, and I'm looking for someone to take control of me."

Chris's mind raced as he tried to process what was happening. He had always kept his personal life separate from his professional life, but something about Phobia's voice made him feel very afraid.

"Listen, Phobia," Chris said firmly, trying to keep his voice steady. "I don't know who you are, or how you got my number, but I'm not interested in this kind of thing. I'm just trying to do my job here."

Phobia chuckled. "Oh, Chris, you're so cute when you're playing hard to get. But let me tell you something – I always get what I want in the end. And right now, I want you."

Chris felt his heart pounding in his chest. He didn't know what to do. On the one hand, he was intrigued by Phobia's offer, and the thought of taking control of someone was always a turn-on for him. On the other hand, he didn't know who this person was, or what kind of trouble he could get into if he agreed to meet her.

"Look, Phobia," Chris said, trying to sound as firm as possible. "I appreciate the offer, but I don't think we should proceed with this. I need to hang up now and get back to work."

Phobia let out a disappointed sigh. "Very well, Chris. I'll let you go for now. But I won't give up that easily. I'll be in touch soon."

With that, Phobia hung up the phone, leaving Chris feeling both relieved and slightly unnerved. He couldn't believe what had just happened, and he wasn't sure how to react. As he sat there, staring at the phone on his desk, his thoughts turned to the last time he had taken control of someone in his personal life.

It had been a few months ago, with a woman he met at a BDSM club. She had been eager to submit to him, and he enjoyed every moment of their time together. But afterward, he felt a sense of guilt and shame that lingered for weeks.

Now, as he thought about Phobia's offer, he couldn't help but feel a twinge of excitement mixed with fear. He knew he shouldn't get involved in something like this again, but the thought of taking control of someone and exploring their fears and desires was a temptation he couldn't resist.

As the day wore on, Chris found himself unable to concentrate on his work. His mind kept wandering back to the phone call from Phobia and the forbidden pleasures she was offering. He tried to push the thoughts out of his mind, but they kept creeping back in, like a persistent itch he couldn't scratch.

Finally, he couldn't take it anymore. He picked up the phone and dialled Phobia's number using the call-back facility, half-expecting her to have already moved on and forgotten about him. But she answered on the first ring.

"Hello, Chris," she said, her voice sultry and seductive. "I knew you couldn't resist me for long. So, are you ready to take control of me and explore your deepest desires?"

Chris couldn't suppress a shudder as he heard those words. At first, he was afraid to say anything he'd regret later, but he found himself speaking before he could stop himself.

"Yes, I am, Phobia," Chris replied. "I'm ready to take control of you."

"Excellent," Phobia purred. "I'll be in your office in sixty minutes. Be ready for me."

With that, Phobia hung up the phone. Chris sat there, staring at his phone in disbelief. This couldn't be happening. He had just agreed to meet a stranger in his office. But he couldn't forget the excitement and anticipation that filled him as he spoke to Phobia. He was already planning what he would do once she arrived.

He took a deep breath and tried to compose himself. His heart was pounding in his chest. He didn't know what would happen when Phobia arrived, but he knew it wouldn't be an ordinary day.

On the other side of Athens in a penthouse apartment belonging to Kappa's cartel, Phobia was getting ready for her meeting with Chris. She decided to call Kappa to explain that she had managed to get an invitation to Chris's office. Kappa was pleased, telling her to be on her guard as Horsman was no fool.

"Should I kill him or just put him out of action for some time?" said Phobia.

Kappa chuckled. "No need to be so violent just yet. Let's see what information you can gather first."

Phobia nodded, understanding Kappa's plan. She would use her charm to get close to Chris and see what valuable information she could obtain. Killing Chris or putting him out of commission would only raise suspicions, and they couldn't afford that right now.

"Got it. I'll play nice for now," said Phobia, a sly grin spreading across her face.

Kappa warned her again to be careful and to not let her guard down.

"Remember, Horsman is a shrewd operative and he didn't get to where he is by being careless."

Phobia assured Kappa she knew what she was doing and ended the call. She spent the next few minutes meticulously planning her approach and going over the seductive techniques she would employ with Chris.

Back in Athens Station, Chris was puzzled. How did a stranger know his private number, and where his office was? From the moment Phobia rang off, Chris had been trawling his memory banks for any hint of where he might have met the woman before. He was sure he hadn't, but where had he seen that name? Then he remembered. Chris grabbed the case file that contained all the reports from the current case and began sifting through the papers.

Bingo, he whispered as his eyes spied Kaliope's report on her visit to the bakery on Milos. The owner called herself Phobia and according to Kaliope, she was beautiful, sultry, alluring, seductive, mysterious, impulsive, daring, fearless, menacing, and oozed sexual magnetism.

Chris looked at his watch, he had fifteen minutes to devise a strategy on how to deal with her when she arrived.

As arranged, at exactly one hour from when Phobia had finished her conversation with Chris, she arrived looking stunning in a black form-fitting dress.

Chris couldn't help but feel his heart racing as he took in the sight of her. She seemed to glide across the room towards him, a predator stalking its prey. He knew he should be cautious, but he couldn't deny the allure of her beauty.

"Hello, Chris," she purred, her voice like honey on his skin. "I've been looking forward to meeting you."

Chris swallowed hard, trying to keep his composure. "Likewise, Phobia," he replied, his voice barely above a whisper.

She smiled, a dangerous glint in her eye. "I've heard so much about you," she said, trailing her finger down the lapel of his jacket. "I hear you're quite the risk-taker."

Chris felt a shiver run down his spine at her touch. He knew he should be wary of her, but he couldn't help but be drawn in by her seductive charm.

"Perhaps," he replied, trying to maintain his cool.

"But I also know how to handle myself in dangerous situations."

Phobia's eyes sparkled with amusement. "Oh, I'm sure you do," she said, her voice dripping with sarcasm. "But the question is, can you handle me?"

Chris felt a surge of adrenaline as he looked into her eyes. He knew he was in dangerous territory, but he couldn't deny the thrill of the unknown.

"I think I can handle anything you throw my way," he said, trying to sound confident.

Phobia chuckled, the sound sending shivers down Chris's spine. "We'll see about that," she said, before leaning in and placing a soft kiss on his lips.

Chris felt a jolt of electricity run through his body at her touch. He knew he was in deep trouble, but he couldn't resist her any longer.

As they parted, Phobia looked at him with a sly smile. "Shall we get down to business?" she said.

"So, Chris," she said, circling around him like a predator. "What do you want from me?"

Chris thought for a moment, trying to choose his words carefully. He knew he had to play his cards right if he wanted to come out of this alive.

"I need your help," he finally said, his voice steady. "There's a job I'm working on, and I need you to spy for me. I know you work for Kappa in some capacity and are close to him. He has taken the Prime Minister's wife prisoner. I want her released unhurt." Chris watched Phobia very carefully as he said this, trying to gauge how she would react now she knew he knew who she was. Either she was going to try and kill him or she would realise the game might be up and acquiesce to his request.

Phobia's face remained stoic as she listened to Chris's request. She took a deep breath before responding, "And why should I help you with this?"

Chris paused before replying, "Because I know who you are, Phobia. And I have connections that could easily send damaging fake information to Kappa if you don't cooperate with me."

Phobia's eyes narrowed at the threat. She leaned in closer to Chris, placing a hand on his shoulder. "You think you have power over me, but you're playing a dangerous game. Kappa doesn't take kindly to threats."

Chris didn't flinch, maintaining eye contact with Phobia, his right hand ready to release the Deringer pistol that was up his sleeve. "I'm not threatening you. I'm giving you an opportunity to do the right thing. You don't have to be Kappa's pawn forever."

Phobia pulled her hand away from Chris's shoulder and stood for a moment as if considering Chris's words. Then, like a snake striking its prey, her hand reached into the thigh length slit of her dress and came out with the six-inch knife she had sheathed there. She lunged forward aiming at Chris's neck, but Chris was even quicker. The Deringer appeared in his hand as if by magic. He fired once, the small hole that appeared in the middle of Phobia's forehead testament to his accuracy.

Phobia, stood there like a statue for a fleeting second as her eyes dulled, then she collapsed in a heap on the floor, into the blood that was spreading around her body.

Chapter 17

On the station platform beneath the Delphi site, Yannis and his men were confident that they were alone and no one was in the waiting room. They entered the room. Suddenly, a group of cartel members burst out from behind the crates, firing their weapons. The soldiers were caught off guard, but they quickly returned fire.

Within the subterranean chamber, a maelstrom of violence erupted. The air throbbed with the deafening roar of gunfire, punctuated by the sharp crackle of automatic weapons and the piercing whine of ricocheting bullets. Muzzle flashes painted the darkness with fleeting, incandescent brushstrokes, illuminating the grim determination etched onto the faces of the embattled soldiers.

Despite their valiant efforts, the outnumbered and outgunned defenders were steadily losing ground. Each echoing gunshot, each fallen comrade, served as a stark reminder of the desperate odds they faced. Yannis, his heart pounding in his chest, his senses overwhelmed by the chaos, knew that retreat was their only option.

"Grenades, lads!" he bellowed, his voice a strained cry amidst the thunderous symphony of battle. He prayed his desperate order would reach the ears of his comrades, a sliver of hope in the face of overwhelming adversity.

A symphony of metallic clinks and hisses filled the air as grenades arced through the smoke-filled chamber, their explosive payloads detonating with concussive force. The ground trembled, a shockwave rippling through the cavernous space as blinding flashes momentarily pierced the darkness. The cartel members, caught off guard by the sudden onslaught, were thrown back in disarray, their ranks momentarily shattered.

Seizing the opportunity, the EKAM squad, their faces grim with determination, regrouped and began a tactical retreat down the platform. They moved with practiced precision, utilizing the massive concrete columns that supported the roof as makeshift shields against the relentless hail of enemy fire.

Yannis, his every sense heightened, led the charge, his heart thundering like a war drum in his chest. Bullets whistled past his head, their lethal trajectory narrowly missing their mark, each near miss a chilling reminder of the fragility of life. Sweat mingled with grime on his face as he fought to control his breathing, desperately seeking a semblance of calm amidst the swirling chaos.

As they reached the end of the platform, Yannis signalled for his team to split up. "You six, take the corridor on the left. We'll take the right," he said, pointing to his six most trusted soldiers.

They nodded in understanding and sprinted towards the corridor, turning left, with their weapons drawn and ready to fire. Yannis and the remaining members of his team headed into the corridor and turned right, hoping to find some cover and catch their breath.

They had only gone fifty metres when they heard gunfire behind them. Yannis turned around, just as he thought, the cartel's men had engaged with the group that headed left up the corridor. Yannis keyed his mike.

"Stephanos," he said addressing the leader of the group. "Do you need help or can you handle the cartel's men?"

Yannis waited for a response, but there was only static on the other end of the line. He couldn't afford to wait any longer, so he signalled to his team to move forward, keeping an eye out for any sign of the enemy.

As they progressed, the gunfire grew louder and more intense. Yannis motioned for his team to take cover behind a nearby wall and peeked out to see what was happening.

To his horror, he saw Stephanos and his team were heavily outnumbered and pinned down by the cartel's men. Yannis knew that they needed to act fast if they were going to have any chance of saving their comrades.

He signalled his team to surge forward, firing their weapons and taking out the enemy one by one. The sound of gunfire was deafening, but they pressed on, determined to save their friends.

As they neared the other group, Yannis saw that several of them were badly wounded and in need of immediate medical attention. He ordered his team to provide cover fire while he and a medic moved in to tend to the wounded. The sounds of battle continued to rage around them as they worked to stabilize the injured.

Suddenly, Yannis heard a deafening explosion and felt the ground beneath him shake. He looked up to see that the corridor behind them had collapsed, blocking their path to the station. Their only route out was back to the descending floor.

Yannis knew that they were in a dire situation. The cartel's men were closing in on them, and they were outnumbered. He felt a flash of anger and frustration at the thought of dying here, so close to completing their mission.

But then he saw the determination in the eyes of his team members. They were soldiers, trained to fight in any situation, and they weren't going down without a fight.

Yannis took a deep breath and rallied his team. "We're not going to die here," he said. "We're going to fight our way out of this. We're going to make it home to our families and loved ones. But to do that, we need to work together. We need to be strong and focused. Are you with me?"

A deafening roar of agreement echoed through the rubble as the team tightened their grip on their weapons. Yannis knew that their only hope was to push forward and fight their way out of the facility.

He instructed his men to utilise their well-rehearsed fall-back tactics. Three of his men would lay down heavy fire, holding up the cartel's men, while the remainder of Yannis's men headed towards their objective.

The cartel's men were caught off guard by the sudden attack and were stopped in their tracks. After half an hour of using these tactics, Yannis's men entered the corridor which terminated with the descending floor. Suddenly the cartel's men broke off the firefight and disappeared into a doorway off the corridor.

Taking advantage of the respite, the men with Yannis in the lead rushed towards the door leading onto the elevating floor. They virtually tumbled through into the room, relieved that they were still alive. Miraculously, they had not lost any of their comrades, but there were three seriously wounded and two walking wounded. Yannis ordered the medic to take care as best he could of the wounded.

One of the men hit the button that started the floor moving towards ground level and the butterfly wall. As they ascended, their communications with the outside world burst into life and the medic was able to call an ambulance for the injured. The moment the ascending floor came to a smooth stop, Yannis hit the switch that opened the butterfly wall.

He immediately called Chris, not only to relay what had happened down in the facility but also to find out if Kaliope had been found. After Yannis had briefed him, Chris told Yannis about Phobia's death before suggesting that they meet in Voula, at the Pasiphae Taverna, Alex's favourite taverna for clandestine meetings. Petros and Pavlina, the owners, not only served the best food in Athens, but they were also discreet.

Unbeknownst to everyone, a silent sentinel had awakened. On the walls and ceilings of the Temple of Apollo, the labyrinthine network of surveillance cameras unblinking eyes had whirred back to life, their lenses capturing every nuance of the recovering EKAM officers, as the hyper-sensitive microphones, once dormant, now hummed with renewed purpose, their delicate membranes vibrating in response to the cacophony below.

In the hushed confines of his office, Kappa, the orchestrator of this elaborate system, listened intently, a sly grin spreading across his face as the conversation between Yannis and Chris fed his twisted sense of satisfaction. But then, Chris's chilling phrase pierced the airwaves, "I managed to kill Phobia."

Kappa's smile evaporated, replaced by a mask of cold fury. His grip tightened around a nearby throwing knife as he leaned closer to the speakers, absorbing every syllable, every inflection of the conversation. A thirst for vengeance ignited within him, a burning desire to inflict upon Chris a fate far worse than death. The wheels of a meticulously crafted plan began to turn in his mind, a symphony of retribution orchestrated with chilling precision.

Chapter 18

Three hours before Yannis and his men escaped the cartel's clutches, Alex and Kaliope were startled to see Phobia by Kappa's side when he came back into the Tudor room. Kaliope couldn't help thinking that Phobia and Kappa were lovers. Phobia's eyes were glowing with the love she obviously had for Kappa. They had been together for almost a year now, and their love had only grown stronger with time. Kaliope's suspicions were true, but they had done their best to keep it a secret from the rest of the cartel.

Alex also noticed the chemistry between the two and couldn't help but feel a pang of jealousy in his heart. Seeing Kappa and Phobia together was a source of pain for him, knowing that he had consigned Gitta to a terrible future and he would never again experience those feelings of togetherness with her.

"I hope you don't mind me intruding?" said Kappa sarcastically. "But I thought you might like to see the consequences of your decision to not accept my offer." As he said this, Kappa picked up what looked like a TV remote controller and pointed it at the false window. The video display changed from the tranquil country scene to a view of the room where Gitta was a prisoner. In horror, they watched as Gitta struggled to stop Mia from pulling her head forward forcing her to put her lips into a pout.

Kappa chuckled. "I'll leave you the remote so you can turn off the video feed when it gets too much for you. Come on, Phobia, my dear, it's time for your visit to Chris Horsman."

Once Kappa and Phobia left them, Alex and Kaliope reluctantly turned to the video screen. Watching Gitta being interrogated and tortured would be doubly dreadful because they would be unable to help her.

They watched as Gitta tried to resist Mia's kiss, but her grip was too strong. She closed her eyes, feeling the warmth of Mia's lips against hers. She felt a strange sensation surge through her body as Mia's tongue forced its way into her mouth, exploring every inch. She pushed against Mia's chest, trying to break free, but it was no use. Mia was too strong, and Gitta was too weak.

As Mia continued to kiss her, Gitta felt herself growing more and more aroused. Her body responded to Mia's touch, and she couldn't help but let out a moan as Mia's fingers trailed down her neck and across her chest.

Kappa now back from the Tudor room chuckled from his seat behind his desk, his throwing knives within arm's length of his right hand. He enjoyed watching the scene that played out before him. He had always known that Mia had a way with women, but he had never seen her work her magic quite like this. Gitta was putty in Mia's hands, and Kappa knew that she would do anything to please her new lover.

"I think it's time to move on," Mia said as she sat back from Gitta letting go of her head. Gitta turned her head to the side, trying to avoid Mia's gaze, but Mia grabbed her chin and forced it back towards her.

"You're going to have to learn to look at me when I'm talking to you, Gitta," she told her.

"When I'm talking to you, you will address me as Queen, do you understand?" she asked.

"Yes, Queen," Gitta replied.

"Good." Mia smiled.

Kappa stood from his chair and walked over to where Gitta was sitting on the chair. He moved behind her and ran his hands over her shoulders savouring the moment of his power over her.

"Do you know why you're here, Gitta?" he asked her.

"No, I don't," she replied.

"We have something special planned for you. Do you remember Takis, my number two?"

"Yes."

"Well, he is on his way over here to see you. Isn't that nice of him?"

Before Gitta could respond, she felt Mia tug on her blouse. She began unbuttoning it slowly, her lips never leaving Gitta's. Mia's hands ran over Gitta's exposed breasts, teasing her nipples as they hardened beneath her touch. She pulled her mouth away and licked her finger before trailing it down Gitta's torso and between her breasts, tracing a circle around each of her nipples, then she moved it down and rubbed the tip of Gitta's skirt.

"I think we should get rid of this," Mia said, tugging at the hem of her skirt.

"No, please," Gitta begged.

Kappa laughed at her defeat. "You're a whore now, make her a whore," he ordered.

Mia pulled Gitta's skirt up over her hips and then she slid it off her legs, leaving Gitta completely naked. Mia sat down on Gitta's lap, trailing her tongue across her breasts, and then neck before kissing her on the lips again.

Gitta threw her head back, breaking the kiss and trying to catch her breath. She looked up at Mia, tears streaming down her face. Her body was reacting, and she knew that she was in danger.

Gitta shook her head, begging. "Please don't do this, I'm begging you."

Mia undid her blouse exposing her breasts, then grabbed Gitta's shoulders, forcing her face against them. "You're going to have to beg louder than that."

Gitta winced in pain as Mia used her knee to force Gitta's legs apart. She knew that she was being punished for refusing to submit to Mia, but she couldn't give in. She would use the strength of her relationship with Alex to resist her.

Gitta tried to push Mia off her lap, but it was no use. Fighting against Mia had only intensified her arousal, and now she was fighting to control her body.

"Please," Gitta moaned, as Takis walked into the room. "Please, help me."

"Bitch!" shouted Takis striding towards Gitta. He stood in front of her, forcing her to have to look up into his angry eyes. "You will pay for messing about with me. Who do you work for?" Of course, Takis knew who she worked for, but Gitta was unaware of that.

"Please, don't hurt me," begged a frightened Gitta.

His hand whipped back, and he slapped her so hard that she felt her head jolt. Gitta held her mouth as her teeth cut into her tongue and she felt blood seep into her mouth.

"You will pay for what you have done." Takis slapped her again.

He turned to Mia and winked at her.

Mia signalled to Raul to help her. He had been watching Mia working on Gitta, twiddling his switchblade in his fingers, impatiently awaiting his turn.

They untied Gitta and told her to lie down on the floor in a star shape. They then tied lengths of rope to her hands and feet. Finally, using a set of hooks in the ceiling and the wall, they managed to hoist Gitta up attaching the ropes around her feet onto the ceiling hooks and the ones on her hands to the wall hooks. She was suspended upside down in a star shape.

She was struggling against the ropes holding her, but it was futile. She had been completely tied up. Mia pulled hard against the ropes tied to the wall, and the suspension device began to spin. Gitta's body was twisted back and forth, sending pain coursing through her.

Gitta screamed out, but Mia ignored her. "This is going to hurt," she said in a voice as cold as steel.

Gitta continued to scream as Mia retrieved a large wooden stick from a box on the floor and raised it over her head. Gitta closed her eyes, waiting for the pain to come.

The blow landed hard against her wrist. Gitta screamed out in pain as the skin broke open and blood began to flow. Mia smiled at the feeling of power the stick gave her. She raised the stick again.

Mia's next move surprised even Kappa. She leaned forward until her mouth was right next to Gitta's ear, and then she whispered, "You are a whore, and I am going to make you mine, bitch." Mia paused her assault on Gitta for a moment, allowing her words to sink in. "I am going to make you regret ever rejecting me."

Gitta's eyes opened wide as her body shook with fear. She was completely at Mia's mercy now. She had no idea how things had spiralled out of control so quickly. She had joined Chris's assignment fully trusting he would watch over her. 'But he failed,' Gitta thought bitterly. Now they were in a lot of danger, and it was all her fault. She felt the tears begin to prick at the corners of her eyes as her mind played back to the past days. Mia's voice gently pulled her back to reality.

Gitta moaned again as Mia's fingers traced the inner slopes of her breasts. She was shocked by how quickly she was becoming aroused. There was only one thing for it she thought to herself, she had no choice but to give in to Mia's advances.

Gitta let out a soft sigh as Mia's fingers brushed against the flesh of her breast, skilfully applying enough pressure to send tingles through her body. Her nipples were beginning to rise to the surface, and Gitta felt herself growing wet as Mia's tongue danced over the soft skin of her neck.

Mia whispered in Gitta's ear, "You are a very beautiful woman, I can see why Alex fell for you. I shall enjoy breaking you."

In the Tudor room, both Alex and Kaliope looked on in abject disgust at seeing what Gitta was going through. Alex especially was feeling guilty, sad, and tearful. He didn't know how long he could stand watching Gitta enduring her pain. He would break long before Gitta, which of course, was exactly what Kappa was banking on.

Kaliope seeing the torment that Alex was going through turned to him and gave him a big hug. Alex held Kaliope tight as if she were the only bastion of sanity around. He began sobbing his head on her shoulder, his body shuddering with each sob.

"No one would think bad of you if you acquiesced to Kappa's demands, Alex," said Kaliope soothingly.

Alex nodded, he was thinking that maybe if he agreed to Kappa's demands, in a day or a few weeks there would be an opportunity to turn the tables on Kappa and get Gitta away from his clutches.

Alex walked towards the security camera in the corner of the room waving his arms frantically trying to attract attention. It worked as two minutes later Kappa came into the room.

"What?" he asked.

"I'll do whatever you ask as long as you stop torturing Gitta," said Alex pleadingly.

"That will disappoint, Mia. Shame, never mind. Let me remind you of the rules. I let you and Kaliope here get on with your lives, allowing my cartel to continue its business and Gitta lives but works for me. You will never see her again. I will allow her to send you weekly video messages so you can be assured she is still alive. Do we have a deal?"

"Yes," murmured Alex.

"Do WE have a deal, Prime Minister!" Kappa shouted.

Alex summoned up as much authority as he could and said, "Agreed, Kappa."

Chapter 19

The Pasiphae Taverna had been a fixture of the Athens suburb of Voula for more than eighteen years and was regarded by most of the Athens elite as having the best home-cooked food on the Athens Riviera. So fashionable was it that many popular Greek singers clamoured to appear on its small dance floor. Built into a rocky escarpment the taverna even in the height of summer was cool. Even though tables had to be booked days in advance, Petros and Pavlina, the owners of the premises, always had Alex's table available, tucked away as it was into a natural alcove in the far corner, away from prying eyes.

Alex was a regular visitor to the Pasiphae Taverna, not just because of the great food, but also because of Pavlina. She had been the love of his life since high school, and though they had both gone on different paths in life, they were friends, even though Alex was now besotted with Gitta, and Pavlina married Petros, they still had a soft spot for each other. Alex always enjoyed Pavlina serving him, and she always did, with a smile that could light up the whole room.

One hot summer night several years ago, before Gitta and Petros came onto the scene after the last customer had left, Alex stayed behind. He had something special planned for Pavlina. As she was locking the doors, Alex grabbed her by the waist and pulled her in for a deep kiss. Pavlina's knees buckled under her and she moaned softly, her hands running through his hair.

They made their way to the nearest table, and Alex pushed the plates and cutlery off while laying Pavlina down. He began kissing her neck, his hands roaming over her body, pulling her dress over her head, revealing a black lace bra and panties. Alex quickly undressed and lay down beside her, stroking her body, kissing her lips, her breasts, her stomach, her thighs, and then up, finding her scent, he entered her gently, his love for her making his passion grow.

They made love like they had never done before. It was a night of passion. Their love was strong, their need for each was other overwhelming, and their passions were uncontrollable.

After they had finished, Pavlina lay in Alex's arms, her head on his chest, her hand running through his hair. They talked about all that had happened to them over the years, their dreams, their thoughts, and their hopes.

They stayed for a long time talking, enjoying the closeness. Eventually, Pavlina said she had to go. She said she had to lock up and get up early to serve breakfast. Alex kissed her on the forehead and said goodnight. That was the first and last time they had made love, Alex was married to his first wife back then, and had just been promoted to minister of justice in the Greek government. He didn't want to jeopardise his marriage or his career, so he stayed away from the taverna for a year. When he went back one evening with his wife, he found that Pavlina had married Petros and they were both very happy. Alex was pleased that she had found happiness and he began to frequent the taverna more often. In time, he became great friends with both

Petros and Pavlina, using the taverna for many over-dinner meetings whenever he wanted a secluded table.

Now, he was greeted at the door of Pasiphae by Petros. "Καλώς ήρθες Alex," said Petros welcoming Alex to the premises, as he kissed him on both cheeks.

"Is anyone else joining you this evening, Alex?"

"Yes, Chris, Yannis and Kaliope."

Petros looked at Alex with a quizzical look on his face, "And the lovely Gitta, will she be joining us later too?"

Alex decided he could trust Petros, so he said, "Let's go to our usual table and have Pavlina join us, then I'll spill the beans on Gitta."

Once they were settled down at the table and pleasantries with Pavlina had been done, Alex said, "Of course, as always you must never mention what I tell you or what you hear at this table, to anyone. Not even your children."

"Of course, not Alex Ενώπιον του Θεού," said Petros invoking the informal phrase, not before God.

So, Alex quickly narrated the bare-bones outline of what had happened to Gitta. He didn't embellish it with any details or mention her torture or the agreement with Kappa, nor did he mention Delphi or Milos, or indeed Aegina Island, a place which he barely believed he and Kaliope had been to.

"Thank you for trusting us," said Pavlina when Alex had finished. "Come on, Petros we have customers to serve," said Pavlina as she took his hand and dragged him away from the table. "I'll bring you some Μεζέδες and wine. Would stuffed vine leaves, taramosalata, tzatziki, olives and bread be okay?"

"Perfect," said Alex.

Just as he said this, Chris, Yannis and Kaliope walked in together. They ordered the same Μεζέδες and wine as Alex, and then Chris asked Yannis to report on his adventures underneath the ancient Delphi site.

"So, there is a railway line underneath Delphi," Chris jumped in as soon as Yannis had finished.

"I never saw a train while we were there. No overhead power wires, neither a third electrified rail along the single track," said Yannis.

"So, it must be diesel or have its electrical power. Did you find out where the line goes?"]asked Chris.

Yannis showed them the cuts and bruises on his arms, evidence of a firefight in a small enclosed space. "No, we had no time or opportunity to investigate. We were fighting for our lives."

"What about you, Alex? The architects' drawings show a railway line underneath the catacombs on Milos also?"

"Yes, we travelled on it," interjected Kaliope before Alex could reply. "The train stopped at a station signposted Aegina Station."

"But," said Alex. "We were somehow drugged before the train journey, so we have no recollection of boarding the train. We awoke shortly before the train entered the station."

Yannis burst out laughing, then grimaced as his laughter caused pain in his rib area. "Are you telling us that there is an underground railway line starting on Milos and ending up on Aegina? Hard to believe that. Besides, it would be impossible to build without anyone noticing."

Kaliope raised her eyebrows and blurted out. "Well, no one noticed the building of the facilities under the catacombs and Delphi, did they?"

"True," admitted Yannis.

"Smoke and mirrors?" suggested Chris looking at Alex.

Alex was thinking about the false window in the Tudor Room. "They kept us in a room which was decorated in the style of the Tudor period. The view from the large window was stunning and quite peaceful. But on closer inspection, it turned out that the window was a video screen. They could have put anything on that video screen and we would have believed it. Smoke and mirrors!"

There was silence for a few minutes as each one of the people around the table tried to comprehend where Alex's comment could be leading them.

"What would you like to eat πεδια?" Pavlina's question broke their revere.

"What do you recommend tonight? asked Alex.

"Stuffed tomatoes and peppers, cooked yesterday but as you know this particular dish tastes much better twenty-four hours after it is taken from the oven."

Alex looked around, everyone was nodding their head.

"Great," said Alex. "We'll have that, lots of feta cheese, a Greek salad and a bottle of your best barrel red wine. Thank you, Pavlina."

Once Pavlina disappeared into the kitchen, Chris said. "You know what you are suggesting, Alex? Something quite extraordinary. It could be that what we believe is happening is not happening where we think it is."

"Yes," interjected Kaliope. "The golden triangle was not a physical triangle but a force. Some of the ancient texts talked about astral planes."

"Astral planes," scoffed Yannis. "Come on, now you are talking about something even more bizarre than an underground railway line."

"No," countered Kaliope. "It could be that what we are seeing and believing *is* something else."

"But," interrupted Alex. "What if it is a physical one, and it is a transport system to someplace on the surface of the Earth, then the only place it could go is Aegina?"

"If that is the case," suggested Chris. "Then whoever has the golden triangle can use it to control this transport system."

"To do what?" asked Kaliope. "To transport people to another place?"

"Maybe," said Chris. "Perhaps to another time, or another location for that matter."

"I would like to know more about the astral plane," said Yannis to no one in particular.

As the group sat in silence, deep in thought, the sound of Pavlina's footsteps echoed on the stone floor. She emerged from the kitchen with a tray piled high with the meal they had ordered, the aroma of hot food filling the air.

"Is everything alright?" she asked, noticing the serious expressions on their faces.

"We're just discussing some theories," replied Alex, tucking into his stuffed tomato. "Nothing for you to worry about."

Pavlina knew when she should be prudent and leave them to their business, she cleared the plates of mezze, before disappearing into the kitchen.

Kaliope cleared her throat, and took a sip of her wine before speaking, "There is a strong possibility that the golden triangle is not a physical object, but rather a force that controls an astral transport system."

Chris's eyebrows furrowed in confusion. "An astral transport system? What do you mean?"

Kaliope took a deep breath before explaining. "It's a theory that suggests there are other planes of existence beyond the physical world we see. The golden triangle could serve as a key to access these planes. Perhaps both, Alex and I were transported to and from what we thought was Aegina, on the astral plane. I don't remember how we got to Kappa's place or how we came back. Do you, Alex?"

Alex thought for a moment, his forehead furrowed as he tried to recall any memory for even the slightest recollection of their journey to the island and back, then said, "No, I don't."

"Don't you need to be trained to journey through the astral plane?" asked Chris.

Kaliope nodded. "Yes, but if the golden triangle is a key, it's possible that whoever holds it can access the astral plane without training."

"That's a dangerous thought," said Yannis, his eyes wide. "Who knows what kind of entities or dangers could be lurking in these other planes of existence?"

"Exactly," agreed Alex. "We need to be careful not to jump to conclusions without concrete evidence."

"But we also can't ignore the possibilities, "said Chris. "We need to investigate further, explore all avenues of this mystery."

The group spent the next hour discussing the implications of their theories and brainstorming ways to gather more information about the golden triangle and its potential connection to an astral transport system. After an hour, they realized they had more questions than answers, but they were determined to uncover the truth, no matter how bizarre it may be.

Suddenly, Chris slammed his fist down on the table causing the Greek coffees and glasses of after-dinner wine to dance over the table. The other three looked at Chris in amazement. He was usually so calm, but today he seemed frustrated, and now it showed.

"There is only one way to solve this. We use technology. We have one satellite and two predator drones at our disposal. The drones can deliver a hefty payload of munitions, but also, they also have powerful infrared sensors that can map the movement of humans up to thirty feet underground, maybe more. The satellite has even more powerful sensors, which penetrate the earth up to fifty feet or more."

Yannis who hated all the astral plane talk, but never imagined that Kaliope was into this spiritual mumbo-jumbo immediately concurred with the use of technology, and said, "Brilliant, let's do it."

"Right," said Chris. Happy now that the conversation had come full circle and that he was on familiar ground. "Where do we deploy?"

"I would suggest that one of the drones is deployed over the Delphi area at the highest possible altitude without compromising the effectiveness of its sensors. We should also keep in place the guards that are on Kappa's payroll," suggested Yannis.

"And the second drone?"

Kaliope chipped in, "Definitely over the Milos Island catacombs."

"Agreed, Kaliope," said Chris. "That leaves the deployment of the satellite."

"If our premise is that there is an underground railway track that connects Milos with Aegina island, perhaps we should deploy the satellite over Aegina for a few days."

"Agreed Kaliope that is my conclusion too," concurred Chris. "Does everyone agree on the deployment targets?"

Everyone around the table nodded in agreement. Alex ordered more wine while Chris got on his phone to talk to the drone pilots. He explained what they needed to do and also arranged that everyone at the table had software transmitted to their phones that would allow them to mirror image what the drones were looking at. At the same time, he texted Barry in Langley instructing him to deploy the satellite on a half-hourly sweep over Aegina. Satisfied with the deployment instructions he returned to their table.

"Για μας πεδια," the four said in unison as they raised their glasses, toasting themselves. Each one was completely unaware that in the next few minutes, they would be fighting for their lives.

Chapter 20

Outside the Pasiphae Taverna, the sun was setting over the sea, its fading light casting a mauve hue over the landscape. The large cicadas which were just beginning to make themselves heard, watched two black SUVs silently pull into the car park area in front of the tavern. Five heavily armed men alighted from each vehicle and strode purposely between the few tables that were occupied by casual customers who were there for drinks, not dinner.

On closer inspection, a casual observer might have realised that five of the customers were not drinking alcohol, only water or a soft drink. They were Alex and Kaliope's bodyguards, with Chris and Yannis's second in commands, all armed and all aware that the former occupants of the SUVs had to be stopped before they entered the taverna.

As the armed men approached, the bodyguards glanced at each other, their eyes betraying the fear that had been building up inside them. They knew that the time had finally come for them to face their worst nightmare. Kappa's men were infamous for their professionalism and ruthlessness.

They rose as one unit from their chairs, hands hovering over their guns, they were ready to act if Kappa's army decided that collateral damage to civilians was better than Kappa's wrath. Besides, they knew he was nearby watching. He had instructed them that Chris Horsman should be taken alive, so that he, Kappa, could perform the coup de gras.

The sound of heavy boots grew louder, and the tension in the air grew thicker with each passing moment. Suddenly, Kappa's men clicked off the safety on their weapons and began to raise their weapons.

Without hesitation, the bodyguards jumped into action, fending off the attackers with a barrage of bullets. They fought as one alongside each other, their movements fluid and coordinated.

The patrons of the taverna ducked for cover, some screaming in terror, while others tried to make a run for the exits, only to be mowed down by the fusillade of bullets screaming through the air.

Inside the taverna, Chris yelled at the others to take cover. They upended their table, not caring about the food and dishes that were sent crashing to the floor. Fortunately, they had all remembered their firearms, Kaliope grabbed hers from her bag, Chris and Yannis from their shoulder holsters and Alex from his waistband.

"Don't worry," said Chris. "Our bodyguards should hold them off, but if one or two breakthrough, we have the firepower and the shelter of this alcove to protect us."

As they crouched behind the makeshift barricade, Chris couldn't help but feel a sense of déjà vu. It was like they were back in Iraq, hunkered down in the middle of a warzone. The sound of gunfire was deafening, accompanied by screams of terror and shattering glass.

But they were trained for this. Chris took a deep breath and steadied his hand as he aimed his Glock at the entrance of the taverna. Yannis and Alex were doing the same, their eyes fixed on the door.

Suddenly, the gunfire stopped. The silence was almost eerie, broken only by the sound of footsteps approaching from outside. Chris held his breath, waiting for the inevitable attack. But to his surprise, the door burst open and a tall, imposing figure strode in.

It was Kappa himself, flanked by his two most trusted lieutenants. Chris felt a shiver run down his spine as he met Kappa's cold, calculating gaze.

Kappa's eyes swept over the scene, taking in the chaos and destruction left in the wake of his men. He smiled, revealing a set of perfect white teeth, before turning his attention to Chris and his companions.

"Well, well, well," he said, his voice dripping with malice. "Look who we have here. Chris Horsman, the man who thinks he could take me down."

Chris didn't respond. He kept his gun trained on Kappa, his eyes locked on his adversary's face. He knew that Kappa was dangerous, but he was determined to take him down, no matter what it took. But today was not the day. He had to think of Gitta. Kappa would have left orders to kill her if he were killed.

"You thought you could stop me, didn't you?" Kappa continued. "But you were wrong, Horsman. Dead wrong."

Chris gritted his teeth, his fingers twitching on the trigger of his gun. He knew that Kappa was toying with him, trying to get inside his head but he wouldn't let him.

"We're not afraid of you," he responded. "I know you think you have the upper hand because you have Gitta as hostage, Kappa, and I know you believe you hold all the cards. But, deep down, you're just as vulnerable as anyone else. You're just a man, Kappa, not a myth." Chris was hoping that the more he prolonged the threats without angering Kappa too much, Yannis would have had enough time to call in the cavalry.

All government mobile "phones had an *"I'm in trouble"* feature, a button just below the volume so it was easy to locate even in the darkness of a pocket. This button, if depressed three times in quick succession would trigger an alarm in EKAM's HQ. The GPS coordinates of the phone calling for help would also be transmitted to guide the response team to the person in trouble. Yannis's index finger found the button and pressed it.

Kappa looked like he wanted to respond, but instead, he lifted his gun, aiming at Chris. Just at that moment, the sound of sirens could be heard emanating from the car park. Then the crackle of small arms fire came from the EKAM officers. Kappa stopped, and turned around, realising that he had been outmanoeuvred. He swivelled back and let off a shot in Kaliope's direction. Yannis was quicker and dived on top of Kaliope; the bullet grazing his shoulder as they both tumbled to the floor.

"This way," Kappa shouted pointing to the tradesman's entrance at the back of the kitchen. Then flanked by his trusted lieutenants, he disappeared into the kitchen closely followed by four of his men who were covering each other as they backed towards the kitchen as fast as they were able. One didn't make it; slumping to the floor covered in blood from a fatal neck wound.

By the time the EKAM officers had reached the tradesman's entrance, Kappa and his men were speeding away in their powerful black SUVs.

"Leave them be, we must clear up this mess and get the injured to hospital. We'll have our day, don't worry about that," said Chris as he watched Yannis scramble up from on top of Kaliope whom he had protected from being shot. Kaliope's skirt had ridden up to her waist revealing her long legs and thong. She sheepishly straightened herself up, looking appropriately embarrassed.

A chuckling Chris said, "You Greeks will take any and every opportunity for some hanky-panky, even as your life is threatened." Both Yannis and Kaliope looked at each other, then back at Chris. Then they all burst out laughing breaking the tension of the last half-hour.

Two hours later, the taverna was back to normality. The injured, dead and blood stains had all been removed. All the bodyguards except for one who had been taken to an intensive care unit, had been killed, and taken to a private clinic funded by the CIA. Of the civilians caught in the deadly crossfire, six had lost their lives and another fifteen were in hospital, two of those in the ICU. Kappa had lost seven men and those too were taken to the CIA's private clinic for autopsies and processing.

Even though it was after ten, for Greeks, the night was young, and the taverna had filled up with customers again, the bouzouki music playing loudly and proudly, while a few customers were showing off their sirtaki dance prowess.

At the same hour, the four were sitting around the conference table in Chris Horsman's office. Now they were able to concentrate on the software that had been installed on their phones. They also had at hand the architects' drawings of both Delphi and the catacombs on Milos. They were tracking the passes of the two drones and the satellite but until now, nothing exciting had been yielded.

"Nothing over Aegina so far. Who is on Delphi right now?" asked Chris.

"I am," said Alex. "Wait, something is happening."

Chris and Yannis switched their phones to the drone over Delphi. They could see that the drone's heat sensors were picking up movement near the station. The sensors were run by clever software developed by the same company that had developed AI Chat GPT. It could analyse the signals it was getting and report whether it was animal, vegetable or mineral. It was also able to learn from its sightings and build pictures of what it saw.

The drone's software had interpreted one of the heat signatures as a train in the station. The other signatures were interpreted as humans, ten in all, boarding the train. There were other heat signatures dotted around the complex which the drone was picking up which had been designated as human.

"Interesting," murmured Chris. "Let's see if the drone can track, excuse the pun, where the train is going." A groan was heard around the table, followed by a couple of seconds of false laughter.

They watched the train pull out of the station, moving at twenty kilometres an hour towards the gaping entrance to the tunnel. The drone tracked its path as it started a long curve to the right. After five minutes or so, they realised that the train was heading back to the western end of the underground Delphi complex. It entered the complex, then stopped a hundred metres in from the point it had entered the complex.

"What the fuck," exclaimed Chris. "The architects' drawings don't show that bit of track at all."

"Are you sure these are the latest drawings?" questioned Kaliope.

"Good point, Kaliope, maybe it's not. I'll get back to Barry."

"There is something odd about those figures," said Kaliope, pointing at the video feed from the drone. "They walk too stiffly to be human, in fact, they walk like robots."

"Robots!" exclaimed Yannis. Then he chuckled. "Next, you'll be telling me that Kappa is an alien."

Chris ignored the comments, as he immediately called the drone pilot and told him to zoom in to the area above where the train had stopped. What they saw made them all take a collective intake of breath, not believing what they were seeing.

Chapter 21

Back in Kappa's luxurious but heavily fortified underground headquarters, Gitta, who had been a prisoner now for several days against her will, realised that she needed to be more strong-willed and resourceful than she had anticipated. Despite being a prisoner, she was granted limited freedom to move around certain rooms within Kappa's villa. Mia, whom Kappa had assigned to always accompany Gitta, was making her feel extremely uncomfortable as she was constantly watched and controlled.

As the hours went by, Gitta became increasingly aware of Mia's unsettling behaviour, as she took advantage of their proximity by finding every opportunity to touch Gitta inappropriately, invading her personal space and testing the boundaries of Gitta's patience. This constant harassment added to Gitta's torment as she struggled to maintain her sanity and find a way out of her nightmarish situation.

Although Mia's unwavering loyalty to Kappa was evident, she found herself inexplicably drawn to Gitta. Mia couldn't help but become mesmerized by Gitta's captivating presence. Every opportunity that presented itself, Mia surreptitiously touched Gitta or gazed deep into her eyes, unable to resist the magnetic pull she felt towards the imprisoned operative.

At first, Gitta was cautious and suspicious of Mia's motives. She knew all too well the dangers of becoming entangled with someone on the other side of the law. However, as time went on and their interactions continued, Gitta began to sense something more beneath Mia's hardened exterior. She recognised a longing for connection and freedom within Mia's actions.

As their interactions intensified and boundaries blurred between captor and captive, an unexpected bond began to form between Gitta and Mia. They found solace in each other's company especially at night when the villa was quiet. They lay side by side in a comforting embrace. Their connection had become a source of strength.

Tonight, as Mia lay in Gitta's arms she whispered, "Gitta, do you ever wonder what life would have been like if we had met under different circumstances?"

Gitta's fingertips gently traced circles on Mia's bare shoulder as she pondered the question. They had been caught in a whirlwind of events, starting from her capture and imprisonment in the secluded villa. Mia, initially tasked with watching over her, had never expected this unexpected connection to blossom between them.

"Yes," Gitta replied softly, her voice tinged with a hint of longing. "I often find myself wondering about different paths we could have taken. It's as if fate has intertwined us in this peculiar dance."

Mia shifted slightly, nestling herself closer into Gitta's warmth. "Do you think we would have found each other outside of these walls?" she asked, her voice filled with curiosity.

Gitta's fingers continued their gentle caress as memories of their encounters flooded her thoughts. "Perhaps," she murmured. "In another life, our paths might have crossed in the unlikeliest of ways. Maybe we would have met at a café, locked eyes across a crowded room, and felt that inexplicable pull towards each other."

Mia let out a soft sigh, her breath tickling Gitta's neck. "And then what?" she whispered, her voice filled with a mixture of hope and longing. Gitta suddenly felt guilty about her relationship with Mia. Although she still loved Alex, she never expected that her strategy of enticing her into believing they could have a relationship would cause her to have feelings for Mia, emotions that she never thought were possible. Could she sustain the relationship she had with Mia at this level and not let it become more intense? It would be difficult she thought. In her mind, she screamed out for Alex to rescue her.

"We would have started with stolen glances and fleeting smiles," she murmured, her voice laced with a touch of wistfulness as she answered Mia's question. "Our connection would have grown stronger with every passing day, until one moment, unable to resist the magnetic pull between us any longer, our lips would finally meet in a passionate kiss."

A shiver ran down Mia's spine at the thought, her body instinctively pressing closer to Gitta's. "And after that?" she asked, her voice barely above a whisper.

Gitta's touch grew more intense as she traced the outline of Mia's jawline. "After that," she breathed, her lips hovering just above Mia's, "Our desires would consume us, leading us down a path of forbidden pleasure."

Mia's heart raced at the intoxicating words, her body humming with anticipation. "Tell me more," she pleaded, her eyes locked with Gitta's.

Gitta's voice dropped to a husky whisper as she painted a vivid picture of their imagined encounters. "In this alternate reality, we would steal moments of stolen passion in hidden corners and secret rendezvous," she murmured, her warm breath grazing Mia's earlobe. "Our bodies would become a playground of exploration and delight, each touch sparking electric currents between us."

Mia's hands instinctively found their way to Gitta's back, fingers tracing delicate patterns over her naked skin. "Yes," she inadvertently gasped, trying not to surrender to the fantasy unravelling before her.

"Where's that bitch, Gitta?" bellowed Kappa from down the corridor. Gitta and Mia sat up in unison.

"Shit, it's him," wailed Mia. "He'll kill me if he finds me here."

Gitta was thinking fast. Poor girl, she was terrified of Kappa. She couldn't leave the room now, he would see her.

"Quick, under the bed and make sure you don't make a sound," Gitta instructed her before turning her attention to herself. How should I play this, what are my options? This was the CIA operative in her, ticking off the options. 'I could try to reason with Kappa, though that's highly unlikely to work. Or I could hide somewhere else in the room, but he's bound to search every corner. Maybe I can escape through the window? No, it's too small and there's no time.' Gitta assessed her options rapidly, her mind racing with adrenaline.

As footsteps grew louder outside the door, Gitta made a split-second decision. She quickly removed her negligee, slipped on a pair of panties, then grabbed a t-shirt and started to put it on, in the hope that Kappa would be a little shocked at the sight of her half-dressed.

The door swung open violently, crashing against the wall. Kappa stormed into the room, his eyes scanning every inch.

"You thought you could hide from me?" Kappa sneered at Gitta.

Gitta pretended to tremble under Kappa's gaze, managing to stammer a response. "I... I didn't mean any harm. I couldn't sleep so I was going to the kitchen to get myself a drink."

"Where's Mia?" questioned Kappa but this time he did not bellow but asked in a low threatening voice.

"I don't know, she doesn't guard me at night."

Kappa's eyes bore through hers as he tried to figure out if she was telling the truth or not. He decided she probably was. He would find her later but now it was time to teach Horsman a lesson and this bitch was going to aid in that. Kappa grabbed Gitta, who had just about managed to put her t-shirt and a pair of shorts on and dragged her out of the room. Gitta had thought about resisting, but Kappa was strong, so it would be foolhardy.

He dragged her up the corridor, into his office, and pushed her forcefully into the chair in front of his desk. Before Gitta could react Takis Penza, who was already in the room, jumped forward and handcuffed both her hands to the chair's wooden arms.

"No, please, what are you going to do?" wailed Gitta, hoping that if they thought she was frightened, they would relax a little, perhaps allowing her to turn the tables - always the optimist. She was already figuring out her options.

"Don't move!" Kappa said with a rough authority in his voice. "Get the video rolling," he ordered one of his lieutenants standing by the door. At that moment he noticed that Takis Penza, his right-hand man was sporting a slight limp.

"Are you okay?" asked Kappa.

Penza pointed to his right leg. "Just a graze, nothing to worry about. What are you planning for this bitch?" he said pointing towards Gitta.

Kappa just smiled as he laid his six ornate throwing knives out on the desk in front of him. "We're going to show Horsman that it doesn't do to tangle with me. He is going to take a fun quiz.. Kappa looked around the room. Where the fuck is Mia?" Once again Kappa's face was distorted red with anger. "Will someone go and find her," he ordered.

Just at that moment, the door to the office crashed open revealing one of Kappa's men roughly handling a writhing Mia who was desperately trying to escape from his clutches. "I found her hiding under this bitch's bed," said the man pointing at Gitta.

"What were you doing hiding under her bed?" Kappa disdainfully emphasised the word "her." "Were you there when I came into her bedroom?"

Mia didn't say a word, she just continued to struggle. Kappa ordered Mia to be tied to the ropes of the pulley on the ceiling. He was fuming now. The loss of Phobia, the failed attempt on Horsman's life and what he saw as a betrayal by Mia, had made him extremely angry to the point of seeing a red mist in front of his eyes. But a flicker of an idea was beginning to form through his anger. There was a way in which he could get Horsman off his back for good. Kappa hit the intercom button on his desk.

"Soula, come in here, will you and get me Horsman on the video phone," he said in a calmer voice than he had shown Mia. Since the demise of Phobia, he had needed a replacement personal assistant. Soula was the daughter of one of his oldest, most loyal lieutenants, and so far, she had proved hardworking.

The ringing tone of the videophone on speaker reverberated around the room while Kappa waited patiently for Chris Horsman to pick up. He was going to make Horsman an offer he couldn't refuse, a choice between torture and death for either Mia or Gitta.

Chris Horsman picked up on the fifth ring after managing to usher Alex out of his office. He knew it was Kappa and was afraid Alex might become upset if Gitta was on the call.

"Yes Kappa, what can I do for you?"

"Watch," said Kappa. He unsheathed one of his knives throwing it in one flowing motion in Mia's direction.

The knife carving through the air, slicing Mia's cheek by mere centimetres as it embedded itself into the wall behind her. She let out a shriek, her eyes widening with terror. Kappa's sadistic grin widened as he watched her tremble in fear as the blood from her wound oozed onto her shoulder.

"Now, Horsman," Kappa's voice radiated with malice as he leaned back in his chair. "Here's the deal. You've been a thorn in my side for far too long. I'm tired of your interference and your pathetic attempts to bring me down."

Chris Horsman clenched his jaw, his hands gripping the edges of his desk. He hated being manipulated, but he knew he had to play along if he wanted to save Mia and Gitta.

"What do you want, Kappa?" Chris forced the words out through gritted teeth, his anger rising.

"I want you to choose," Kappa sneered. "You have one hour to decide which one of them dies. Chris's heart pounded in his chest as he stared at the screen displaying the terrified faces of Mia and Gitta. His mind raced, searching for a way out of this impossible situation. He couldn't bear to lose either of them, but he knew he had to think quickly.

"Time's ticking, Horsman," Kappa's voice taunted him through the speaker. "Who will it be? Mia or Gitta?"

Chris clenched his fists, his knuckles turning white. He took a deep breath, trying to steady his trembling hands. Sweat dripped down his forehead as he glanced from Mia to Gitta, their eyes pleading for him to make the right choice.

"Remember, one hour or they both die." Kappa cut the connection.

Chapter 22

As soon as the connection with Kappa successfully closed, Chris quickly made his way to the operations room. There, he re-joined his team of Alex, Yannis, and Kaliope who were all intently studying an array of monitors surrounding them. One monitor in particular had captured their full attention – it displayed a live video feed from a Reaper drone that was circling above the ancient site of Delphi. The high-definition footage showed robotic arms skilfully manoeuvring crates from the entrance of the underground complex to waiting lorries parked on a maintenance road just outside the perimeter of the site. The team watched in awe as the precision and speed of the robots were displayed on the screen before them.

"Who have you around there, Yannis?" asked Chris.

"There's a team of five officers standing guard, scanning the comings and goings at the Temple of Apollo. The cartel continues their operations, harvesting the precious white substance from the delicate butterflies. As soon as the temple closes to the public at eight o'clock, a figure enters with a bag reminiscent of the one given to Gitta. They swiftly pluck fifty cocaine filled butterflies off the wall, stuffing them into the bag before slipping away undetected to everyone else except for my men. It is a routine that plays out every night, like clockwork, under the watchful gaze of my officers stationed outside."

"The same person every night?" asked Chris.

"No," replied Yannis.

"Okay, can you get your men to discreetly disable one of the lorries themselves? Once they've done that get them to open a crate and see what's inside. Don't touch the robots, I don't want someone getting suspicious when the robots stop working," warned Chris. "We can't shut down the operation at the Temple of Apollo yet. We have to get Gitta back first."

"What can I do?" asked Alex, fearing he would be asked to stand down while the others had all the fun.

"You have an important assignment, Alex. In the morning, take two of Yannis's best men and Kaliope to Karagianis's office. Find out if he has a more recent copy of the architects' drawings of the catacombs below the ground."

"And if he refuses or denies their existence, what shall we do then?"

"I'll give you a warrant authorising you to confiscate his hard drives." Chris paused, then said, "But once he knows that we know he is in league with Kappa, his political survival instincts should kick in, and you won't need the warrant. Make sure you are at his door first thing in the morning just in case Kappa has had time to warn him, and Karagianis deletes or takes the hard drives."

"Check this out!" shouted Kaliope, pointing at the screen that was showing the video stream from the satellite, which was now passing directly over the Temple of Aphaia, on Aegina. "Look what the big bird is picking up."

They all turned to look at the monitor Kaliope was pointing at.

"Well I'll be darned," uttered Chris, at the same instant that Alex uttered a few choice words.

The state-of-the-art satellite, equipped with powerful infrared sensors, was meticulously mapping out an underground complex. Despite not being as expansive as the catacombs or Delphi facilities, the satellite revealed a sizeable dwelling beneath the surface. The main area consisted of a grand central room, surrounded by smaller rooms connected by narrow corridors. One of these corridors led to a separate building that resembled a bustling railway station, complete with platforms and tracks stretching off into the distance. Following the tracks revealed their northern path towards the coast, where they eventually faded into obscurity.

The four were speechless for almost a minute, each deep in their own thoughts at what they were seeing.

"My apologies, Alex," said Chris, "I doubted you were on Aegina, but it seems there is a tunnel under the sea, and a train track running from Milos Island to Aegina, and possibly to Delphi too."

"So, the lines on Aegina disappear because they are at a depth at which the satellites sensors cannot detect them?" asked Yannis.

Chris said, "That's a good assumption, but I still can't believe that they could build tunnels between Milos, Aegina and Delphi, without anyone knowing about it."

"If you mean, Kappa, he most likely didn't," said Kaliope. "Someone else did." She was looking down, doodling on a page in her notepad.

"Well, if Kappa didn't do it, then who did?" asked Alex, his voice laced with frustration. Meanwhile, Chris and Yannis were both fixated on the object that Kaliope had been absentmindedly doodling. As they took in the intricate details of her creation, their eyebrows raised in unison to show their disbelief. It couldn't be real, could it? Surely, Kaliope had just been watching too many Sci-Fi movies. But as they studied the drawing more closely, they couldn't deny what their eyes were telling them - it was a flying saucer. The sleek design and otherworldly symbols etched into its surface made it seem like something out of a dream or nightmare. But here it was, in Kaliope's sketchbook, looking as though it belonged in a museum exhibit on alien spacecraft.

"You mean.....?" said Alex.

Without missing a beat, Kaliope interjected with a burst of curiosity, "Yes, why not? Have you ever heard of Erich von Daniken and his ground-breaking book, Chariots of the Gods?" Her eyes sparkled with excitement as she continued, "Do you recall the theories he put forth about ancient civilizations being visited by extra-terrestrial beings? Imagine if these intricate tunnels and underground complexes were not created by humans at all, but instead by a highly advanced alien civilization."

The room fell into silence once again as the weight of Kaliope's suggestion settled upon them. The implications were staggering. If von Daniken's theories held any truth, it meant that everything they thought they knew about human history could be turned on its head.

Chris was the first to break the silence, his voice filled with a mix of scepticism and curiosity. "But if we follow that line of thinking, why would the aliens build these complex networks of tunnels? What would be their purpose?"

Kaliope looked up from her doodles, a mischievous smile creeping onto her face. "Well, according to von Daniken, they were used as transportation systems for the aliens themselves."

Alex stared at Kaliope, his mind racing with thoughts and possibilities. The idea that ancient extra-terrestrial beings could have been responsible for the tunnels and underground complexes seemed both absurd and fascinating at the same time. He had heard of Erich von Daniken's controversial theories before, but he had always dismissed them as mere speculation.

Chris, Yannis, and Kaliope exchanged glances, their eyes filled with excitement and curiosity. It was as if a door to a new realm of possibilities had been opened before them, and they were eager to explore its depths.

Kaliope closed her notepad with a satisfied smile. "Think about it," she said, her voice filled with conviction. "The technology we find in these ancient sites is far beyond what humanity could have achieved at those times. The precision, the intricacy... It's almost otherworldly."

"But how do we prove it?" Chris asked, his voice tinged with scepticism. "We can't simply rely on speculation and theories. We need concrete evidence."

Yannis, always the practical one, spoke up. "We should conduct further investigations. Explore these underground complexes ourselves. See if we can find any artefacts or remnants that could support Kaliope's theory."

Alex nodded, his mind already racing with plans and possibilities. "We'll need to gather a team of experts in archaeology, geology, and perhaps even extra-terrestrial studies. We'll need to document everything meticulously and present our findings to the scientific community."

"No!" Chris said rather forcefully. "You are forgetting about Kappa, Gitta and now Mia. They are our priority. Proving claims of alien interference and searching those tunnels and the complex can be done once Kappa is in custody and his cartel destroyed."

Kaliope chimed in, her eyes sparkling with excitement. "And what if we find something truly ground-breaking? Something that could change the course of human history, while we are rooting out Kappa?"

Chris sighed, a mix of caution and anticipation evident in his voice. "We need to proceed with caution. If it's true we can't let this knowledge out into the public domain until Kappa has been snaffled. But if we do find something... as hard as it might be we put a lid on it until the time is right."

The room fell into silence once again as each of them revelled in their thoughts. Then Alex cut the silence voicing his concern that unless they got some hours of shuteye they wouldn't be able to function efficiently. It was now almost midnight so they had a maximum of six hours sleep at best. Chris agreed, putting his thoughts to one side and putting on his leader's hat he reminded them that they had his full trust in whatever decisions they had to make tomorrow.

"Right, off you go, get a good night's sleep and good luck tomorrow," said Chris, as he shook each of them by the hand.

As the minutes ticked by and the pressure mounted, Chris couldn't help but constantly glance at his watch. He only had fifteen minutes left before he needed to give his decision to Kappa, and every second seemed to slip away faster than the last.

Just as the weight of his impending decision started to settle on his shoulders, his phone rang. He let out a small sigh of relief at the distraction. "About time," he muttered to himself after checking the caller ID.

It was Barry, no doubt wondering if he had made up his mind yet. Chris though couldn't resist teasing his friend a little, especially since Barry was usually so punctual. "You're cutting it fine, Barry," Chris scolded.

"Sorry, Chris," Barry replied, trying to sound apologetic. "But it was damn difficult spotting an entrance to the Aegina complex. It was so well hidden that I had to borrow a satellite from the United Kingdom."

Chris's anxiety rose at the mention of the Aegina complex. "Good news, I hope?" he asked tentatively.

Barry let out a chuckle. "Of course, it is. We managed to negotiate fifteen minutes of full zoom with the UK spy satellite, which means our video had a resolution of just six metres."

Chris breathed a sigh of relief at the confirmation that their mission was a success. "Send me the coordinates, Barry. I have a helicopter on standby to take me to Aegina."

"Will do," Barry replied efficiently. "The entrance is located right in the centre of the Temple of Aphaia, where the steps lead up to the upper area. The satellite detected steps descending beneath the temple, so there must be some sort of mechanism to open them." He quickly sent over the coordinates through their secure communication system. "Good luck, Chris. And keep me posted if you can."

"Thanks, Barry." Chris ended the call and took a deep breath. This was it - the moment he had been waiting for. Excitement and nerves mingled within him as he prepared to embark on the next phase of their mission.

Chapter 23

Chris punched in Kappa's mobile number.

"I was beginning to think you had bottled out of a decision, Horsman. You only just made it before the hour was up. Who do you want to die?"

Kappa turned his video phone so that Chris could see both Gitta and Mia. A small trickle of blood was running down Mia's cheek so it was obvious that Mia's knife wound hadn't been treated yet. Gitta seemed unharmed, to which he was thankful.

"I won't let you do this," Chris growled, his voice filled with determination. "I won't let you control me anymore."

Kappa's eyes narrowed, a flicker of surprise crossing his face. The audacity of Chris's defiance seemed to momentarily catch him off guard.

"What are you babbling about, Horsman?" Kappa sneered, his voice dripping with contempt. "You think you can defy me? You are nothing! Just a pawn in my game."

"Fine," Chris spat, meeting Kappa's gaze with unwavering determination. "If I have to choose, then I choose myself."

Kappa's laughter filled the room. "Oh, how noble of you! But it won't save you from making a choice."

Chris smirked, his eyes glinting with defiance. "You misunderstand. I choose myself to save them both."

Confusion flickered across Kappa's face before giving way to anger. "What are you scheming, Horsman?"

Chris put his head closer to the screen on his video phone, his voice cold and calculating. "I challenge you to a game, Kappa. If I win, you release Mia and Gitta unharmed. If you win, you can have me as your pawn forever."

Kappa's eyes narrowed, a dangerous smile playing at the corners of his lips. "Very well, Horsman. I accept your challenge. But remember, the consequences of losing will be far worse than you can imagine."

Chris felt relieved for the moment, later he would feel the anxiety, but for now he had bought himself, Gitta and Mia time. "I'll come to your headquarters to play the game, Kappa." Then he added, "Of course, only if that is good for you."

Kappa roared with laughter. "How are you going to come to me, you don't know where I am?"

"Oh, but I do!" Chris exclaimed, a sly grin on his face. "See you in thirty minutes." With that, he cut the connection and made one more quick call before striding confidently towards the helicopter pad on the roof of the building. As he approached, the unmistakable silhouette of an Airbus H160 came into view - the quietest helicopter in the world. Its sleek white exterior shimmered in the sunlight, blending seamlessly with the clear blue sky above. No one would hear him arrive in Aegina.

Chris clambered aboard, noting with a satisfied nod the six US Marines who were already buckled in and ready for take-off.

"All set, sir?" asked the pilot, snapping to attention as Chris settled into his seat.

"Flight time to the Temple of Aphaia estimated thirty minutes," he replied briskly, his mind already focused on the mission ahead.

"Go!" commanded Chris, and with that, the powerful blades of the helicopter began to slice through the air with a steady rhythm.

As they soared above the sprawling city below, gradually shrinking into tiny dots, Chris gazed out of the window and let out a deep breath. The hum of the engine muted any attempts at conversation, giving him a moment of solitude to contemplate the gravity of his task. He couldn't afford any distraction as he prepared to confront his greatest challenge yet. The fate of Gitta and Mia rested on his shoulders and he was determined not to fail them.

The helicopter soared over the sparkling Aegean Sea, the waves glistening like diamonds in the moonlight. Chris's eyes were fixed on the horizon, the Temple of Aphaia drawing closer with every passing second. The ancient ruins stood majestically on a hilltop, its weathered columns a testament to a forgotten era.

He now believed that within those sacred walls lay the key to unlocking the secrets of an ancient power, a power that could change the course of history.

As the helicopter descended towards a clearing near the temple, Chris could feel his heart pounding with anticipation. He couldn't ignore the weight of responsibility that now rested upon him. Gitta and Mia had entrusted him with their lives, believing in his ability to unravel the mysteries that surrounded them. Failure was not an option.

The helicopter touched down with a gentle thud, stirring up a cloud of dust that hung in the air for a moment before dissipating into the breeze. Chris unbuckled himself and stepped out onto the firm sun-hardened ground. He told the marines to follow him as he led them towards the steps which led to the upper platform. They needed to find the mechanism which opened the steps and revealed the entrance to Kappa's facilities below ground level.

With the precise coordinates from the satellite mapping in hand, Chris and the marines swiftly located the hidden mechanism. A section of the stone steps slid upwards, revealing a small vestibule with ancient, moss-covered stone steps leading deeper underground. The mechanism itself was a small piece of stone, barely the size of a brick, nestled into the bottom step. From a distance, it seemed to blend seamlessly with the surrounding stones, but upon closer inspection, its edges were worn and chipped from years of use. With a gentle push inward, a faint click echoed through the air, followed by a deep rumbling sound reminiscent of a garage door opening.

The opening revealed ancient stone steps descending into the darkness, Chris and the marines exchanged wary glances. Chris turned to them and said, "You know what to do. When I send the go signal, you call in the Reaper drone which is on standby up there somewhere. Make sure you are outside of the blast area before it unleashes its missiles. Otherwise, wait half an hour and if I haven't appeared, come and get me."

The unmistakable scent of damp earth filled the air, mingling with a faint aroma of aged parchment as Chris slowly descended the stairs. It was as if he were stepping into a hidden world, a forgotten realm buried beneath the surface. With each careful step, his boots whispered against the worn stone, creating a symphony of anticipation. The narrow passage gradually widened, revealing an expansive underground chamber. The walls, adorned with intricate carvings depicting long-lost civilizations, told tales of forgotten kings and mythical creatures.

Illuminated by the flickering glow of his tactical flashlight, Chris ventured deeper into this subterranean labyrinth. The silence was deafening as he pressed on, navigating between towering pillars that seemed to support the weight of history itself. Chris marvelled at the sheer scale of the underground complex. Who could have built it? Could Kaliope's theory be true? Too many unanswered questions.

Suddenly, he reached a T-junction. The left tunnel was similar to the one he had just walked down, it looked very tired and very old. But the right tunnel was ablaze with modern lights, clad with plastic walls, and air conditioning ducts in the ceiling which threw welcome cool air into Chris's face. Just a few metres from the T-junction was a set of metal double doors with card-key access on the right-hand wall. Before Chris could think through how he was going to get through the doors, they silently swung inwards revealing two of Kappa's lieutenants carrying AK-103 assault rifles on their shoulders. Chris breathed a sigh of relief. He was carrying a gun, a Glock, but it was no match for an AK if he had to use it in earnest. One of the men beckoned Chris to follow them. The surroundings were now very plush, the corridor was carpeted with a deep pile of blue carpet, the walls were wood panelling and between the walls and ceiling indirect lighting offered a soft glow to the surroundings.

As they made their way through a series of doors, Chris followed the two men until they finally stopped at a large, ornate door. With a flourish, one of the men opened the door and stepped back to allow Chris to enter the room. Inside, he was met with a sight that left him both intrigued and disturbed.

The room was Kappa's expansive office, and sitting behind his grandiose desk was Kappa himself. Beyond him, Chris could see Gitta tied to a wooden chair, her once-polished appearance now dishevelled and worn. The richness of the room seemed out of place compared to the helplessness of its current occupants. And just beyond Gitta, hung from the ceiling by ropes, was the unfortunate Mia. The wound on her cheek had closed, but it was clear that without proper treatment, she would be scarred for life. Behind her stood Takis Penza with a whip in his hand. It didn't need much thought to understand who the whip was for.

"Come on in, Horsman," said Kappa welcomingly. "Please, take a seat," he added, gesturing towards a chair in front of his desk. "So, what's your proposal? Oh, by the way, on your way down here you were scanned several times. We know you're carrying a Glock."

Before answering Kappa, Chris took a moment to smile reassuringly at Gitta and Mia. He hoped it would give them some sense of comfort and encouragement amidst this tense situation. "Just to keep you honest, Kappa," said Chris calmly. "I have a squad of six marines stationed above us, ready to come down and escort Gitta, Mia, and myself out at my signal. Or," he added with a slight smirk, "The Reaper drone circling overhead can direct its missiles towards the entrance of this complex and kill all of us."

Kappa scoffed haughtily at Chris's words. "A bit melodramatic, Horsman," he claimed with bravado in his voice. But Chris could see the surprise in Kappa's eyes, and it gave him a sense of satisfaction. Penza took a step forward and then stopped seemingly waiting for Kappa's command to hurt someone. Kappa signalled with the flat of his hand, making a downward movement, indicating to Takis to calm down. Inside Kappa wasn't calm, he was wondering how Horsman had found his headquarters so quickly. If things became too close to home, he could move to the secondary location on the other side of the island.

"So, what are we playing, Horsman?"

"Right," said Chris confidently. "The game we shall play is Bridge. I'll partner with Gitta, and Takis will be your partner. I'll even throw in the cards." Chris said as he threw two packs of pristine cards onto Kappa's desk.

Kappa's eyes narrowed as he considered Chris's proposal. What Horsman couldn't possibly know was that before he became a drug baron, he had been a very competent bridge player who had played for the Serbian international bridge team. A sly smile emerged on his face, revealing a glimmer of amusement. "Very well, Horsman," Kappa said, leaning back in his chair. "Let's play."

Chris and Gitta exchanged cautious glances, their hearts pounding with a mixture of anticipation and anxiety. Kappa gestured towards the small round table positioned in the corner of the room, inviting them to take a seat. As they settled into their chairs, Gitta opposite Chris and Takis opposite Kappa, Mia took a chair and sat behind Gitta, her worried gaze never leaving Chris.

The room fell silent except for the faint sound of shuffled cards as Kappa began to deal the first hand. The atmosphere was thick with tension, each player acutely aware that this game held far more than just the fate of a few hands of cards.

As the first game progressed, Chris couldn't help but admire Kappa's skilful playing. His partner Penza played with surprising tenacity, and Gitta, the opposite played with the utmost concentration.

Chris couldn't help but admire Kappa's and Penza's skillful playing. Gitta sitting opposite him played with utmost caution and concentration.

"Final rubber," said Chris, slurring a little more than he had in the previous rubber. He and Gitta had agreed that Chris would gradually pretend that he was becoming more and more tipsy. Chris felt that Kappa might begin to be more relaxed and not notice Chris's sleight of hand.

"Your deal," said Kappa, grinning like a Cheshire cat.

"Sure," said Chris, as he fumbled to pick up the pack of cards on his left, shuffled them with great difficulty and then passed them to Kappa on his right for him to cut them. As he took the cards off the table he feigned a sneeze, by bringing a handkerchief up to his face with his right hand, while at the same time switching the pack to his left hand. Unbeknown to the others around the table the pack he switched to his left hand was a doctored pack hidden from view behind the hanky, and the original pack stayed hidden in the hanky. It was done so quickly that no one realised what had happened.

After pocketing the hanky and the pack, Chris dealt the cards from the doctored pack. He made heavy weather of the deal fumbling cards here and there but not enough for Kappa to call for a re-deal. The hand he dealt were as follows.

GITTA
C 76532
D –
H 6543
S T987

TAKIS	**KAPPA**
C -	**C** KJ9
D JT9	**D** AK
H T9872	**H** AKQJ
S 65432	**S** AKQJ

CHRIS
C AQT84
D Q8765432
H -
S -

Chris slurring said, "Seven clubs."

Takis glances at Kappa not knowing how to respond. Chris pretended not to notice when Kappa made a small movement with the flat of his hand.

"No bid," said Takis a little nervously.

Gitta wondering what Chris was up to, stared at her cards as she quietly said, "No bid."

Kappa with a smirk on his face immediately responds, "Double." Then stares at Chris as if challenging him to redouble, convinced that the alcohol which Chris had drunk had gone to his head, and Kappa was about to acquire Gitta and Mia.

"Look, I've got a pretty good hand here," slurred Chris. "How about a side bet?"

Kappa almost jumped up and down with glee. "What do you think Takis, shall we take a punt, the CIA must be loaded?"

"Yes, boss. How many zeros should we bet?" asked Takis, hoping Kappa knew what he was doing. His own hand did not have any clubs. Kappa must have pretty good clubs to have doubled.

"How about a nice round five million dollars, Horsman?"

Chris's brow furrowed as he put on his thinking face. "I don't know," he said slurring his words. "Okaaaay, let's do this. I agreeee!" He leaned across the table holding out his hand. Kappa took it. "Agreed!

Kappa let out a chuckle barely able to contain himself.

"Redouble," said Chris in a much stronger voice than before, and with no hint of a slur. Kappa's eyes widened as he looked at Chris's glass of whisky, which was still half covered by a napkin. Chris reached out picked up the glass and put it to his lips. Kappa still staring at the glass, realised he had been duped. Horsman's glass still had the same amount of whisky in it, as when he received it from the waiter.

Chris smiled at Kappa, then led the two of diamonds, which he ruffed in dummy with the two of clubs, over Kappa's king of diamonds. Kappa said nothing but it was slowly dawning on him that something wasn't quite right. Chris then finessed the three of clubs from the dummy, in response, Kappa put up his jack of clubs which Chris took with his queen of clubs. Chris again led a low diamond which he ruffed with the five of clubs in dummy, trapping Kappa's ace of diamonds.

Kappa groaned when he realised that Horsman might take the thirteen tricks he had contracted. He watched in dread as Chris finessed the six of clubs from dummy to which Kappa put up his nine of clubs, and Chris won the trick with his ten of clubs. Kappa looked aghast as he suddenly realised that Takis had no clubs support and Horsman must be sitting with the ace, and queen of clubs and so will be able to finesse dummy's clubs through his own clubs. There was no defence against this at all. He was going to lose five million dollars.

Chapter 24

As the morning sun cast its golden rays over Syntagma Square, Dimitri Karagianis couldn't help but relish in the grandiosity of his dreams. The prospect of the Golden Dawn party ascending to power was like a beacon of hope, shining brightly amidst the chaos and uncertainty that plagued Greece.

Karagianis clenched his fists, feeling the weight of anticipation building within him. He had dedicated his life to this cause, tirelessly spreading his ideology and rallying supporters across the nation. It was time for their moment to shine, their chance to reshape Greece in their own image.

His eyes shifted from the panoramic view outside to a stack of papers on his desk, filled with meticulously crafted plans and strategies. Victory seemed within reach; all that remained were the final steps. Dimitri knew that he needed more than just support from loyal followers; he needed the people's trust. He had to convince them that his vision was not one of hate and division, but rather a path towards a unified right-wing government that embraced both the not-so-well-off, but also the well-off.

He smiled to himself as he thought about the grandeur of his plan. The secret underground complexes that had once been hidden from the world would in the near future, be transformed into magnificent tourist attractions. Milos and Aegina, with their breathtaking natural beauty and hidden wonders, would become the crown jewels of Greece.

With Kappa's support, he had managed to secure the necessary funding for the ambitious project. The construction crews would soon be hard at work, transforming the vast underground caves into a mesmerizing labyrinth of tunnels and chambers. They would be adorned with intricate carvings, vibrant murals, and awe-inspiring statues that depicted the rich history and mythology of not only Greece, but also of the advanced alien civilization that had chosen Greece as the earthly birthplace of learning and democracy.

News of their undertaking would spread, excitement would ripple through the nation. People from all corners of Greece eagerly awaiting the day when they could explore these subterranean marvels. Families would save every euro they could spare, dreaming of being among the first to witness the ethereal beauty that lay beneath their feet.

Apart from the lavish tourist attractions, his partnership with Kappa had born fruit for his party. It had become the source of vast sums of money with which, apart from maintaining a lavish life style, enabled him to bestow gifts and favours to the poorest families in the land. A sort of Greek Robin Hood in a weird kind of way. The revenue of millions of dollars – the currency of drugs – would transform Greece's economy into the fastest growing in Europe and little Greece would be a giant again.

A soft tap on his door broke his revere.

"Come in," he shouted, as he sat down in the chair behind his desk.

The door to the anteroom where he held his meetings softly opened and one high heeled elegant foot slid into view followed by a bare leg which went on and on. With a mischievous smile on her face, the woman gracefully sauntered into the room. Her raven hair cascaded down her shoulders, framing a face that seemed to hold secrets yet to be discovered. As she approached, the scent of roses filled the air, intoxicating his senses.

"Good evening," she purred, her voice velvety and seductive. "I hope I'm not disturbing you."

His heart quickened at the sight of her, captivated by her mysterious allure. "No disturbance at all," he replied, his voice almost a whisper. "In fact, your presence is most welcome."

She glided towards him, her movements as enchanting as a waltz. The room seemed to dim in her presence, casting a halo of shadows that danced along the walls. His eyes traced the curve of her lips, unable to look away.

"I've heard whispers of your remarkable talents," she continued, her voice filled with intrigue. "They say that you possess the power to bring dreams to life."

He leaned back in his chair, his interest piqued. "Indeed," he replied, a hint of a smile playing on his lips. "But how did you come to know of such things?"

The woman's eyes twinkled with mischief as she circled him, her fingers gently grazing the edge of his desk. "I have my ways," she teased, her voice laced with secrets. "And I've come seeking your assistance."

Curiosity burned within him. "What is it that you desire?"

Her gaze locked onto his, intense and unyielding. "I seek to turn the tides of fate," she confessed, her voice filled with determination. "To rewrite the story that has already been written."

A surge of excitement rushed through him, for he knew that rewriting destiny was no simple task. It required a delicate balance of skill and daring. "And how do you propose we accomplish this?" he asked. She sauntered closer, the scent of roses growing stronger with each step. Her eyes gleamed with a mixture of hope and desperation. "I believe in the power of words," she said, her voice quivering with conviction. "I've heard that you possess the ability to infuse life into every sentence, to create a world where everything is possible."

He pondered her words, his mind spinning with possibilities. As an expert in fiction, he had crafted countless tales and breathed life into characters who had captured the hearts of readers far and wide. But this request was different. It required him to rewrite the very fabric of existence itself.

A smile tugged at the corners of his lips as he glanced at the woman standing before him. There was an air of determination about her, an unwavering belief in defying fate that mirrored his own rebellious spirit.

"I accept your challenge," he declared, his voice resonating with quiet resolve. "Together, we shall rewrite destiny."

The woman's lips curled into a wicked smile as she stepped closer to him, her piercing green eyes locking onto his. She moved lithely, perching on the edge of the desk next to him, and with a flick of her wrist, the slit in her dress fell open revealing that she wore nothing underneath. Karagianis's jaw dropped as he took in the sight of her perfectly toned thighs and the enticing curve of her pubic mound. His mind raced with thoughts - he didn't even know her name, but here she was, offering herself to him. Could this really be happening? He was no stranger to beautiful women, but this was something else entirely.

As she stood up, she deftly slipped off the straps of her dress, letting it fall to the ground at her feet. With each step closer, she brought herself inches away from Karagianis who remained rooted to his chair. She noticed beads of sweat forming on his forehead and gently wiped them away with his own white handkerchief from his jacket pocket, tantalizingly close to his skin.

"Look at me," she whispered huskily, not as a demand but an invitation. And without hesitation, Karagianis met her gaze, feeling a primal desire burning within him. He couldn't believe his luck - a literary partnership turned passion igniting before his very eyes. This was uncharted territory for him, but he was more than willing to explore every inch of it with her.

Her hand reached out to brush a loose strand of hair from his face, her touch sending a jolt of electricity through his body. He could feel the heat radiating off her, igniting a fire within him that he hadn't known before.

"I want you," she murmured, her voice barely above a whisper.

He swallowed hard, trying to find the words to respond. But all coherent thought left him as she leaned in closer, her lips meeting his in a passionate kiss. He could taste the sweetness of her lipstick, feel the softness of her skin against his own. It was intoxicating, overwhelming.

She pulled away, leaving him breathless and wanting more. Her eyes gleamed with mischief as she reached down to unbutton his shirt, revealing the toned chest beneath. She traced her fingers over his muscles, a small smile playing on her lips as she felt him shiver under her touch.

"Wait," she whispered, as she placed a perfectly manicured finger against his lips, "Before we go on to seal our physical partnership, we must seal our business relationship. I would like to see the architects' drawings that you have on your private server, relating to the catacombs on the island of Milos. And of course, Aristeidis's Diary. You have the only copy in existence I believe. They will form the basis for the beautiful words you are going to write."

Karagianis was taken aback by her sudden shift in demeanour, her request catching him off guard. The allure that had enveloped the room seemed to dissipate, replaced by a sense of unease. He had expected their encounter to be one of passion and creative collaboration, not a transactional exchange of information.

Slowly, he regained his composure and regarded her with a mixture of curiosity and caution. "Why do you need those architectural drawings and the diary?" he asked, his voice tinged with suspicion. "And what do they have to do with the words I am meant to write?"

The woman's eyes bore into his, a flicker of impatience crossing her face. "Those catacombs hold ancient secrets," she replied, her voice laced with urgency. "Secrets that have the power to unlock the very essence of our story. The words you write will only come alive if they are woven with the truths hidden within the drawings and diary."

Karagianis hesitated for a moment, weighing the risks and rewards of divulging such information. The catacombs on the island of Milos were renowned for their enigmatic history, rumoured to hold cryptic symbols and hidden passages. They were the perfect source of inspiration for his writing, but to share the papers meant exposing a truth that could alter the course of their partnership.

He locked eyes with the woman once more, searching for sincerity in her gaze. There was a vulnerability in her expression, an unspoken plea that resonated deep within him. Perhaps this exchange was more than just a transaction; it held the key to unlocking a narrative beyond their wildest imaginations.

Karagianis's hand trembled slightly as he reached into the dark depths of his desk drawer, retrieving a small, inconspicuous USB drive. His voice remained steady, but there was a hint of hesitation in his resolute nod. "Not on a server, but this contains everything you seek," he said, his eyes meeting hers with a mix of fear and trust. "But remember, with great power comes great responsibility."

The woman before him, tall and confident with a teasing smile on her lips, took the USB drive from his hand. Her fingers brushed against his in a delicate touch, sending shivers down his spine.

In the anteroom next to Karagianis's office, two figures leaned in closer to listen. Alex and Kaliope had heard enough. It had been Kaliope's idea to involve the woman, Alya - one of her three best undercover operatives who reported directly to her.

Alya was born in Alexandra, to Greek and Egyptian parents. She grew up learning to belly dance and became quite skilled at it before moving to Athens with her family. Kaliope spotted her unique seductive abilities when visiting the pole dancing club where Alya worked. Without hesitation, she recruited Alya for her select band of seductresses who all worked undercover, infiltrating crime organizations, drug gangs, and even the Albanian mafia.

In a matter of minutes, Alya had slyly managed to retrieve the coveted flash drive from Karagianis - a task that Alex and Kaliope could have spent hours attempting without success. To them, Alya was not just an operative, but a valuable asset with a skillset that proved invaluable time and time again.

As Alex and Kaliope entered the room, they were met with two surprising sights. Firstly, Alya sat calmly in Karagianis's chair, still completely naked but wearing a satisfied smile on her face. And secondly, Karagianis's complexion had turned ashen, drained of all colour as he realized he had been outsmarted.

In an attempt to regain control of the situation, he blustered, "Prime Minister, you've arrived just in time. This woman has stolen something of great importance to me." He pointed accusingly at Alya. "Shall I call security?"

Kaliope interrupted his protests with authority. "No need, Dimitri. This woman is working with us."

Karagianis stammered in confusion, "I-I don't understand..."

"There's no need for you to," retorted Kaliope sternly. "You are under arrest for drug trafficking and terrorist activities. Please remain seated until EKAM officers arrive."

Alya finally stood up and began to get dressed as Kaliope took charge of the situation with confident efficiency. The room was tense with anticipation as they waited for reinforcements to arrive and take Karagianis into custody.

Two hours later, the only sound in the Maga Maximo in Athens was the faint hum of fluorescent lights and the occasional shuffle of papers. In Mega Maximo's conference room, Alex and Kaliope were bent over blueprints of the catacombs on Milos Island and an ancient drawing of the underground complex on Aegina. They anxiously awaited Chris and Gitta's return from their adventure to Kappa's headquarters on Aegina, and they hoped Yannis could join them after overseeing the progress at the Delphi site with his team.

Alex's laser pointer illuminated certain areas of the blueprints as he spoke, his voice filled with excitement. "These are incredibly valuable pieces of information," he declared. "Take note here - this is where German U-boats would enter the catacombs during World War II." He then shifted his focus to another section of the blueprint. "And look here, a tunnel that leads under the sea towards Aegina island - most likely the same one we travelled through by train."

Kaliope, who was stationed at the other end of the conference table with her own set of blueprints, gasped audibly. "This goes beyond anything I could have imagined, sir," she breathed out. "What I see here has the potential to change history as we know it."

Intrigued, Alex joined her at her end of the table and examined the drawing she was referring to. "My god," he exclaimed in disbelief. "You're absolutely right. This discovery could have a massive impact."

Chapter 25

While Chris was playing mind games with Kappa in his underground villa on Aegina, Yannis and his team of fifteen highly trained officers were scouting the northern entrance of the ancient site of Delphi. As Chris had ordered, they did not interfere with the robots who were diligently loading cases of military grade weapons onto waiting trucks just outside the gates.

Realizing that he and his team could not be in two places at once, Yannis swiftly formulated a plan. He instructed his team to deploy a number of advanced drones under their control to follow the trucks.

These drones were equipped with state-of-the-art technology, including artificial intelligence, that allowed them to calculate the optimum speed, and height to transmit accurate clear video footage. With their uncanny ability to mimic human behaviour, they began tailing the trucks while relaying real-time information back to Yannis and his team.

Each team member had a small screen on their forearm about the size of a quarter of an iPad. The screen streamed information in real time, from deployed drones, satellites, and their command centre. So, each member of the team received the same information as their team members. Gone were the days when a squad of soldiers would have to rely on one person in their team to relay information to them.

Yannis found himself increasingly fascinated by Kappa's robotic companions. Their flawless execution of tasks and unwavering dedication impressed him beyond measure. Yet, as their interactions continued, subtle doubts began creeping into Yannis's mind – could there be more to these robots than just mere machines?

Yannis had witnessed the extraordinary capabilities and unexpected emotions displayed by these advanced robots. He considered the possibility that true humanity might extend beyond flesh and blood, encompassing a genuine desire to protect, care, and sacrifice for others.

With those thoughts in mind, Yannis left his men at Delphi, impressing upon them that they should stay hidden and observe only. Whatever the robots did they should leave well alone. An EKAM helicopter picked him up from the old town of Delphi just a few kilometres away, and within an hour at exactly eleven o'clock in the morning, he was touching down onto the Maga Maximo helipad.

"Welcome, Yannis," greeted Alex as he walked into the conference room. "We've been busy studying the architects' drawings that Alex and Kaliope retrieved from Karagianis's office."

"Yes, I heard on the radio that Karagianis had been arrested and was now in a cell at our headquarters."

Kaliope walked over to Yannis and gave him a quick kiss on his lips. "We have the evidence that he has been collaborating with Karras and perhaps even acting as a silent partner. Come over here," she said, pointing to where Alex, Gitta and Chris were studying one of the drawings.

Five minutes later, Yannis, like the other four, found himself captivated by the mysterious theory that had been circulating amongst themselves, that the ancient Greeks had been aided by extra-terrestrial beings who had left behind advanced robots or even androids to assist them in their technological advancements.

Determined to uncover the truth, Alex had invited a great friend of his, Pericles Brudo, a professor of ancient history at Athens University, to study the drawings. Armed with his extensive knowledge of Greek history and a relentless pursuit of answers, Pericles sat at one end of the conference room at a small table, studying ancient texts, and deciphering cryptic symbols.

The drawings they had found on the flash drive showed, without a doubt, the mythical existence of the Golden Triangle - a network of underground tunnels connecting the islands of Milos, Aegina, and Delphi - was not a myth at all, but very true. The tunnels were not the only structures under the Aegean. At intervals of twenty kilometres, there were structures that according to Pericles's ancient texts, held the key to a hidden truth that could change the course of humanity forever.

Notated on the back of the architects' drawings that displayed the facilities underneath the catacombs on Milos, were lists of items the archaeologists had unearthed. Ancient artefacts, hinting at advanced technology far beyond their time. The storage facility held secrets of a lost civilization capable of space travel and interstellar communication. The notes were signed by Dr Elena Marlowe, a recognised and prominent archaeologist who twenty years ago disappeared, left a husband and three children utterly heartbroken. Yannis remembered that there were strong rumours that she had stumbled on something so profound that historians' view of history would be severely challenged.

Her notes suggested that the cryptic chambers, they stumbled upon were not just relics of the past, but clues to a world far ahead of its time. The storage facility held secrets so extreme that they could shake the very foundations of modern understanding. Among the artefacts were intricate devices that seemed to harness cosmic energies, inscriptions detailing celestial maps leading to distant galaxies, and remnants of what appeared to be communication devices capable of transmitting messages across vast cosmic distances.

Along the underwater tunnels to Aegina, scientists had also discovered complex machinery with intricate designs reflecting a level of sophistication never seen before. The facilities here seemed to be a hub for manufacturing components essential for space exploration.

Then, underneath Delphi, scientists had stumbled upon what appeared to be launch pads for futuristic spacecraft. The air in the conference room crackled with anticipation as the six people in the room realized the monumental significance of these sites.

"But where are these architects and scientists now?" questioned Alex.

"Dead," answered Chris and Yannis in unison. "When I first joined EKAM, I read a report concerning the disappearance of several prominent archaeologists and scientists, including Dr Elena Marlowe. The report concluded that it was a coincidence and that there were no indications that the missing persons were working on the same project or for the same sponsor."

"Do you think it was Kappa who got rid of them?" asked Kaliope.

"We don't have enough evidence to charge him, but he most certainly had something to do with it," said Yannis.

"If all of this actually exists, Greece will become the most important country on the planet," mused Alex to no one in particular.

"We should explore everything that's on the drawings once we have finished with Kappa."

"Yes, Gitta, we should. But it's not going to be easy. He will be waiting for us," said Chris.

"Surely we have got more firepower?"

"Maybe we have Alex, but he knows every nook and cranny in the underground complexes. We don't, and you can bet your life he'll use it to his advantage," suggested Chris.

"I'd love to go with you when you deem it safe for civilians," said Pericles Brudo. "Who is this Kappa fellow? You mention him a lot."

"The less you know the better my good friend," said Alex taking his friend by the arm. "You'll be the first academic I'll call on when it's safe to explore the complexes. You'd better go now and thank you for your input. Maria, my secretary has a non-disclosure agreement for you to sign in her office." Alex put his arm around Pericles shoulder as he led him to the door. "Goodbye, my friend."

Once Pericles had left the room, Chris took charge. "Right, we need to plan our assault on Kappa's empire. Let's mind-map the options and then work towards a majority vote on the one that gives us the greatest chance of victory."

"Agreed," said Yannis, eager to contribute. "But something has been bugging me about those robots loading the trucks in Delphi."

Chris raised an eyebrow, "What is it?"

"They look like robots but they don't move like robots, they move more like humans, like us."

"Do you think they are androids, Yannis?" asked Chris.

"Yes, I do."

Kaliope and Alex were looking at the drone footage from the Delphi surveillance drone. "I think he is right," said Alex. "Look at this footage," Alex said, pointing at the monitor.

They all gathered round the monitor watching closely the movements of the robots. It was Gitta who broke the silence. "So, humanity has found itself bestowed with an unusual gift: androids, left behind by the enigmatic aliens. These androids, sleek and sophisticated, obviously possess advanced artificial intelligence, and are probably programmed with a singular purpose - to assist and serve humanity. Kappa found them, and somehow harnessed them to undertake mundane physical work, not anything monumental, so he can't know how advanced their AI circuitry is."

"How do you know they only do mundane tasks?" asked Alex, his eyes having that quizzical look that Gitta found so endearing.

"I don't but I'm guessing that if they did more than mundane tasks Kappa would have harnessed that sort of power to build his business at a much faster pace. Besides, Mia did not mention such a use for the androids - which she called robots by the way - but she did mention something which seems to blur the lines between master and servant."

"What was that?" Chris said, his ears pricking up.

"Mia told me that on two occasions that she knows of two different androids actually raped two of Kappa's female staff."

"They actually raped the women or tried to rape them?" questioned Chris, a disbelieving look on his face.

"Actually raped! They both succeeded in penetrating their vaginas and leaving their seed."

Kaliope stared at Gitta, nor daring to believe what she had just heard. Her voice quivered as she asked, "Do you believe Mia?"

"Yes, why would she lie about that? According to Mia both women became obviously pregnant, then quite suddenly disappeared."

"Killed?" asked Yannis.

"I asked the same thing but Mia didn't know, but when I asked her how they stopped the androids, she told me that before they could try to stop them, they stopped themselves, and as if nothing had happened and got on with their previous mundane tasks."

"So, are these androids truly under human control, or are they still puppets dancing to the strings of their alien creators? Are these androids saviours or silent invaders, here to guide or to manipulate?" mused Kaliope.

"How can we find out?" asked Alex.

"There is only one way and that's to search through the underground complexes, and we can only do that when we have defeated Kappa," said Chris.

They all nodded their heads in agreement, before turning back to the monitor showing the live drone feed. Just at that moment, quite unexpectedly one of the androids put down the package it was carrying, turned and looked up at the drone. It was as if the android was staring into their eyes as they watched the monitor. They all said afterwards that at that moment they had felt disorientated, feeling a low buzzing in their ears for a few seconds, just before the monitor went black.

Yannis immediately called the officer he had left in charge at Delphi.

"What happened?" asked Yannis when he had got him on the phone.

"We don't know. One moment the drone was completing a reconnaissance run, then next moment it fell out of the sky!"

Yannis didn't know what to say for a second, then he recovered his composure and said, "As you were, stay vigilant and I'll be out there in a few hours. Meanwhile get another drone on station. Report back to me when it's in position."

Yannis closed the call then turned to the others "What the hell is going on?"

Chris's voice trembled as he spoke, his eyes fixed on the android in the corner of the monitor. "I think one of these damn things just showed its true colours." He turned to face Yannis, his expression grave. "We need to shut down the Temple of Apollo operation now that we have Gitta back."

Yannis's eyes widened in shock. "You mean that android that looked up at the drone's camera just destroyed it?" His mind raced with fear and disbelief. "I thought it had malfunctioned, not been shot down."

Chris shook his head. "I don't know what happened. All I know is that this could be much bigger than we ever imagined." The weight of his words hung heavily in the air, sending a chill down everyone's spine.

As they processed Chris's analysis, a haunting question lingered: were these androids being controlled by some sinister force from within the underground complexes forming the infamous golden triangle? Fear and suspicion crept over them like a suffocating fog, trapping them in a web of uncertainty and danger.

Chapter 26

On Aegina, Kappa was hunched over his desk, plotting a ruthless assault. The news of Karagianis' arrest had sent shivers down his spine. He quickly summoned Takis to his office, a grave expression etched on his face.

"How many EKAM officers are stationed at the Delphi site?" he barked.

Takis paused, his mind racing as he calculated the numbers. "Around fifteen to twenty," he replied cautiously. "But they seem content just watching the androids perform."

Kappa grunted in acknowledgement before moving onto more pressing matters. "And the butterfly wall? Is it still operational without any interference?"

"For now, but we've lost our leverage after Gitta's and Mia's retrieval," Takis admitted, regretting the words as soon as they left his lips. He braced himself for Kappa's wrath.

But instead, Kappa's grin widened menacingly. "We have a backup plan," he declared. "There's a hidden exit further up the mountain, connected to the railway tunnel under Delphi. It's an exact replica of the Temple of Apollo, complete with butterflies. And no need for any construction work."

Takis couldn't hide his surprise. "I never knew that" he confessed.

"Need-to-know basis, my friend," Kappa replied cryptically. "But now we must focus on taking down Horsman and reclaiming Gitta and Mia before Horsman and Yannis Spanos arrive with their heavy firepower." His eyes gleamed with determination. "It's time to utilise some of the weaponry left behind by our extra-terrestrial visitors."

Takis couldn't believe what he was hearing. The rumours about the mysterious tunnels connecting Delphi, Aegina, and Milos were true after all. But there was no time to dwell on it now.

"I'm with you, boss," he said.

Kappa's sharp, intense gaze flicked over Takis, assessing his loyalty with a nod of approval. "Good. Gather our most skilled and trusted men and prepare for the assault," he ordered, his voice exuding authority.

They huddled together over several maps, spread out on Kappa's expansive desk. The dim light of the room cast deep shadows across the intricate lines and symbols on the maps, adding an air of urgency to their discussion. "We must be careful not to put all our resources in one location, Takis. We cannot risk being caught off guard by a surprise attack from Horsman's men while we are making our move on Mega Maximo where the Prime Minister and Gitta will be." Kappa's brow furrowed in concern, clearly strategizing every possible scenario.

Takis nodded in agreement, his eyes scanning the maps as he visualised their plan coming to life. He pointed at different locations on the maps representing Milos, Aegina, and Delphi facilities, indicating where some of Kappa's men should be stationed. "Here and here on Milos, here at the entrance to Aegina complex, and in Delphi, at the Temple of Apollo, the northern exit where the androids load up, and the backup entrance up the mountain."

"How many men can we muster altogether?" Kappa asked.

"Sixty," Takis replied confidently.

"And how do you suggest we split them?" Kappa leaned in closer, eager to hear Takis' plan.

After a moment of thoughtful consideration and some mental calculations, Takis responded. "As far as we know, they only have knowledge of the Temple of Apollo and Aegina sites. So, I propose we station ten armed men at each of those locations and five men at each of the others. That would leave us with twenty-five men to take down the Mega Maximo. What do you think?" The tension in the room was palpable as he awaited Kappa's decision.

Kappa's eyes glazed over as he leaned back in his chair, lost in thought. His right hand rested on the six knives strapped to his belt, each one secured in its own leather sheath. After a minute or so of contemplation, he leaned forward with determination. "Go for it Takis," he said, his voice low and steady. "I trust you to do a good job." He paused briefly before continuing. "Will you personally visit the three storage facilities, hidden beneath the sea between here and Milos, and see what weaponry we can use to give us an edge?"

Takis nodded confidently. "Yes, boss," he replied, already planning out his strategy in his mind.

Takis left Kappa's office with a sense of purpose, his mind already racing with strategies and plans. He couldn't shake off the weight of responsibility that now rested on his shoulders. The fate of their entire operation seemed to hinge on his ability to secure advanced weaponry from the hidden storage facilities. He had already decided on the ten men he would take with him to search the storage facilities under the Aegean Sea. After briefing them over the phone, he arranged to meet them on the railway station on Milos the next day at seven in the morning.

Chapter 27

At seven, the next morning, Takis and his team boarded the train at the Milos complex having programmed it, as it was a driverless train, to stop at the first storage facility of the three they planned to search.

The train ride was silent, the tension in the air almost suffocating as Takis and his team mentally prepared themselves for what lay ahead. The first storage facility was rumoured to hold some of the most advanced weaponry left behind by the extra-terrestrials, and they knew that retrieving these weapons would be crucial for their upcoming assault on the Mega Maximo.

As the train came to a stop in front of a seemingly inconspicuous building twenty kilometres from Milos, Takis and his men quickly disembarked, scanning their surroundings for any signs of danger. With their weapons at the ready, they cautiously approached the entrance, which was concealed beneath a camouflage net blending into the rocky wall of the tunnel.

Takis signalled for one of his men to check for traps while he examined the security system guarding the entrance. It seemed outdated, but Takis knew better than to underestimate their adversaries. With skilled precision, he disabled the security measures and entered the code that was only known to a few of

Kappa's lieutenants, the heavy door slid back with a hiss revealing a dark corridor leading underground.

The air inside was musty and stale, with a metallic tang that made Takis' nose wrinkle in distaste. The faint hum of generators echoed through the narrow passageway, indicating that the facility was still operational despite being hidden from plain sight for so long. As they ventured deeper into the underground complex, Takis and his team passed rows of storage units containing various crates and containers, all waiting to be explored.

Their footsteps echoed off the concrete walls, creating an eerie symphony of sound that seemed to follow them as they navigated the labyrinthine tunnels. Every shadow seemed to hold a hidden threat, every creak of metal a warning of potential danger lurking in the darkness.

Takis led his team with determined strides, his hand never straying far from the weapon holstered at his side. He trusted his men to cover each other's backs, but he knew that in the world they operated in, trust could be a deadly luxury.

Finally, they reached the central chamber of the facility, a massive room filled with rows of high-tech vehicles of every sort. None of the strange transports had wheels but all had what looked like guns on their roofs, probably laser, or energy weapons Takis wagered. There were over three hundred of these vehicles in the huge chamber which was far larger than a Boeing seven-four-seven hanger.

It was obvious that there was no individual weaponry in this facility, so Takis led his team back to the entrance where he reset the security measures before inputting the codes to close the heavy door. They boarded the train, waiting while Takis re-programmed it to stop twenty kilometres further down the track at the next storage facility.

A few minutes later, the train glided to a stop opposite another huge door embedded in the rocky walls of the tunnel. Once again Takis disabled the security measures, placed his eye two centimetres in front of the retina reader and waited. Nothing happened at first, then slowly the giant door began to move majestically upwards disappearing into the ceiling of the tunnel. Takis and his team's eyes widened in awe at the sight before them. Before them was a cavernous space completely empty except for one object – a spacecraft.

The sleek black coloured craft, hovering just three metres off the ground, was the size of three large cruise ships. It was a bulbous shape similar to a giant tadpole without a skinny tail. All its portholes were dark – it was obviously unmanned. Takis and his team stepped gingerly into the facility, their boots making faint clicking noises as they walked towards the craft. As they neared it, a faint humming seemed to emanate from it. They reached the spacecraft but none of the men dared move underneath it lest it move down and crush them. They touched its exterior, whatever metal it was made of was cold to the touch.

Suddenly, the humming sound started to diminish and as it did the craft began to slowly descend until it settled on the surface of the hanger, for in essence, that was what the cavernous space was, a spacecraft hanger. They stood back looking in awe at the craft, both in an excitement tinged with a fear of the unknown. One of the men that owned a private plane and had been flying for over ten years said, "I'd love to see the cockpit of this beauty. I wonder how easy or difficult it is to fly?"

"You probably just need to talk to it," said Takis laughingly. "Just like Google or Alexa."

They all chuckled at Takis' humour, immediately breaking the tension that had been hanging in the air.

"C'mon," said Takis as he led them away from the spacecraft. "There are no weapons here of use to us. Let's go to the next storage facility."

Fifteen minutes later, they were standing in another massive storage facility which was jam packed with extremely high-tech weaponry, unlike anything they had ever seen before. His team spread out, each member carefully examining the advanced weaponry laid out before them. Plasma rifles, energy shields, and sleek black suits that seemed to blend into the shadows beckoned to them, promising power and protection in equal measure.

Takis approached a particularly intricate device that hummed softly with latent energy. It resembled a compact handheld cannon, its design unlike anything he had ever seen. As he reached out to touch it, a voice echoed through the chamber, causing them all to freeze in place.

"So, you've found your way here at last."

Takis whirled around, his hand instinctively moving to his sidearm as a figure stepped out of the shadows. It was a woman, her features obscured by the dim lighting but her voice carrying a tone of authority that demanded attention. She wore a sleek black suit similar to the ones displayed in the chamber, with a symbol embroidered on the shoulder that Takis recognized as the insignia of the extra-terrestrials.

"Who are you?" Takis demanded, his grip tightening on his weapon.

The woman raised a hand in a calming gesture. "I am Astra, guardian of this facility. I have been tasked with ensuring that our weaponry does not fall into the wrong hands."

Takis studied her carefully, noting the way she moved with precision and grace, like a predator ready to strike. "We are not your enemies," he stated firmly. "We seek to use these weapons to overthrow the heads of government who reside in the Mega Maximo building in Athens." He immediately regretted what he had said. "The government is corrupt and the people are weary of the taxes they impose on everyone, even the poor."

Takis knew that their mission had just taken an unexpected turn. Astra's presence signalled that their task was not going to be as straightforward as they had hoped. He exchanged a quick glance with his team, silently communicating the need for caution and diplomacy.

“We understand the gravity of our request,” Takis began, his voice steady. “We may not have been on your radar, but our fight is real, and the people are suffering under the oppressive regime of Mega Maximo,” he lied. “We need these weapons to level the playing field and bring about change for the better.”

Astra remained unreadable, her gaze penetrating. After a moment of tense silence, she spoke again. “I will test your worthiness. Follow me.”

With a nod from Takis, his team fell into step behind Astra as she led them deeper into the facility. The corridors grew darker, illuminated only by strips of LED lights along the walls. They passed by more advanced weaponry, each piece deadlier than the last. Takis couldn’t help but feel a twinge of unease at the thought of what these weapons were capable of in the wrong hands. Astra led them to a high-security chamber at the heart of the facility, where a single pedestal stood with a shimmering orb hovering above it, emitting a soft, pulsating light.

“This is the Orb of Ascendance,” Astra announced, her voice reverberating in the chamber. “It holds untold power and knowledge, but only those deemed worthy may harness its true potential.”

Takis exchanged wary glances with his team, uncertainty flickering in their eyes. They had not expected to encounter such a mystical artefact in their mission to acquire weapons for their cause. But they knew that backing out now was not an option.

Astra turned to face them, her gaze piercing through their defences. "To prove your worthiness, each of you must approach the orb and face your inner truth. Only then will it reveal its secrets to you. Choose wisely, for the orb sees all."

Takis felt a surge of mixed emotions as he stepped forward, his team following suit. As he neared the Orb of Ascendance, a sense of foreboding washed over him. He knew that this moment would be a test of not just their resolve but also their innermost selves.

With a deep breath, Takis reached out a hand towards the pulsating orb. The moment his fingers made contact, a flood of memories and emotions coursed through his mind. Visions flickered before his eyes, memories long buried rising to the surface.

He saw himself as a young boy, playing in the streets of Athens, filled with dreams of a better future. He saw the faces of his loved ones, those he had lost to the cruelty of the heroin and other drugs he had sold onto the streets of Athens, the people that he had needlessly murdered, and worse of all the women he had raped, cheated and abused. And he felt a burning desire deep within his soul, to kill Astra. He felt that she had a resolve to fight for justice and freedom at any cost. Her cost would be her life!

As the visions faded, Takis gripped his rifle tighter, noting that the others were doing the same. He felt a sense of pride that these nine men would follow him even if it meant that they might die. Takis knew that they had crossed a line they could never return from. He could see the determination in his team's eyes, a reflection of his own resolve to see their mission through to the end. Astra watched them with a knowing look, her expression unreadable.

"You have seen your truths," she said, her voice filled with a mixture of caution and curiosity. "Now, you must choose your path."

Takis exchanged a glance with his team, a silent agreement passing between them. They had come too far to turn back now, their cause too important to abandon. With a nod to Astra, Takis spoke the words that sealed their fate.

With a commanding shout, Takis ordered his men to raise their weapons and aim them at Astra. Nine soldiers stood in formation, their guns trained on the cloaked figure before them.

Despite the surprise in her eyes, Astra's composure remained unshaken. "You have chosen your path," she stated calmly, "Now, you must face the consequences of your choices."

A tense silence hung in the air as Astra stood motionless, surrounded by armed men. Suddenly, Takis fired a round from his rifle, followed by the others. The bullets hit Astra's black armoured suit with a loud clang before ricocheting back towards the attackers. They fell one by one, their bodies battered and bruised, until only Takis was left standing.

Confusion and fear etched onto his face, Takis stammered, "How-why... why am I not dead like the rest of my men?"

Astra's lips curled into a small grin as she revealed her true identity. "We don't interfere with other cultures," she explained. "We try to help them, as we helped your race over two thousand years ago."

Still uncertain and bewildered, Takis turned to inspect his fallen comrades. To his surprise, they were slowly beginning to stir and groan as they attempted to get up. "They're alive," he exclaimed, "But how?"

"We are not human," Astra replied simply.

Puzzled and amazed, Takis watched as Astrid opened a panel in the pedestal of her orb and revealed a video screen showing their attack in ultraslow motion. He saw their bullets being caught by Astra's lightning-fast reflexes and being redirected back towards them at a much slower speed.

"We have learned to harness the properties of light," Astrid explained. "We can move at incredible speeds, faster than your eyes can see."

In a flash, Astra was gone, leaving Takis and his remaining men to contemplate their choices and the power of those they had underestimated.

Chapter 28

Chris slowly emerged from his sleep, the remnants of dreams fading as he tried to pinpoint the sound that had awoken him. His ears strained, and then it clicked - the sound of water hitting tile. The shower was on in the en suite. A smile crossed his face as he remembered last night, a welcome break from the constant work and planning to defeat Kappa.

In a moment of trust and closeness, Chris had offered Mia the safety and comfort of his apartment. And now here she was, serving him up a delicious meal last night, and now washing away any traces of stress or worry with her beauty and grace. As he lay there, he couldn't help but feel grateful for this unexpected and wonderful interlude in their dangerous lives.

With a contented sigh, Chris allowed himself a few more moments to bask in the warmth of the morning sunlight filtering through the curtains. He could hear the soft hum of Mia's voice as she sang a tune he couldn't quite place, her melodic notes intermingling with the sound of the running water. Slowly pushing himself up from the bed, Chris swung his legs over the edge and stood up, stretching his arms above his head.

Padding softly across the carpeted floor, he approached the door to the en suite and leaned against the frame, watching Mia through the frosted glass shower door. She had her eyes closed, face tilted up towards the cascading water, a look of peaceful serenity gracing her features. Chris couldn't help but admire her in this unguarded moment, her usual tough facade stripped away to reveal vulnerability and beauty.

As Mia reached for the soap on the shelf, her eyes flew open abruptly, meeting Chris's gaze through the misted glass.

A flicker of surprise crossed Mia's face before a mischievous grin appeared, her eyes sparkling with amusement. Chris felt a rush of warmth at the sight of her playful expression, the tension that had been building in his chest melted away instantly. Without breaking eye contact, Mia slowly reached for the shower door handle and pushed it open, the steam billowing out around her in a swirl of fragrant mist.

"Enjoying the view?" she teased, her voice laced with humour as she stepped out of the shower, droplets of water glistening on her skin like liquid diamonds.

Chris chuckled softly, a smile tugging at the corners of his lips as he shook his head in mock exasperation. "I could ask you the same thing," he replied, his tone light and teasing.

Mia's laughter rang through the bathroom, a melodic sound that filled the air with joy and lightness. She wrapped herself in a fluffy towel, her movements graceful and effortless. Chris couldn't tear his eyes away from Mia as she dried herself off, the towel clinging to her curves in a way that made his heart race. He cleared his throat, trying to push away the sudden surge of desire that had him rooted to the spot. Mia shot him a knowing smirk, her eyes dancing with mischief as she sauntered over to where he stood.

"Like what you see?" she purred, her voice low and suggestive. Chris swallowed hard, feeling the heat rise to his cheeks as he struggled to find a clever retort.

Before he could form a coherent response, Mia closed the distance between them, her fingers trailing lightly down his chest. Chris shivered at her touch, electricity sparking in the air around them. With a soft chuckle, Mia tilted her head up to look into his eyes, her gaze intense and unwavering.

"Care to join me for round two?" she whispered, her breath warm against his skin. Chris felt a rush of desire as her fingernails light as a feather, circled the head of his penis. He tried to speak, but before he could answer Mia, her lips were pressing against his.

His mind cast back to last night when soon after they had finished the meal which Mia had ready for him when he arrived at his apartment, she had said, her face flushed with wine as a flirty look lit up her face, "Why don't you pour us a couple of drinks while I take a shower, Chris darling?" Chris watched her as she walked towards the bathroom undoing the belt of her skirt, then effortlessly stepping out of it as it fell to the floor. He was mesmerised by the sway of her hips which she accentuated as she walked.

Then as she reached the bathroom door she turned around facing him, her fingers very slowly and deliberately undid the buttons on her shirt exposing her bra-less breasts. She smiled teasingly, turned and disappeared into the bathroom leaving her shirt in a rumpled pile on the floor.

Ten minutes later as Chris was pouring a couple of whisky sours she called out, "Chris, hurry up! I don't want to miss the end of my shampoo playlist!"

He nearly dropped the shaker, a delighted grin spreading across his lips. "You mean there's more?" he asked, knees weakening at the thought of what else she might have planned.

Mia giggled, the sound as sweet and invigorating as the drink she so eagerly anticipated. "Of course, there's more," she replied, her voice sultry and enticing. "Why do you think I left the playlist on?"

Chris set the shaker down, the ice clinking against the sides as he handed her the drink. "You're a master of manipulation," he murmured, a hint of admiration in his voice.

Mia's eyes sparkled with mischief. "And you're a quick learner," she countered, with a playful smirk. "Now, come on. Let's see if you can keep up with my playlist."

Chris's heart pounded in his chest as he followed her into the en suite, the sound of water still echoing in the room. He set the drinks on the counter, their glasses clinking together softly as he stepped closer to Mia, who had turned off the shower and was now wrapped in a plush towel.

"I'm ready for round one," Chris said, his voice low and filled with desire. Mia's lips curved into a seductive smile, her eyes never leaving his.

"Then let's make it a night to remember," she whispered, stepping closer and pulling him into a passionate kiss. Their lips met, tongues entwining in a fervent dance, and Chris felt his body respond to her touch, his desire for her growing stronger with each passing second. What followed was indeed the most passionate night he had ever had in his life.

Now, as they passionately pressed their lips together, their tongues entwining, Chris deftly undid her towel, letting it fall onto the floor. He lifted her up, her legs wrapped around his waist, and carried her into the bedroom. They tumbled onto the bed in a loving tangle of arms and legs before Mia pressed Chris down onto his back then mounted him cowgirl style.

As Chris confided in Mia later that day, round two was even better than round one.

Chapter 29

As Chris and Mia revelled in each other's company, the carefully laid plans from the previous evening were set into motion by Alex, Gitta, Kaliope, and Yannis. They had discussed multiple options for infiltrating Kappa's underground complex, fully aware of the importance of destroying their operations without damaging any artefacts left behind by extra-terrestrials.

The option which had the most traction was for a team to infiltrate the Delphi site to cause a distraction, then once they had fully engaged Kappa's men, a team at the Milos site would commandeer the train and advance towards Aegina, stopping on the way to search the three giant storerooms.

Chris with Mia, would lead a team of ten marines to the ancient Temple of Aphaia on Aegina under which was the location of Kappa's headquarters. The plan was that once the other teams were engaging Kappa's men, Kappa would have a minimal security detail protecting him.

Yannis was to lead a team of twenty EKAM officers into the Delphi underground site, entering it through the ancient Temple of Apollo. Their mission was to capture any armed resistance they encountered, but Alex had also given them strict orders to use 'Kokkinos,' the code for lethal force, if necessary.

The team were now waiting for the green light from Chris, to begin the mission. Kaliope in her capacity as Home Secretary, was to organise police search teams tasked with seizing any suspected drug distribution centres, which Mia had red flagged in her briefings to Chris.

At the same time, Alex, together with Gitta would lead another group of thirty EKAM officers on Milos island. Accompanying them were two scientists and an archaeologist; the scientist, Pericles Brudo, a dear friend of Alex's and the other scientist the renowned Rosita Drosos. The archaeologist was none other than the prominent Greek expert Lidia Filitas, who had excavated numerous ancient sites including the Minoan Palace at Knossos. The team had been helicoptered to Milos and were now waiting for the go ahead from Chris to enter the secret passage down to the train station. They were ready to face whatever challenges lay ahead.

Chris with a team of ten marines had made his way to Aegina, not far behind the advanced team of technical experts, who had taken over one of the small hotels in the capital. Here the technicians had set up monitors, satellite and drone links, communication links to all the teams, including body cam feeds, and drone pilot rooms for the pilots controlling the "reaper" (predator) drones. Those personnel monitoring the monitor feeds could potentially see and talk to every one of the mission participants. Chris had left no stone unturned.

A clock somewhere in the distance struck twelve, and Yannis's heart raced as he was finally given the green light to enter the Temple of Apollo. His team, moved swiftly towards the main door. The site of Delphi was eerily quiet, closed off to tourists and giving off an unsettling aura. The only sound breaking through the silence was the unlocking and pulling back of the heavy wooden doors.

With weapons at the ready, the team cautiously made their way through the outer chamber and into the inner sanctum. The tension was palpable as they advanced, expecting an ambush from Kappa's men somewhere within the complex. But so far, there had been no resistance.

As they reached the wall of butterflies, where animated ones fluttered with mechanical wings, Yannis noticed something was off. In between where the ones carrying the white powder should have been, there were blank spaces.

"Looks like we've disrupted their cocaine distribution," Yannis shouted enthusiastically to his team, who all murmured their agreement. Moving towards the control panel on the wall, Yannis deftly pressed the green button, causing the wall to begin rotating open.

But just as it was barely one meter open, Yannis abruptly halted it. "Check for booby traps," he ordered, his senses on high alert. One of his officers shone a flashlight into the dark space beyond, revealing potential danger lurking in the shadows. As the flashlight's beam illuminated the empty space, Yannis could make out tripwires crisscrossing the room and pressure-sensitive plates scattered across the floor. It was a maze of traps, designed to incapacitate or kill anyone who dared to venture further into the depths of the temple.

Yannis's mind raced as he assessed the situation. They were running out of time, and Kappa's men could appear at any moment. He knew they had to tread carefully if they were to navigate through the treacherous path ahead.

"Expo, I need you to use your expertise to disarm these traps," Yannis instructed his bomb disposal expert, his voice firm and unwavering. Expo nodded in understanding, his eyes scanning the intricate network of mechanisms before him.

With shaking hands and a racing heart, Expo carefully dismantled each trap with lightning speed. His movements were precise and calculated, fuelled by the urgency of the situation. The air was thick with tension as the team held their breath, knowing any wrong move could mean their demise.

Sweat dripped down Expo's forehead as he finally stood up, giving a sharp nod to Yannis. "It's safe to proceed," he confirmed in a low voice, masking the fear that still lingered inside him. The team erupted into relieved cheers and gave Expo grateful high-fives before gathering around Yannis as he checked the controls. Every second felt like an eternity as they waited for the verdict.

At last, Yannis let out a sigh of relief as he found no signs of tampering on the controls. With a deep breath, he pressed the 'down' button and braced himself for what was to come. The floor jolted and groaned but continued to descend smoothly, inching closer to the unknown darkness below.

As they reached their destination less than a minute later, everyone held their breath once again until the floor came to a smooth stop. The danger may have passed, but the adrenaline was still coursing through their veins.

Yannis peered out of the small window set in the door that opened out to the complex. All seemed quiet, but Yannis knew that Kappa must be aware that they were entering the complex. The corridor leading down to the station was empty save for doors strung out at regular intervals. Each one having the potential to harbour a nasty surprise behind it.

As they cautiously made their way down the corridor, every creak of the floor beneath their feet sounded like an alarm bell in the silence. Yannis led the way, his hand hovering over the weapon holstered at his side. Expo followed close behind, his senses on high alert for any sign of danger.

Chapter 30

In the depths of the Pentagon, Barry Lightfoot, Balkans Station Chief, sat in his office, his eyes fixated on a monitor displaying a live feed from Echo 137, a redirected reconnaissance satellite. The footage showed something that made him question his own sanity - robots, emerging from an underground tunnel at the ancient site of Delphi. Each robot carried a large box as they marched towards parked trucks with a precision that could only be described as mechanical.

His breath caught in his throat as he struggled to comprehend what he was seeing. Robots? In Greece? Also, the revelation that the original drawings were over two thousand years old sent a sudden chill down his spine.

Turning to his team, who were huddled around architectural drawings taken from several computer servers, copies of which had been sent to Chris Horsman. "Check those Delphi drawings and switch your monitors to Echo 137." He knew that if Chris found out about the hacked copies, he wouldn't be happy.

As they studied the map displayed on the big screen, gasps echoed through the room. The robots were exiting from an underground complex hidden beneath the ancient site of Delphi with an efficiency that left the team in awe. Each member shared their findings, piecing together the incredible scope of these hidden complexes.

Barry's voice cut through the shocked silence, "Nothing we've seen or heard leaves this room, understood?" This was information that needed to be taken to higher authorities. How had these underground structures remained hidden for so long?

For hours they pored over the drawings, coming to a startling conclusion - these underground complexes under Delphi, Milos, and Aegina were not created by humans. If these drawings truly dated back thousands of years, then the level of technology required was beyond anything known to the ancient Greeks or the Romans.

Barry made up his mind. He paged his secretary and requested a meeting with Chuck Harris, the head of the CIA and his direct boss. The presence of these advanced underground facilities had to be brought to light before Chris's actions could potentially expose them.

As Barry made his way to Chuck's office he reflected on the conversation he had just had with Chris Horsman. Chris had explained their strategy of a three-pronged attack on Kappa's underground domains. Barry had objected to the attack on Delphi and also the incursion on the island of Milos. Particularly, as the Greek Prime Minister was going to lead it. Barry had no objection to the attack on Kappa's underground villa on Aegina. Chris countered that Alex was an adventurer and it was more of a scouting mission than an attack. Besides, he argued Alex had Gitta and thirty EKAM officers to prevent him getting into harm's way. Barry tried to dissuade Chris from his strategy, even attempting to pull rank, but Chris was adamant that as he was the man on the ground, he should use his strategy.

Five minutes later, Barry was in Chuck Harris's office, and Chuck was intently studying the architects' drawings spread out over his large desk.

Barry thought that Chuck's face was more weathered than the last time he had seen him, definitely more jowly. And that paunch and ill-fitting suit was a dead giveaway to his liking for good food and fine wine. But Barry could see that Chuck's eyes were sharp and assessing, showing off his intelligence.

Every now and then, Chuck would look up a look of astonishment on his face. Barry watched Chuck closely, noticing the flickers of surprise in his eyes as he took in the intricate details of the ancient drawings. "Barry, this is... unprecedented," Chuck finally spoke, his brow furrowed in thought. "If these underground complexes truly exist and were built with advanced technology thousands of years ago, we need to handle this situation delicately. It could change everything we know about history."

Barry nodded in agreement, knowing the gravity of the situation. "Chris has already initiated a plan to infiltrate these underground sites, but I believe we need to reassess our approach. The potential implications of what we've discovered cannot be overstated. I've warned him that his strategy is not a good one and could lead to needless deaths – even the destruction of extra-terrestrial technology. There is no way a small country like Greece can keep a lid on this, let alone exploit any discoveries they make."

Chuck leaned back in his chair, tapping his fingers on the desk thoughtfully. "We must tread carefully, Barry. The knowledge contained within those structures could be immensely powerful and dangerous if misused. We need to consider all possible outcomes before taking any further action. We have to take this to Protos, it's that fucking important."

Barry leant forward. "The president? Are you sure it needs to go that high, Chuck?"

"Just think what would happen if the Russians or the Chinese got wind of this. They would both go out of their way to court Greece, probably offering them billions of dollars for a piece, not a small piece but a large piece of the pie," said Chuck.

Barry understood the urgency of the situation as Chuck's words sank in. The implications of such advanced extra-terrestrial technology falling into the wrong hands were too dire to ignore. If other countries caught wind of what lay beneath the surface of Greece, it could spark an international race for power unlike anything seen before.

Nodding solemnly, Barry made the necessary arrangements to prepare a briefing for Protos. As he and Chuck delved deeper into the details of their discovery, a sense of unease settled over them both. The weight of this revelation was heavy, and they knew that every decision from this point forward could shape the course of history.

Their meeting with Protos was set for later that day, at about the time Yannis was entering the Temple of Apollo with his men, giving them little time to gather all the relevant information and formulate a plan of action. As they parted ways, Barry couldn't shake the feeling of being on the brink of something monumental. The fate of humanity seemed to hang in the balance.

At four o'clock, Barry and Chuck were ushered into the Oval Room in the White House. The President was sitting behind his desk wearing his usual navy coloured tailored suit. His silver hair combed back not distracting from his ruggedly handsome face, from which a pair of piercing blue eyes looked up from reading papers, as Barry and Chuck entered the room.

"Good afternoon, Mr. President," Chuck and Barry said in unison.

"Good afternoon, gentlemen," the President smiled disarmingly, stood up and walked around to the front of his desk, where he sat on its edge, crossing his feet showing off his immaculately polished expensive shoes. "What have you got for me?"

Barry cleared his throat, feeling the weight of the information he was about to impart on the President. "Mr. President, we have uncovered evidence of advanced underground complexes beneath ancient Greek sites - Delphi, Milos, and Aegina. These structures appear to have been built with technology far beyond anything known to ancient civilizations. And there's more, sir.

The drawings we've discovered suggest that these complexes may not be of human origin."

Chuck interjected, "The potential implications of these discoveries are immense. If this technology falls into the wrong hands, it could tip the balance of power on a global scale. We believe it is imperative that the United States takes control of this situation before other nations become aware of what lies beneath the surface in Greece."

The President's expression shifted from curiosity to amusement as he absorbed the information. "This is... extraordinary," he murmured, his eyes narrowing with intensity. "We need to act swiftly and decisively. Chuck, I need you to put together a team to assess the situation on the ground in Greece. I take it that you haven't told Barry about Omega?"

Chuck looked shocked by what Protos had admitted. "No, sir…I didn't know I had the authority to disclose this."

"Don't worry, Chuck," said the President with a grin on his face. "Now, Barry, what I'm going to tell you must never leave this room, okay?"

Barry wondered what he was about to be told. "My lips are sealed," he said.

"We've known about the underground complexes in Greece for more than a decade now. When I say we, it's a small group of people. Apart from myself, it's Chuck here, also Angelina Ferris, who like me has Greek roots. Also, Kappa "the milkman" Galatas, the drug lord and Dimitri Karagianis, the president of the Golden Dawn party. What do you say to that?"

"Does Chris know?" asked Barry, trying to suppress any emotion. This was astounding. So, Chris and Alex Kalfas were trying to bring down one of the members of Omega.

"No," said the President emphatically. "He must be converted to our way of thinking. From what you have told me, you should include him and his team. They will be useful because they have been on the ground for some weeks now. They also have the drones and satellites programmed for the terrain you will face. That way you will hit the ground running. We cannot allow this information to fall into the wrong hands. Time is of the essence. But if anyone shows that they are not loyal to Omega's values, then they will be eliminated. This is too important to the western world to be shared east of Europe."

Barry and Chuck exchanged a knowing glance, understanding the gravity of the President's words. "We're on it, Mr. President," Barry replied with determination. "We'll assemble a team and head to Greece immediately."

As they left the Oval Room, Barry turned to Chuck. "We need the best of the best for this mission. People we can trust with their lives and with this critical information."

Chuck nodded in agreement. "I know just the team, and they are already in the Middle East." They both knew that this mission would be unlike anything they had ever faced before. The fate of not just one nation, but the entire world rested on their shoulders as they embarked on this unprecedented journey into the depths of ancient secrets hidden beneath the Greek soil.

Chapter 31

At twelve o'clock midday, Chris gave the green light to Yannis and Alex ordering them to commence their missions.

"Good luck, keep safe." Just as he had uttered this, his cell phone beeped. Not recognising the number, he was tempted to let it ring, but as the area code was Washington DC he decided to answer.

"Horsman," he answered with a feeling of trepidation.

"Chris, where are you? I've got Chuck on speaker here," said Barry eager to have Chuck do the talking.

Chris's antenna was buzzing. To bring Chuck into this operation meant only two things, the CIA wanted a piece of the action or they were intent on shutting it down. Which was it? "Hi Barry, are you going to shut me down?" asked Chris thinking that it was better to meet Barry head on.

"Of course not," intervened Chuck over the speaker phone. "We want to help."

"What sort of help, intelligence, resources or marines?"

There was a deep chuckle from the other end of the phone. "A little sensitive, are we, Chris? We had to take this up to Protos himself and he doesn't like the idea of the Greek government sending a team into areas where there may be high-tech equipment left behind by extra-terrestrials. He feels that this could be another Area 51 situation, a secret kept from the world for over twenty-five years. He doesn't feel that Greece could handle their situation on their own and word would inevitably get out, then we would get Russia and China poking their noses in. So, he wants you to stop Alex Kalfas from entering the catacombs on Milos island."

"Too late!" interjected Chris. "He has already entered the catacombs."

"Can't you reach him?" asked Barry.

"No signal down there."

Chuck's brows furrowed in concern as he processed the information. The situation had escalated faster than they had anticipated, and they were now faced with a critical decision. "We need to act quickly," Chuck urged, turning to Barry with a determined look. "If Alex Kalfas has entered the catacombs on Milos island, we have to get to him before it's too late. This is our chance to prevent any further interference and secure the extra-terrestrial technology."

Chris knew the urgency of the situation as he listened intently over the phone. Time was of the essence, and every moment counted in their race against forces that sought to exploit the otherworldly secrets hidden within the ancient structures. But he was annoyed, more than that, he was angry. For years, he had been warning Barry and Chuck about the escalating drug problem in Greece. Every time he brought the subject up he would get the same answer '*do it yourself, we trust you.*' Well, now because they smelt a pot of gold at the end of the rainbow, they want in.

"I'll do everything in my power to reach Alex and ensure his safety," Chris affirmed, his tone filled with determination which he didn't feel. "But, I'm still going to attack Kappa's hideout and take him out. It's time his drug cartel is destroyed."

Chuck sighed then nodded in agreement, his mind already racing ahead to formulating a plan of action. "We have alerted a team of marines based in the Middle East, they will arrive on Milos in eight hours. We are speaking to you from a military plane half way over the Atlantic. Our estimated time of arrival is five hours from now."

"I'll arrange for a helicopter to transport you both from Athens airport to Milos. I'll join you there."

"Okay, thanks, Chris. Good hunting," Chuck closed the connection, then turned to Barry. "Let's hope we get to Alex and Chris before any major damage is done. Kappa is an important asset and the Secretary of State has promised him immunity if he gives us the information we want."

No sooner had he finished his conversation with Chuck, Chris had called the CIA headquarters in Athens arranging for a helicopter pick up at Athens airport for Chuck and Barry to transport them to Milos island. 'Hopefully, I'll still be alive to meet them there,' he wryly said to himself.

He had earlier instructed one of the marines, aided by Mia to open the entrance to Kappa's lair. Now the steps leading down to the underground complex were in full view.

As Chris made his way down the ancient steps leading to Kappa's underground complex, he couldn't shake off the sense of foreboding that clung to him like a heavy shroud. The air was thick with tension as he navigated through the dimly lit passageway, his senses were on high alert for any sign of danger.

If Kappa knew they were coming, he was playing a waiting game, holding his cards close to his chest. Chris remembered from the last time he had come down this passageway that the danger area would be the fork at the end of this tunnel. They approached a door on their right. Chris, who was in the middle of the phalanx of marines, called out to the man on point to stop. Chris moved up to the door and tried the handle.

"Locked," he announced. "There is a hum of machinery in there, must be some sort of generator. Take a listen, captain." The captain who was the point man put his ear to the door.

"I agree with your assessment, sir, but I feel we should station a couple of men outside the door just in case."

Chris nodded in agreement with the captain's suggestion, knowing that it was crucial to proceed with caution in such a high-stakes environment. He gestured for two of the marines to take up position outside the door, their trained eyes scanning the corridor for any signs of movement or danger.

As they continued down the passageway, the sound of machinery grew louder, reverberating off the ancient stone walls and creating an eerie atmosphere that set everyone on edge. The captain led the way, his senses sharp and alert as they approached the fork in the tunnel. He knew that this was where their path would diverge, leading them deeper into the heart of Kappa's underground lair.

Suddenly, it dawned on Chris why the sound of machinery was louder. He signalled to the captain to stop.

"My god," exclaimed Mia, as she too, realising that the sound of the machinery was emanating from the open door behind them, had turned around. Behind them were twelve heavily armed men, while the two marines whom they left to guard the door were lying prone on the floor.

The metallic tang of fear filled Chris's mouth as he realized their blunder. The air, thick with humidity just moments ago, condensed into a suffocating weight around them. The armed men, shadows against the low lighting, advanced like mechanical reapers, their assault rifles glinting in the low light of the tunnel.

Mia pressed closer to Chris, her knuckles white, her gaze flickering between the approaching figures and Chris's face. It was a silent plea - a desperate hope for a plan, a flicker of escape.

"Drop your weapons," the order barked, cold and devoid of humanity. Chris locked eyes with the captain, a silent conversation passing between them. A curt nod, a shared breath held. Guns thudded to the dusty ground, followed by the reluctant clicks of the marines reluctantly mirroring their leaders. This was a gamble, a desperate bid for time in the face of overwhelming odds.

"We don't want trouble," Chris forced a calmness that felt brittle on his tongue. Every fibre of his being screamed to fight, but reason clawed its way back. Understanding the situation was paramount. "We're here to talk."

The leader studied Chris, suspicion etched into every line of his face. His grip tightened on the weapon, a silent threat coiled and ready to strike. "This is Kappa's domain. Outsiders are not welcome here."

Chris held the leader's gaze, searching for a chink in the steely armour of his resolve. "We come in peace," he began, his voice taut but steady. "There's a way to resolve this without bloodshed. We offer a solution, not a threat."

The leader's face twitched, a flicker of doubt momentarily breaking the icy facade. "Kappa negotiates with no one," he growled, reasserting his authority. "You've trespassed, and there will be consequences."

Panic gnawed at Chris's insides. Time was a luxury they couldn't afford. An idea, reckless and desperate, flickered to life. He had to act fast, before diplomacy turned into a bloodbath.

"We may not have Kappa's trust," Chris said, his voice firm but laced with a sliver of hope, "But perhaps we can earn it. Let us speak with him. A peaceful solution benefits everyone."

The armed men exchanged a tense glance, the weight of the decision hanging heavy in the air. A moment stretched into an eternity, punctuated only by the ragged gasps of fear. Finally, the leader grunted, a single, reluctant nod.

"You may see Kappa," he rasped, the words laced with a hidden threat. "But your weapons stay here. No one enters his quarters armed."

"Where are the rest of Kappa's foot-soldiers?" asked Chris. "I hope they are not waiting around the corner to ambush us."

The leader hesitated before replying, "We've got problems in Delphi and Milos, probably something to do with the Greek authorities, EKAM no doubt. So, there are only a couple of Kappa's closest lieutenants with him, and of course, us." As he spoke his men let their guard down slightly, their weapons more pointing to the floor than at the marines.

Chris's mind roared. Disarmed, defenceless – this was a trap within a trap. But as the leader spoke, revealing Kappa's depleted forces, a sliver of opportunity emerged. A prearranged signal, a desperate gamble they'd discussed before entering this viper's nest.

A subtle shift. Chris feigned a step to the left, momentarily blocking the captain from view. In a single, hidden movement unseen by the enemy, the captain reached for a concealed pocket. A glint of metal – a last-ditch defence, a flicker of hope against a tide of danger.

The captain clutched the object, its smooth surface was a promise of a desperate fight for survival. The stage was set. The dance with death was about to begin.

With a single deft motion, the captain swung his arm releasing the stun grenade on an arc that took it to within a yard of the group of armed men. In the enclosed space of the tunnel, the crack of the grenade was deafening. Chris's men had time to cover their ears with gloved hands, but the armed men not knowing that was a stun grenade coming towards them, threw themselves onto the floor to try to avoid the expected blast from the explosion. They were still lying on the ground with burst eardrums completely unaware of what was going on, when Chris's men disarmed them and tied their hands with plastic ties.

Chris and his team quickly secured the incapacitated armed men, their training kicking in as they swiftly disarmed and restrained them. The tunnel echoed with the groans of the fallen, still dazed from the unexpected stun grenade. Chris could feel the tension crackling in the air, a palpable mix of fear and relief as their risky plan had paid off.

The captain's eyes met Chris's across the chaos, silent communication passing between them. They couldn't linger here – time was of the essence, and more dangers lurked in the shadows of Kappa's underground lair. With a decisive nod, Chris gestured for his team to move forward, deeper into the heart of the labyrinthine tunnels.

Their footsteps echoed in the dimly lit passage, each one a drumbeat of determination against the lingering spectre of danger. Mia walked close to Chris, her trust in him unspoken but unwavering. She had seen his leadership tested time and time again, always rising to the occasion.

The tunnel loomed ahead, its darkness tinged with a sense of foreboding. Chris and the captain approached the fork cautiously, adrenaline coursing through their veins as they prepared for a potential ambush. Both men gripped stun grenades tightly in their hands, ready to throw at a moment's notice.

As they neared the fork, their footsteps fell silent and their mouths went dry with fear. Every sense was heightened, straining to catch any hint of danger lurking around the corner. With a nod from Chris, both men hurled their grenades into the tunnels, shutting their eyes, bracing themselves for the blinding flash and load bang that would follow. After two seconds, they cautiously peeked around the corners - only to find both tunnels empty. A wry chuckle escaped Chris's lips at the underwhelming outcome.

Before them stood heavy doors leading to the Tudor Room as Chris, and Alex before him, liked to call it. They entered the room cautiously, not knowing if it was empty or not. To Chris's relief it was. He gestured to the captain to follow him.

The captain stopped dead in his tracks when he was able to view the room in its full glory.

"My god, Chris, this room is so beautiful. It must have cost a fortune to decorate in this style."

"It did."

Then the captain noticed the huge window taking up most of one wall. "I didn't realise we were above ground again. That is a beautiful tranquil scene. Which part of the island are we on?"

Chris couldn't help but chuckle. "Go over to the window," he said laughingly. After a moment or two at the window, the captain turned around and looked at Chris, a look of astonishment on his face. "That's technology of the highest order. I've never seen or heard of anything like it. It's IMAX, 3D and super 4K all rolled into one."

"Yes, it's another marker that for an extra-terrestrial hand not far from here."

They stopped at the heavy double doors, the entrance to Kappa's office and beyond the facilities that housed Kappa's men in the sort of luxury they would find it hard to find in a five-star hotel. The doors beckoning like a gateway to an unknown world. Mia joined them at Chris's signal, while the captain instructed his men to stay on guard at the fork. Together, they pushed them open and stepped into Kappa's office, unsure of what awaited them inside.

Chapter 32

The smell of cigars and tension hung heavy in the air as they stepped into Kappa's office. Chris's eyes swept the room, searching for any sign of the elusive criminal mastermind. He could sense the captain's apprehension, both of them realizing the enormity of the task ahead.

Kappa's office was a sea of shadows, the murky light barely illuminating its contents. On one side of the room, Kappa's large, ornate desk loomed ominously, a testament to the wealth and power of its occupant, who was sitting behind it. A thick cloud of smoke from his cigar obscured any view of the other side of the desk. On the desk were Kappa's knives, their blades even in the shadowy gloom shone brightly, his left hand hovering near them. To his right, a Glock pistol was lying on the desk well within reach of his right hand, and an open laptop in front of him. Chris figured that the Glock was loaded with a seventeen-bullet magazine.

As the cigar smoke began to dissipate, Chris could make out Takis Penza standing on Kappa's right and on his left two men who Chris had never seen before.

Kappa looked directly at Mia. "Ah, the turncoat!" he almost spat the words out. Then a broad smile lit up his face. "But my dear, you look quite striking this evening."

Mia said nothing as she edged a little closer to Chris. She looked into the darker recesses of the office, her fears allayed when she saw that there was no one else lurking in the shadows. Takis laughed out loud when he saw this. "A little nervous, are we, bitch?" he said as he continued his laughter. "You'd better be because Raul will be here soon."

"Okay enough," said Chris. "If he comes he'll be arrested too."

This time it was Kappa's turn to laugh. "And how do you propose to do that, Horsman?" he asked.

"I've got ten marines outside your office listening to our conversation. As soon as the captain here gives the orders they'll be in here double quick."

Just at that moment, the doors at the back of the office burst open and Raul walked in. The moment he saw Mia he screamed, "You traitorous whore," and rushed towards her, his face contorted into a malevolent rictus.

Mia's training kicked in as she swiftly sidestepped Raul's lunge, her movements fluid and precise. With a deft twist, she disarmed him of the knife he had drawn from its sheath, her eyes locked onto his with unwavering focus. The room seemed to blur around them as they engaged in a deadly dance of skill and survival.

The tension in the room was palpable, a thick fog of adrenaline and danger hung heavy in the air. Mia and Raul circled each other like predators, their every move calculated and precise. Raul's face contorted with rage as he launched himself at Mia once more, fuelled by a desire for vengeance.

Mia, however, was not one to back down. She met his attack with a fluid grace, her movements mesmerizing in their fluidity and precision. The room seemed to spin as they continued their deadly dance, their lives hanging in the balance with each passing moment.

Raul lunged at Mia once more, but she was too quick for him. She grabbed Raul's knife from the floor, then with a swift twist of her wrist, she sent her knife flying into his neck severing the artery. Raul stood, a look of astonishment on his face as he watched his blood spurt onto his clothes. Then his legs seemed to buckle as he collapsed onto the floor and lay still.

Takis made a move to come around the desk but Kappa put his arm out and stopped him. Suddenly, there was a dull mechanical sound from the doors leading into the room where the marines waited and the doors that Raul had used to enter the office. Chris and the captain glanced at each other, "What's going on, Kappa?" Chris shouted fearing the worst.

Kappa laughed "Too late, Horsman your marines won't help you now. I've just made this office a safe room. Steel shutters are covering all the doors. No one can get in or out!"

A cold sweat broke out on Chris's forehead as he realized the gravity of the situation. Kappa's laughter echoed in the room, filling the air with an oppressive sense of hopelessness. The marines outside were trapped, just like them.

Mia's eyes widened in terror as she watched the steel shutters close over the doors. She looked at Chris, searching for any sign of hope or a plan. But Chris's expression was grim, his mind racing as he tried to come up with a way out of this impossible situation.

Kappa chuckled, savouring the moment. "Well, well, well. It seems our little game is over, Horsman. You and your men are stuck in here with me and my loyal crew. We'll see who comes out on top."

As the laughter faded, the room fell into a tense silence. Chris knew that they were running out of time.

"Perhaps, before we kill you, Takis can give you an account of his close encounter of the third kind, which he had this morning. A taster to show you what you will be missing when you're dead. Not that I believe everything he told me. Go on, Takis, tell them," commanded Kappa, grinning all over his face.

Takis moved around to the front of the desk, then sat perched on the edge facing Chris, Mia and the captain. Takis leaned forward as if for emphasis.

"It started this morning on Milos. I was there with ten of my best men, tasked by Kappa to search the three huge undersea warehouse type buildings…."

"Hasn't anyone ever searched those buildings before today?" interrupted Chris.

"Not that we know of," lied Takis.

Chris looked quizzically at Kappa. "So, Dr Marlowe never set foot in the complex below Milos?"

Kappa looked decidedly uncomfortable at that question. "Why would she want to visit Milos?" retorted Kappa.

"Why indeed – how did you know Dr Marlowe was female if you've never met her?"

Kappa's laugh echoed through the dimly lit room, his deep voice resonating with a hint of sinister satisfaction. The corners of his mouth curled into a sly grin as he addressed Horsman, taunting him with the knowledge that there was no escape from their clutches.

"You got me, Horsman," Kappa admitted, leaning back in his chair with an air of casual confidence. "As you'll never get out of here alive, I'll confess all."

Horsman's jaw tightened as he bristled at Kappa's nonchalance. "What did you do to the woman who found this place?" he demanded, his voice tight with fury.

"That bitch wanted to tell the world what she had found," Kappa chuckled, his eyes gleaming with malicious glee. "She and her scientist friends had all signed a non-disclosure agreement but were willing to break it for the good of mankind." He leaned forward, relishing in the power he held over Horsman. "So, I had them disappear."

Horsman's fists clenched at his sides as he fought back the urge to lunge across the table and strangle Kappa. "You murdered them, you mean. Have you ever seen what they saw?" he pressed, determined to uncover the truth.

"No," Kappa replied smoothly, feigning innocence. "We never had the codes to open the storage facilities until late last night when they were text to my cell phone. I sent Takis down there this morning with the codes, and ten men to see if we could use the advanced technology weapons the extra-terrestrials had left behind to attack Mega Maximo, the prime minister's home. But I guess he got more than he bargained for."

His smile faltered as he remembered Takis' report. "Oh, he found the weapons alright," Kappa continued, his voice growing quieter as he reached the end of his tale. "Also, the vehicles and a huge craft that Takis thinks is a space vehicle. But..." His voice trailed off, his face contorted with disbelief.

"But what, Takis?" Horsman urged, desperate for more information.

"An alien being," Takis whispered, his voice barely audible over the heated argument that had broken out among the group. Kappa's booming voice filled the room as he accused Takis of lying about an encounter with a supposed extra-terrestrial.

"Takis took ten men with him and he alone came back!" Kappa yelled, slamming his fist on the table for emphasis. "This so-called alien was a woman, disguised to look human! And now Takis expects us to believe that she killed our men without ever laying a hand on them? I see right through his lies."

Takis pleaded with Kappa, fear evident in his trembling voice. "Boss, please, believe me. I wouldn't do something like that. It really was her and that orb thing."

Chris, always level-headed and logical, interjected. "Describe this woman to us, Takis."

A sly grin spread across Takis' face as he recalled the mysterious woman's alluring appearance. "I could carry a torch for her. She was tall and slim, with striking features," he began, before quickly correcting himself. "Well, no torch anymore after seeing what she's capable of." He shuddered at the memory of her deadly abilities. "She moved strangely, almost gliding along the floor."

"How did she kill your men, Takis?" Chris probed further, determined to uncover the truth.

"She caught our bullets and threw them back at us," Takis replied quietly, his confidence faltering in the face of scepticism.

Kappa burst into laughter at Takis' explanation, joined by his two lieutenants who found the whole situation ridiculous. After several moments of uncontrollable laughter, Kappa managed to compose himself. "Come on now, Horsman," he chortled. "You can't seriously believe this fantasy about a bullet-proof woman from outer space?"

But Chris met Kappa's gaze steadily, his expression unwavering. "I believe him," he declared firmly. "And now it's time for you to come clean, Kappa. You're under arrest."

The room erupted into chaos as Kappa's laughter turned into a furious outburst, his once jovial expression contorted with anger. "You think you can take down me and my crew?" he roared, his words echoing off the walls. "We are untouchable, unstoppable!" But Chris stood his ground, ready to bring Kappa and his criminal empire to justice. The tension in the room was palpable as the two men locked eyes, their battle of wills raging on.

Kappa let out a boisterous laugh, his entire face lighting up with a wide grin. "Tell you what," he said, "I'll make you a deal!" Chris scoffed in response. "You're hardly in a position to negotiate, Kappa. What could you possibly offer the Greek and American governments in exchange for your illegal activities?" But Kappa was undeterred. "I'll give up my drug business and shut down my underground facilities in exchange for turning them into a theme park."

At first, Chris couldn't contain his laughter at the absurdity of the proposition. His chuckles echoed through the tension-filled room, breaking through the thick air like a breath of fresh air. Even Kappa's smug facade faltered for a moment. Wiping away a tear from his eye, Chris composed himself enough to speak again.

"A theme park? You want to turn your illegal labs into a tourist attraction?" The thought of it sent shudders of suppressed laughter through the room, even the captain struggled to maintain his stoic expression.

But Kappa seemed unfazed by their reactions. On the contrary, he seemed to grow even more confident as he continued his pitch. "Think about it," he exclaimed, "It will be more than just a theme park - it will be a museum displaying exhibits from both the past and the future! And if Takis's claims are true about extra-terrestrial beings, we could even offer flights to their planet! Imagine the thrill of exploring interstellar space, educational tours, and gift shops filled with unique memorabilia!" However, Kappa's grand vision only caused Chris's laughter to escalate into full-blown guffaws.

Finally, managing to catch his breath, Chris wiped away tears of mirth and looked at Kappa with incredulity. "You must be out of your mind," he said between laughs. "There's no way the Greek and American governments would ever agree to such a deal, let alone let you make contact with extra-terrestrial beings."

But Kappa remained undeterred, his smug grin never wavering. "Come on, Horsman," he continued, leaning forward and resting his elbows on the table. "Let's make the best of this situation. You can't kill me or my crew, so why not negotiate? I can offer you a golden ticket to a future where your government is in our debt. Where we have a hand in shaping humanity's destiny, and you'll have a front-row seat to the greatest show on Earth. And I'll even provide you with technology to defend against any other countries trying to take over the underground facilities." Kappa's words hung in the air as he waited for Chris's response.

Chris stared at him for a long moment, considering his options. He turned to the captain, supposedly seeking his opinion before deciding, but in reality, using up precious minutes. The rest of the room was silent, all eyes were on Chris. Glancing at his watch, he realized that Yannis should be arriving soon if he had successfully taken control of the Delphi facility. Looking back at Kappa, Chris pointed towards a bank of monitors on the wall behind him. "Are those security feeds?" he asked.

"Yes," replied Takis.

"Turn them on," commanded Chris. "Let's see what's happening around the facility." He knew why Kappa had kept them off - he didn't want Chris to see how many men he had and their locations. But Chris wanted Kappa to see something else - the resources he had above ground near the temple.

"I'm sorry," said Kappa with false conviction. "The monitors aren't working." However, Kappa couldn't hide the fact that on his laptop were three active feeds - one from Delphi - which had been down for an hour - one from Milos where Alex and his team were stationed, and one from the tunnel where Chris and the marines had entered Kappa's headquarters.

As Chris was about to call Kappa's bluff, a deafening explosion rocked the room. The heavy doors, and the metal shutters, behind which were the captain's men, were blown into splinters and debris, obscuring Kappa's Tudor room in a cloud of dust and smoke. Chris, Mia, and the captain all turned towards the commotion, looks of shock and astonishment etched on their faces as they trained their guns at the now visible doorway opening.

As the dust began to settle, they could just make out a familiar figure standing amidst the chaos where the doors once stood.

"Yannis!" Chris exclaimed with relief. "I was getting worried."

Yannis stepped towards them with confidence, giving a salute to the captain and a playful wink to Mia before embracing Chris in a hug.

"They're gone," Mia shouted excitedly, pointing to Kappa's desk. Chris turned to see what she was pointing at and felt his heart sink.

"Shit," he exploded. "Where the fuck did they go?"

Sure enough, Kappa, Takis, and the two lieutenants were nowhere to be found.

Chapter 33

The fluorescent lights of the Milos base cast a sterile glow on the twenty marines, their faces grim under their helmets. Alex had handpicked the man, Makis Trakas, that was to lead the EKAM officers, a grizzled veteran with a cybernetic eye, who was at home barking orders, his voice could be heard in the largest of underground chambers. Beside him stood Gitta, her blonde hair pulled back in a tight braid, her features fixed with a mix of excitement and apprehension. Their mission was to search the colossal storage facilities scattered under the sea between Milos and Aegina, as well as capture or neutralise any of Kappa's men along the way.

With a hiss and a groan, a section of the concrete wall lurched upwards, revealing a sleek, metallic train car. Its obsidian shell gleamed under the harsh lights. The marines filed in, their boots clanging on the cool metal floor. Alex and Gitta took the front carriage, a tense silence hanging heavy in the air.

The train smoothly moved forward, as it accelerated at an unnerving pace. Milos, now a paradise island, had hidden its secrets well, housing a labyrinth of tunnels carved out of the volcanic rock that stretched from the island itself to the island of Aegina. The rhythmic swish of the train was the only sound as they hurtled through the darkness.

Twenty kilometres later, the train slowed to a halt. The heavy doors still open since the earlier visit that day by Takis Penza and his men, revealed a sight that stole the breath from Alex's lungs. The cavernous space stretched as far as the eye could see, its high ceiling lost in the shadows. Rows upon rows of metallic structures, unlike anything Alex had ever seen, filled the chamber. They pulsed with an otherworldly light, an alien hum resonating through the vast space.

"By the gods of the Greeks," Gitta whispered, her voice barely audible over the hum.

Each structure was a monument to a bygone civilization, a testament to technology so far beyond human comprehension that it felt like peering into the heart of a god. Weaponized pods, sleek and menacing, glinted in the dim light. Razor-sharp blades extended from hovering platforms, their edges shimmering with an unnatural energy. In the distance, colossal walkers loomed, their metallic forms dwarfing the EKAM officers.

A sense of awe, tinged with fear, washed over Alex. These were the tools of unimaginable wars, a power that could reshape the galaxies. The weight of responsibility settled on his shoulders. Securing these weapons was paramount. If they got into the wrong hands, they could negatively tip the scales in the fight against terrorist threats.

"Go ahead," said Alex nodding his head towards Makis.

Makis straightened, his gaze hardening. "Alright men," he boomed, his voice echoing in the vast chamber. "Secure the facility. Let's make sure these bad boys don't get into the wrong hands."

The EKAM officers buzzed with activity, their initial awe giving way to focused efficiency as they began cataloguing and securing the weapons. Alex, however, couldn't shake the feeling of something more being present. He felt a pull towards a shadowed doorway at the far end of the vast chamber.

"Gitta," he called, his voice cutting through the metallic hum. "You coming?"

Gitta, meticulously recording data from a hovering energy blade, looked up. "What is it?"

"There's another room," Alex said, already heading towards it. "Something doesn't feel right about leaving it unexplored."

Gitta hesitated for a moment, then followed, her hand instinctively going for the Glock pistol holstered on her hip. The doorway led into a smaller, oddly serene chamber. Unlike the weapon storage, this room was bathed in a soft, bioluminescent glow emanating from strange flora lining the walls. The air buzzed with an electric thrum, carrying faint chirps and clicks - recordings perhaps, or whispers of a lost civilization.

In the centre of the room stood a pedestal, upon which rested a smooth, obsidian sphere. It pulsed faintly, its surface swirling with nebulous light. Beside it, lay a series of intricate metal rings, etched with swirling patterns that seemed to shift and flow under the bioluminescent light.

Further down the room, Alex spotted a collection of what appeared to be tablets, made from a material that resembled polished bone. They were covered in strange symbols that resembled constellations more than any alphabet Alex knew. Next to them, a series of glass vials held shimmering liquids that pulsed with an inner light, their properties unknown.

"This... this isn't a weapons storage," Gitta whispered, her voice filled with a reverence Alex hadn't heard before. "This is a library, a museum. A glimpse into their world."

Alex felt a pang of regret. They were soldiers, not scientists, here to secure weapons. But these relics – they held the history of a race, a window into a civilization both terrifyingly advanced and hauntingly beautiful.

A low, mournful cry echoed through the chamber, emanating from a holographic panel embedded in the wall. It flickered with images of a lush, vibrant world unlike anything on Earth. Towering crystalline structures pierced the sky, while strange, winged creatures soared through vibrant clouds. The image faded, replaced by the stark emptiness of space and a single, shattered planet.

Silence descended upon the chamber. The EKAM officers, who had followed them in, stood transfixed by the holographic display. The weight of the alien civilization's demise hung heavy in the air.

"They weren't the first," Alex finally said, his voice low. "And they won't be the last. We need to learn from their mistakes."

He looked at Gitta, his gaze meeting hers. They had come for weapons, but they had found a story. A story that could hold the key to the survival of the earth, and maybe, just maybe, to understanding the universe a little bit better.

The silence stretched on, broken only by the soft hum of the alien flora. The weight of the holographic message settled on Alex and Gitta like a physical burden. These weren't just weapons; they were a legacy, a cautionary tale etched in the remnants of a lost civilization.

"We need help," Gitta said finally, her voice firm. "Scientists, historians, Xeno linguists. We can't decipher this on our own."

Alex nodded, his mind already racing. Back at base, they had access to secure communication channels. He pulled out a small, encrypted device and with a few taps, established a connection.

"This is Alex Kalfas requesting immediate priority contact with Dr Anya Sharma and Professor Chen," his voice crackled through the speaker. "This is a Code Alpha situation. Repeat, Code Alpha."

Code Alpha was reserved for discoveries of paramount importance. Back at the Milos base, the message would have sent alarms blaring.

The wait felt like an eternity. Finally, a woman's voice filled the speaker, tinged with urgency. "Prime Minister, this is Dr Sharma. What's the situation?"

Alex explained their findings in a rapid burst - the vast arsenal, the alien library, and the haunting holographic message. There was a stunned silence on the other end, then a flurry of questions.

"We need you here, Doctor," Alex concluded. "And anyone else you think can help us understand what we've found."

"We're on our way," Dr Sharma replied, the urgency in her voice palpable. "But be warned, Prime Minister. This could change everything we thought we knew."

With mixed emotions, Alex ended the call. He knew Dr Sharma was right. This wasn't just about securing weapons anymore. They had stumbled upon a treasure trove of knowledge, a doorway to understanding a civilization both terrifying and awe-inspiring.

Turning to Gitta, Alex nodded. "We head back to base. Time to bring in the big guns, the scientific kind."

The train ride back to Milos was a sombre affair. The EKAM officers, initially excited about the prospect of acquiring powerful weaponry, now carried a sense of foreboding. The knowledge of a lost civilization, their advanced technology and their ultimate demise, hung heavy in the air.

As they emerged from the tunnel network into the sterile white corridors of the Milos base, a new kind of battle awaited them. This time, the fight wouldn't be waged with bullets and bombs, but with the tools of science and the human spirit's unquenchable thirst for knowledge. The fate of humanity, perhaps even the galaxy, might just hinge on their success.

The arrival of Dr Sharma and her team brought a shift in energy to the Milos base. Lab coats replaced fatigues, and excited chatter filled the hallways in place of hushed strategizing. Alex knew his role was shifting. While he'd led the mission with military precision, the labyrinthine nature of this new discovery needed a different kind of expertise.

Dr Sharma's team was a motley crew - seasoned archaeologists with a penchant for deciphering lost languages, theoretical physicists who spoke fluently in quantum mechanics, and biologists with an almost unnerving fascination for the potential of alien DNA. Alex, and the Marines by extension, found themselves on the periphery, their mission was to get the scientists and their equipment to the storage facility as quickly as possible and leave them alone to decipher everything in the alien library.

As Alex and Gitta waited for the loading of their scientific equipment, Alex couldn't resist checking his phone for any important messages. His heart raced as he read a text from Chris, causing anxiety to wash over him.

"Gitta, listen to this. Chris just informed me that his boss has escalated the knowledge of what we have found all the way to the President himself. The CIA and Secretary of State, Angelina Ferris, have been ordered to get involved. And they've even sent a unit of marines stationed in the Middle East to escort them through the underground tunnels."

Gitta's eyes widened in shock. "Are we going to wait for them?"

Alex shook his head firmly. "No way are we waiting. Chris will meet them here in two hours, then they can follow us into the tunnels using the second train."

Thirty minutes later, the obsidian sleek metal train silently glided out of the Milos base station, heading towards the first of three colossal storage facilities. As they arrived at the facility, their scientific equipment was unloaded and taken to the alien library, which quickly became a hive of activity. The holographic message had confirmed their suspicions - this was indeed a storehouse of incredible knowledge. But its operating system was far more complex than anything human technology had ever achieved. It would take weeks to decipher the alien code and numerical systems.

Finally, Alex decided it was time to move on to the second storage facility. Leaving the excited scientists behind, he gathered Gitta and the EKAM officers for the next stage of their mission: searching the facility while flushing out any of Kappa's men along the way. Excitement buzzed through them as they discussed what they might find. The architects' drawings and notes from Alex's friend Pericles Brudo spoke of futuristic vehicles and enormous spaceships stored within these facilities. What wonders awaited them at this next location?

Chapter 34

The moment of realization hit Chris and Mia like a rogue wave. One second, they'd been welcoming Yannis into the plush office, the tension of first introductions easing under Kappa's deceptively jovial grin. The next, the room was empty except for the faint tang of expensive cologne hanging in the air.

"Where did they go?" Mia whispered, her eyes darting between the heavy mahogany door – still solidly closed.

Chris, his sharp military instincts kicking in, crossed to the door in three long strides. "Door's still locked," he confirmed, his voice tight. Panic threatened to coil around his chest, but he forced it back. Panic wasn't an option when dealing with a man like Kappa.

They turned their attention to the window. It was triple glazed, the kind designed to resist storms and intrusion. There was no way anyone had slipped out, not from this high up. Then he realised he had been fooled again by a piece of amazing technology. They were underground, but for a moment he had thought they were in a tall office building.

"There must be another way out," Yannis said, his voice tinged with a tremor he couldn't quite hide. Chris had a hunch the young man wasn't used to seeing his enemy vanish into thin air.

"Scan the room," Chris instructed, his mind racing. Hidden panels, secret compartments - he'd encountered them all during his years with Task Force Athena.

They started a frantic yet methodical sweep of the room, searching for the impossible. Mia pulled at the heavy silk drapes lining the walls, Chris ran his hands along the ornate bookshelves, while Yannis checked behind the imposing desk.

Nothing.

A prickle of unease ran down Chris's spine. Kappa was the kind of man who always had a trick up his sleeve, an escape route, a backup plan. This felt like more than a power play- a meticulously orchestrated move in a far more dangerous game.

Just then, Mia gasped. She was crouched near a framed map of the Mediterranean. "Look," she pointed, her voice barely above a whisper. A section of the map, depicting the coast of Greece, was slightly raised, and the paper crinkled in an unnatural way.

With a surge of hope and a growing sense of dread, Chris reached out and peeled away the edge of the map. It revealed a smooth, metallic panel and a small, biometric scanner.

Kappa always had a flair for the dramatic.

Chris exchanged a grim glance with Mia. The biometric scanner was confirmed. Kappa was playing a dangerous game, and they'd just been forced onto the board. He placed his thumb on the sensor, a mix of resignation and adrenaline coursing through his veins.

There was a soft click, and the hidden panel slid aside, revealing a dimly lit corridor. The smell of damp concrete and something metallic pricked at Chris's senses.

"We don't have a choice," he said, turning to Mia. "But before we move down that tunnel, tell us what happened at Delphi, Yannis?" Chris turned to face Yannis.

Yannis gathered his thoughts before answering. "It was all pretty much of an anti-climax, really. The only real danger we faced was the mines in the room behind the butterfly wall. Our Expo managed to make them all safe without any trouble."

"That must have been a heart in the mouth situation." Yannis nodded, determination warring in his eyes. Chris knew he wouldn't abandon him, not even if his own life was at risk.

"Go on," Chris urged.

"We reached the lower level without further mishap, then made our way down the main corridor towards the train station."

"And you met none of Kappa's men at all?" said Chris.

"None at all," said Yannis. "The place was eerily quiet. And that was puzzling until we reached the train station and entered its goods storage area. Kappa's men were neatly lined up on the floor – I think we counted thirty-three bodies..."

Chris interjected, "You mean dead bodies?"

"Yes."

"Who killed them?" asked the captain.

"The robots," explained Yannis. "They too were lined up along the back wall. Each with a pile of weapons taken from Kappa's men on the floor in front of them."

"Robots or Androids?" queried Chris.

"Androids, I believe. They didn't seem to mind that we were armed. It's as if they knew we were friendly. They must be somewhat sentient to behave that way."

"Well, it's nice to know that Kappa's force of armed men has been reduced," mused Chris. "Let's go!"

Mia squared her shoulders, her usual quick wit hidden behind a mask of resolve. "Lead the way, captain."

With the captain in front, they stepped into the darkness. The corridor was narrow, the walls rough and unfinished. It sloped subtly downwards, leading them further into the unknown depths beneath Kappa's luxurious office.

They walked in silence, Chris's instincts on high alert. Every squeak of their shoes, every echo against the concrete seemed amplified in the confined space. After what felt like an eternity, the corridor opened into a small, circular room bathed in a cold, fluorescent light.

A single, metal chair sat in the centre, facing a large video monitor on the far wall. The screen flickered to life, revealing Kappa's face, creased in a calculated smile.

"Ah, Horsman, so good of you to join me," his voice boomed from hidden speakers, a mocking edge to his tone. "Welcome to my inner sanctum."

Chris clenched his fists, the urge to smash the screen almost overwhelming. "Cut the theatrics, Kappa," he growled. "What do you want?"

Kappa's smile widened. "Patience, Captain. Answers come at a price. Let's just say, this is an opportunity for... collaboration. Shall we begin?" He gestured towards the empty chair.

Chris looked back at Mia and Yannis. He knew he didn't have a choice. This was Kappa's game, and they had to play, whether they liked it or not. He settled into the chair, the cold metal biting into his back. He fixed his gaze on Kappa's projected image.

"Let's hear it then, Kappa," he said, his voice flat. "What's this opportunity you have for us?"

"It's not an opportunity, it's a surprise." The game had just gotten a lot more complicated, and there was no telling who'd make it out as the winner.

A gasp echoed in the room. Chris and Mia spun around, while Yannis's hand instantly went for his weapon. A section of the wall, previously seamless, slid open to reveal a hidden corridor. Two figures emerged, their presence electrifying the air.

It was Angelina Ferris, Secretary of State, her expression as steely as ever. And beside her, Chuck Harris, the notoriously enigmatic Head of the CIA. Angelina, although now in her mid-fifties was still slim with a graceful posture owing this to her lifelong hobby of yoga and dance. Even though she had been traveling for over eleven hours, her silver-streaked hair was still in a neat chignon. Her striking blue eyes bore into Kappa's face which was still showing signs of the surprise at her entrance.

In a measured voice, she said, "Kappa," her voice cut through the tension, "You've played this game long enough. It's over."

The image of Kappa on the screen wavered; his smug mask cracking. "Secretary Ferris, how... unexpected."

"Unexpected is my middle name," Ferris retorted, her stride confident and unhurried as she approached the chair opposite Chris. Harris followed, a silent sentinel. "Now, you were saying something about an opportunity?"

Chris exchanged a stunned look with Mia. The CIA head and the Secretary in this forsaken bunker with them? Things were getting stranger by the second.

Kappa coughed, attempting to regain his composure. "Indeed. It seems our... associate has had a change of heart." His eyes flicked towards Harris with barely concealed disdain.

Harris cleared his throat. "Kappa has agreed to provide full disclosure. Names, networks, operations - the whole nine yards. In exchange for a plea deal, naturally."

Stunned silence filled the room. Kappa, the ghost, the puppeteer, turning on his own organization? Chris felt his gut twist. It was a desperate gamble, but it could be the break they needed.

"And why should we believe him?" Yannis challenged, his voice rough with scepticism.

Ferris smiled thinly. "Because we made him an offer he couldn't refuse. Besides, we have certain ways of ensuring his story holds water."

A cold dread settled in Chris's stomach, chilling him to the core. He knew what Ferris meant, and the thought sent shivers down his spine. The CIA's methods were notorious for their lack of gentleness. But if it meant cracking this whole damned thing open...

"So, Chris," Ferris said, turning her keen eyes on him. "Are you ready to join Omega with us?" Her gaze seemed to probe the very depths of his resolve.

"What is Omega?" Chris asked, the name unfamiliar and mysterious to him.

"Operation Omega is our attempt to contact the extra-terrestrials who built the underground complexes and left behind a trove of advanced technology. We want to claim this weaponry for ourselves, for America," Chuck explained, his tone confident and determined. "We have an elite squad of marines making their way from the Middle East as we speak."

Chris couldn't help but feel a sense of disbelief at what he was hearing. And Kappa, could it be possible that he was a part of this too?

"Is Kappa also a member of Omega?" he asked, though deep down he already knew the answer.

"Not only is he a member, but here in Greece, he is its leader," Ferris replied matter-of-factly.

Chris turned to look at Kappa, who simply shrugged his ample shoulders and flashed a sly smile.

"And who is the overall leader of Omega?"

"The President himself," Ferris stated, causing Chris's jaw to drop in shock. "In fact, the last two presidents have both been leaders of Omega. Chuck and Barry are also members. So, are you in?"

After a moment of hesitation, Chris weighed his options carefully. He knew that Mia's safety and her importance in taking down Kappa's organization were on the line.

"I'm in," he declared, glancing at Mia and seeing the determination in her eyes as well. "And Mia is too. But we have unfinished business to take care of first."

Chris turned to the captain and gave his orders. "Take your men and arrest Kappa. If Takis or any of Kappa's lieutenants are present, bring them in too. Take them all to EKAM headquarters in Athens. Yannis, you go with them. And if they resist, shoot to kill."

Kappa's face on the video screen went from smug to surprise, then horror as Chris spoke. "You can't do this, Horsman! I'm protected by Omega, the President of the United States, and Angelina Ferris."

"Wrong!" Chris shouted back, his voice rising in anger. "You are under Greek jurisdiction now, and Alex Kalfas has given me the authority to lock you up. Yannis, charge Kappa with drug smuggling, murder, and kidnapping Gitta Lehrer. That should keep him behind bars for the rest of his life."

The captain and his team disappeared through a sliding panel door and reappeared on the screen thirty seconds later, with Kappa in handcuffs between two marines. Gunshots could be heard before Yannis appeared again.

"Sorry, Chris," he said solemnly. "We had to shoot Takis; he pulled a gun on us."

"Is he dead?" Chris asked.

"Yes."

"Too bad," Chris muttered, a satisfied look on his face.

Then Chuck turned his attention to Chris. "So where exactly is Alex? I've heard he comes from a family of senior CIA operatives and that even as a prime minister, he's drawn to danger like a moth to a flame. Fancies himself as a modern-day Indiana Jones, does he?"

Chris couldn't help but laugh at the image of Alex wielding a whip as a weapon.

"Have you seen or heard from the extra-terrestrials?" said Chris.

"Unfortunately, not yet," Ferris replied with a grim tone. "We have been tracking them for years. Declassified documents, intercepted communications, we are the only group in the world with ambitions to contact these beings. We believe hidden within the underground facility lies the key."

"But why all the secrecy?" Mia chimed in, furrowing her brow in confusion. "If there's proof of extra-terrestrial life, wouldn't the world have a right to know?"

Harris let out a heavy sigh. "In an ideal world, yes. But can you imagine the chaos and panic that would ensue? The power struggles that would occur? Omega believes it's better to control the narrative and secure whatever technology we can before anyone else knows what's out there."

Chris felt a chill run down his spine. "Didn't Kappa tell you what his second-in-command saw and experienced this morning? According to him there is definitely an alien presence down there."

"Yes, he did, briefly, we only just arrived before you did. But we want to experience this first-hand. Where is the prime minister?" Ferris said with a worried frown on her face.

"He's taken some scientists down through the Milos entrance to the undersea storage facilities."

"He's the wild card," Ferris said. "An impulsive adventurer. But his scientific connections run deep, and we in Omega believe he can be an asset. However, if he is not on our side and doesn't agree to keeping this from the rest of the world, he will be eliminated. This is far too big to have rogue agents running loose."

"I'm sure Alex wouldn't let the cat out of the bag without authority," said Chris, trying to keep as much belief in his voice as he could.

"I hope so," said Ferris without much conviction.

The revelation hung heavy in the air, twisting Chris's stomach into knots. Omega wasn't just some rogue faction, they were a shadow government, hell-bent on a dangerous gamble. And Alex, the friend he'd known since childhood, was caught in the crosshairs. Chris thought about his friend Petros who had been savagely murdered on Milos whilst on an undercover operation in Kappa's organisation. He knew, deep down, he couldn't endorse Omega but now was not the time to challenge it. He would wait and bide his time.

"We need to get to Milos," Mia said, her voice clipped and urgent. "We need to warn Alex."

Ferris nodded. "Chuck, assemble the extraction team. We move in thirty minutes. Horsman, you're coming with us. Your local knowledge will be vital."

A surge of adrenaline coursed through Chris. His loyalty to Alex warred with a deep-seated distrust of Omega's motives. Was Alex truly an asset, or a liability? And what did they mean by 'eliminated?'

As they hurried towards the surface, the bunker's oppressive walls seemed to close in. The world outside felt starkly different - the sun blinding, the breeze on his skin an unexpected relief.

Chapter 35

The chopper ride to Milos was a whirlwind of tense silence. Ferris and Harris were lost in their thoughts, strategizing, weighing the risk of intervention. Chris stared at the sea, the same waters that hid the labyrinth below, now a battleground for an unimaginable future.

Upon landing, they were greeted by a scene of controlled chaos. The marines from the Middle East had arrived, and now in full tactical gear they swarmed the area, securing the perimeter. A makeshift command centre had sprung up, scientists buzzing around monitors, their faces etched with a mixture of awe and dread.

"Where's the Prime Minister?" Ferris demanded, cutting through the noise.

A young marine pointed towards the station. "Left on the train, Ma'am. Entered the access tunnel about an hour ago."

Chris's heart hammered in his chest. Sixty minutes. Alex could be anywhere within the complex by now. They didn't have the luxury of time.

Ferris wasted no words. "Horsman, Mia, with me. Harris, you hold the fort here. Get the marines ready, tell them to stand by. I'll take ten with me just in case there is trouble."

The descent to the station was a claustrophobic blur. The air grew stale, the only sound was of their rapid footsteps echoing against the ancient stone. With every meter, the weight of what they were walking into pressed heavier.

Finally, they emerged into what looked like an ordinary modern railway station, its scale the same as any in Europe. It had two platforms with a waiting room on each platform. They looked to be built out of wood, but on closer inspection they would have found it was built from a metal unknown on earth and made to look like wood. There was a train standing on one of the platforms. A sleek black train made of obsidian, some might say, a healing train, and they wouldn't be far wrong.

Chris led the party onto the train, and then he and Mia went forward to the front cab. It was empty except for a console on which there was a touch screen and next to that a red button. The touch screen had four numbers on it, one, two, three, and four. Chris assumed correctly that they referred to the stops, the three storage facilities and Aegina. The red button was probably some sort of emergency stop which he hoped he would never have to use. The thought of being stuck in a tunnel under the Aegean was too much to bear.

Chris pressed the number one on the touch screen. Without a sound, the train slowly moved out of the station, then picked up speed as it took them into the unknown towards the storage facility that held the advanced alien vehicles that they hoped Alex and Gitta were still cataloguing.

Chris's hope was misplaced as Alex's team had left a couple of EKAM officers guarding the massive storage facility, even though they knew that there was a very slim chance that any of Kappa's men would turn up.

As they entered the third and largest storage facility, Alex and his team were immediately struck with a sense of awe at the sheer size of the building. Its grandeur was unlike anything they had seen before. Unlike the other two facilities, this one felt sturdy and impenetrable, like a fortress rising up from the ground. It was as if they were standing at the base of a reverse iceberg, with much more hidden above than what could be seen by the naked eye.

Alex's estimates put the ceiling at an astonishing height of one hundred and thirty meters, towering over them like a giant among men. He couldn't help but wonder how close they were to reaching the surface of the Aegean Sea above them. Their eyes were drawn to the only thing occupying this massive space - an immense space vehicle, hovering gracefully, despite its bulk, about five meters above the floor. Its exterior was made of black obsidian, contrasting sharply against the white walls of the building. It seemed almost otherworldly in its presence, catching and holding their attention with its mysterious allure.

There didn't seem to be any obvious windows or entrance ports on the vehicle, however, it was so big that they could not see if there was a bridge or control room of some sort on the top of the vehicle.

Gitta was the first to break out of their collective mind-blowing trance. "What the fuck, this is beyond words, Alex. Not even Star Trek had space vehicles this big."

"I know. This must be at least half a kilometre in length and a hundred metres high. It's phenomenal, it really is."

Gitta grabbed Alex's hand. "Can you comprehend that this craft has been here for over two thousand years? It still looks brand spanking new."

Alex laughed. "Yes, it looks as though it was built yesterday."

As they approached the space vehicle, a low hum filled the air, vibrating through their bones and creating an almost ethereal atmosphere around them. The team exchanged wary glances, unsure of what to make of this unexpected discovery. Alex took a cautious step forward, his eyes never leaving the craft as if drawn to it by an invisible force.

Without warning, a door on the side of the vehicle slid open soundlessly, revealing a dimly lit interior that seemed to stretch far beyond its physical confines. A soft glow emanated from within, beckoning them closer with an irresistible pull.

Alex felt a surge of both fear and curiosity coursing through him as he hesitantly crossed the threshold into the unknown. The rest of the team followed suit, their footsteps echoing eerily in the vast expanse of the spacecraft hanger.

Inside the spacecraft, they were greeted by a sight that left them speechless - intricate control panels adorned with alien symbols, pulsating lights casting an otherworldly glow over the interior.

"Do you think this is the control room, Alex? "asked Gitta.

"I don't think so, we can't see outside the craft," said Alex.

The air inside the spacecraft hummed with a strange energy, making the hairs on the back of Alex's neck stand on end. He reached out a trembling hand to touch one of the control panels, the smooth surface cool to the touch. As his fingers made contact, a surge of images flooded his mind - visions of distant galaxies, swirling nebulas, and planets unlike anything he had ever seen.

With a gasp, Alex staggered back, his heart pounding in his chest. The rest of the team looked at him with concern, but there was a glint of excitement in their eyes. They were standing at the threshold of something extraordinary, and despite the fear that gripped them, they knew they couldn't turn back now.

As they explored further into the spacecraft, they discovered chambers filled with strange artefacts and advanced technology beyond their comprehension. It was clear that this was no ordinary vessel – it was a gateway to worlds beyond their wildest imaginations.

They came across a chamber that seemed to be sleeping quarters, with strange, pod-like structures lining the walls. The pods were made of a smooth, translucent material that shimmered in the dim light, giving off an aura of tranquillity and mystery.

Gitta approached one of the pods tentatively, drawn to it by an inexplicable force. As she reached out to touch its surface, a soft hum filled the air, and the pod slowly opened, revealing a figure lying inside.

It was unlike anything they had ever seen - a being with delicate features and skin that seemed to glow from within. Its eyes were closed in peaceful slumber, and its chest rose and fell rhythmically, as if in a deep state of meditation.

Alex and the team exchanged astonished looks, their minds struggling to comprehend the sight before them. Who was this being? Where did it come from? And most importantly, what was its connection to the ancient spacecraft they now found themselves inside?

Before they could ponder these questions further, the being stirred, its eyes fluttering open to reveal irises the colour of a distant galaxy. It regarded them with a mixture of curiosity and wisdom that seemed to transcend language. Without speaking a word, the being rose from the pod gracefully, its movements fluid and purposeful.

Alex felt a wave of calm wash over him as the being approached, a sense of recognition tugging at the edges of his consciousness. It stopped in front of them, its gaze locking with Alex's in a way that felt both intimate and all-encompassing. In that moment, it was as if time itself had come to a standstill.

The being raised a hand, palm outstretched, and Alex instinctively reached out to meet it. As their fingertips made contact, a surge of memories flooded Alex's mind - memories that were not his own, or maybe they were. Visions of ancient civilizations, cosmic battles, and a bond that spanned aeons cascaded through his thoughts like a torrential river.

"My name is Astra," said the being in a voice which was soothing and warm, reminding Alex of the sound of a becalmed sea lapping against a Greek shore.

"The ancient Greek word for stars," said Alex. "Is that a coincidence?"

"No, as you saw in the myriad of memories I showed you, we have been here on earth since the fifth century BC."

"Down here all this time?" Alex found it difficult to comprehend what Astra had told him. Were these people - he couldn't bring himself to call them aliens anymore – responsible for the numerous UFO sightings over the years?

"Yes," said Astra reading Alex's thoughts.

He stumbled back, overwhelmed by the sheer magnitude of what he had just experienced. The being regarded him with a knowing look, as if understanding the weight of the memories that had been unleashed within Alex's mind.

"You carry the legacy of our past," Astra spoke, her voice resonating within the chamber in a melodic tone that seemed to echo through time itself. “It is time for you to remember who you are and the role you play in the grand tapestry of the universe.”

Alex felt a sense of purpose stirring deep within him, a connection to something far greater than himself. He looked at his team, seeing a reflection of awe mirrored in their eyes.

“We are here to awaken the dormant powers within you,” Astra continued, her presence radiating a sense of ancient wisdom and unfathomable power. “The time has come for you to embrace your true destiny and fulfil the prophecy that has been written in the stars since time immemorial.”

The spaceship resonated with a soft hum, emanating from the glowing orb that appeared before them. It pulsed with a rhythmic light that illuminated Astra’s serene features. “Alex,” the alien began, its voice a melodious chime, “Our arrival on this planet predates your recorded history by millennia. In the year 500 BC, as you measure time, we landed on the island you now call Milos."

Alex, stood rooted to the spot, a cocktail of disbelief and fascination coursing through him. “Milos? But that’s where...”

“Yes,” Astra interrupted, its ethereal eyes seemingly reading his thoughts. “That is where we first encountered the progenitors of your civilization. The Greeks, a vibrant people with an insatiable thirst for knowledge. We saw in your ancestors a potential far beyond their rudimentary understanding of the universe.”

"Where do your people come from?" asked Alex, his mind still swirling with the energy of the colours and sounds that Astra had flooded his mind with. Gitta had moved closer to Alex and taken his hand, while the others stood transfixed by the tableaux before them.

Astra's journey had begun aeons ago, in a galaxy far removed from the Milky Way. Their civilization, the Astraea, had reached a pinnacle of technological and spiritual advancement, their thirst for knowledge rivalling the brightest stars. But their galaxy, once teeming with life, was slowly dying, its stars fading, its planets cooling.

The Astraea, driven by an unyielding spirit of exploration, embarked on a grand exodus. They constructed massive vessels, arks of knowledge and life, designed to traverse the vast expanse of the cosmos. Astra, a scholar with an insatiable curiosity, was chosen to be part of this momentous voyage.

Their journey was long and arduous, spanning generations of Astraea. She explained that the Astraea's average lifespan was over two hundred years. They navigated through nebulae and black holes, encountering wonders and perils beyond imagination. Their ship travelling at the speed of light, covering great distances, using worm holes to jump from one galaxy to another. They visited countless worlds, some barren and lifeless, others teeming with exotic flora and fauna.

Astra marvelled at the diversity of life, the myriad ways in which evolution had shaped these beings. She observed creatures with crystalline skin that refracted starlight, sentient plants that communicated through bioluminescent pulses, and aquatic beings that navigated through the depths of methane oceans.

But despite the wonders they encountered, none of these worlds resonated with the Astraea's purpose. They sought a civilization on the cusp of intellectual awakening, a species with the potential to grasp the wisdom they offered.

After centuries of searching, they stumbled upon a pale blue dot, a planet orbiting a yellow star in a spiral arm of the Milky Way. Earth, in the year five hundred BC, was a world of burgeoning civilizations, each with its own unique culture and worldview.

The Astraea observed the Egyptians, with their intricate hieroglyphs and monumental pyramids. They witnessed the rise of the Persian Empire, a vast domain stretching across continents. They even encountered the enigmatic Indus Valley civilization, with its advanced urban planning and mysterious script.

But it was the Greeks, a relatively young civilization nestled on the shores of the Aegean Sea, that captured Astra's attention. They were a people of boundless curiosity, with a passion for philosophy, art, and science. Their cities were bustling centres of intellectual discourse, where ideas clashed and new concepts were born.

Astra saw in the Greeks a reflection of her own people, a thirst for knowledge that transcended the mundane. She observed their philosophers debating the nature of reality, their poets crafting verses that captured the essence of the human spirit, their mathematicians unravelling the secrets of numbers and geometry.

It was then that Astra knew they had found their destination. The Greeks were at a crucial juncture in their evolution, a time when the seeds of wisdom could take root and flourish. And so, the Astraea made their presence known, not as conquerors, but as mentors.

They shared their knowledge of the cosmos, of mathematics, of philosophy. They taught the Greeks the secrets of astronomy, engineering, and medicine. They guided their hands in the creation of magnificent temples and statues, inspiring them to reach for the heavens.

And as the Greeks flourished, so did the Astraea's legacy. Their wisdom echoed through the ages, shaping the course of human history. And Astra, the young scholar who had once embarked on a journey of discovery, found her true purpose in nurturing the potential of a nascent civilization.

"But why Milos?" Alex asked, his voice barely above a whisper, unable to fully comprehend what Astra had just related to him. "It's... it's just a small island."

Astra's form shimmered, morphing first into the woman form that Takis had encountered earlier that day, and then into a holographic projection of the Aegean Sea, highlighting a radiant point. "Milos," she explained, "Is a nexus of potent energies, a conduit between your physical realm and the dimensions we traverse. We discovered that the energy conduits extend from

Milos to the island of Aegina and then on to the site that you call Delphi.

"The golden triangle," whispered Gitta.

"Yes," replied Astra. "We used Milos as a base, a haven from which we could discreetly interact with the blossoming minds of ancient Greece."

"Interact? How?" Alex's curiosity was piqued.

"We didn't seek conquest or control. We were, and remain, explorers, seekers of knowledge. We shared insights, planted seeds of wisdom, nurtured the nascent potential of those we deemed worthy."

The holographic image transformed again, cycling through portraits of familiar figures - Pythagoras, Socrates, Plato, Pericles. Each face, Alex realized, bore a subtle resemblance to his own.

"These men," Astra continued, "Were more than just philosophers, poets, and statesmen. They were conduits of our knowledge, vessels for ideas that would shape your world. And Alex, you are their direct descendant."

Alex's heart pounded in his chest. "Descendant? But how?"

Astra's voice softened. "Pericles, your ancestor, was more than a political leader. He was a visionary, a man with an open mind and a burning desire to elevate his people. We saw in him the potential to carry our legacy forward."

The orb's glow intensified, casting an ethereal light on Alex's face. "We did not simply share knowledge, Alex. We intervened on a genetic level, ensuring that the spark of our intellect would continue to burn brightly within your lineage."

Alex reached up to touch his face, as if expecting to find some alien mark. "I... I don't understand."

"You are a child of two worlds," Astra said. "Your DNA carries the imprint of our wisdom, the essence of our understanding. You are the culmination of a two-thousand-year experiment, Alex. You are the bridge between our civilizations."

A wave of emotions washed over Alex – awe, disbelief, and a profound sense of responsibility. He had been chosen, not by chance, but by design. The future of both his world and Astra's rested on his shoulders. The weight of it was almost unbearable yet exhilarating at the same time.

With a gentle touch, the being transferred a surge of energy into Alex, causing his entire body to tingle with newfound power. It felt as though a dormant part of him had been awakened, a fire ignited deep within his soul that burned brighter than ever before. Images flashed before his eyes, guiding him towards a path he had never imagined possible.

As the energy settled within him, Alex turned to face his team, a newfound determination shining in his gaze. "We have a mission," he declared, his voice steady and resolute. "We are meant to unlock the mysteries that Astraea have left us in the undersea complexes and use their immense power for the greater good of all beings on this earth."

Astra looked at the EKAM officers who were standing aimlessly behind Alex and Gitta. It was as if they felt that Astra was looking at them. Her eyes locked onto theirs, although each of them found themselves looking into her eyes, in reality she was only looking at one of them. The officers felt a slight buzz in their heads which seemed to be suggesting that they leave the ship. They obeyed as one, exiting the ship, then lining up at the entrance to the hanger, guarding the facility.

Gitta and the team of scientists they had with them nodded in agreement at Alex's words, their hearts filled with a sense of purpose that transcended any fear or doubt they may have harboured before. Together, they began to explore the spacecraft with a newfound sense of clarity and understanding, deciphering alien symbols and activating long-dormant systems with ease. They never thought to question how they now completely understood the systems.

Chapter 36

The train's interior lights flickered as it accelerated through the tunnel. Mia stood beside Chris, her hand resting lightly on his arm, her eyes fixed on the tunnel's darkness rushing past the window. The only sound was the low hum of the engine and the swish of the train against the tracks.

"How long do you think it'll take?" Mia asked, her voice barely audible.

Chris shrugged. "No idea. We never made this trip before."

Mia squeezed his hand. "Just glad to be out of that bunker."

He returned the squeeze, a silent reassurance in the face of the unknown. The journey seemed endless, but eventually the tunnel began to brighten, revealing a vast, dimly lit cavern ahead. As they drew closer, Chris's breath hitched.

The cavern was a subterranean hangar, its sheer scale taking his breath away. Row upon row of sleek, otherworldly vehicles gleamed in the low light, their forms unlike anything he had ever seen. Each one seemed to pulse with an eerie energy, hinting at the incredible power they possessed.

The train slowed to a halt beside a platform, its doors sliding open with a hiss. Chris and Mia stepped out, their senses overwhelmed by the spectacle before them.

"This is it," Chris whispered, his eyes scanning the hangar. "The weapons systems."

Mia's hand instinctively found her sidearm. "Where's the spaceship?"

"I don't know," Chris admitted. "But we need to find Alex and Gitta, if they are here."

"The spaceship is in the third hanger," said Ferris. "Kappa told me that Takis had seen it when he came here."

She signalled to the ten marines to follow them into the hanger. They began to cautiously explore the hangar, their footsteps echoing in the cavernous space. The vehicles varied in size and shape, some resembling sleek fighter jets, others like armoured tanks with bizarre appendages. Each one seemed to radiate an alien intelligence, their smooth surfaces devoid of visible controls or instrumentation.

As they ventured deeper into the hangar, they noticed a ramp leading down to a room on a lower level. Chris exchanged a nervous glance with Mia before cautiously descending. The air grew cooler as they went, the humming of the vehicles growing fainter.

The lower level room was bathed in a dim, eerie glow emanating from strange symbols etched into the walls. At the tablets that were on pedestals, were Alex's team of scientists led by Dr Sharma, working feverishly to decipher everything they could. Chris, Mia and Ferris wondered around the chamber, their eyes wide with a mixture of wonder and apprehension.

"It's a library," said Dr Sharma. "A historical narrative going back millions of years."

"Have you found anything of significance? Where does this equipment come from? What does it all mean?" asked Ferris.

"We have," said Dr Sharma. "The underground complexes were built by an alien race called the Astraea. We believe from what we have deciphered that they come from a distant planet not in the Milky Way but another galaxy several light years away."

Dr Sharma paused, her voice hushed with a mixture of excitement and awe. "The Astraea were a highly advanced civilization, far beyond anything we could imagine. They were explorers, scientists, philosophers, and they left behind an incredible wealth of knowledge. They also left behind something which we can't quite understand yet, but it looks as though they somehow transferred the DNA of Pericles, one of the important ancients from the golden age of Greece, down through the ages to maybe the present day."

Chris, Mia, and Ferris exchanged glances, their minds racing. A library millions of years old, filled with secrets from another galaxy – it was almost too much to comprehend.

"But why here?" asked Mia. "Why Earth?"

Dr Sharma shrugged. "We don't know for sure yet. But we believe they had a profound interest in our planet and its life forms. Perhaps they saw potential in us, or perhaps they simply found us fascinating. Or, they wanted to give the human race a jump start and picked the ancient Greeks."

Ferris, ever the pragmatist, cut to the chase. "What about the equipment? The technology?" She feared that all this talk about favouring the Greeks, and transferring knowledge to them as the chosen ones, would undermine Omega's aim of taking over the equipment, using it as a deterrent against future security issues, particularly from Russia and China.

"Ah, that's the most intriguing part," said Dr Sharma with a spark in her eyes. "The Astraea were experts in energy manipulation. They harnessed the power of the cosmos in ways we're only beginning to understand. Their technology is breathtaking."

She gestured towards a massive, pulsating sphere in the centre of the chamber. "That, for example, is a quantum energy reactor. It could power an entire city for centuries."

Mia gasped. "And you can operate it?"

Dr Sharma chuckled. "Not yet. But we're learning. The Astraea were meticulous in their documentation. They left behind detailed instructions, almost like a user manual for the universe. However, even with that it will take months, maybe even years for us to operate it."

Chris stepped closer to the reactor, his hand reaching out as if to touch it. "This could change everything," he murmured.

"Indeed," said Dr Sharma. "If we can unlock the secrets of Astraea technology, it could revolutionize our world. Clean energy, interstellar travel, medical breakthroughs. The possibilities are endless."

But as the team delved deeper into the library, they began to uncover a darker side to the Astraea. Their history was not without conflict. They had faced wars, betrayals, and even extinction events. And they had left behind warnings, cryptic messages about threats from beyond the stars.

One tablet, in particular, caught Dr Sharma's attention. It spoke of a cataclysmic event that had forced the Astraea to flee their home world. It spoke of a malevolent force, a 'shadow' that sought to consume all light and life.

"Could this be why they came to Earth?" wondered Ferris. "Were they seeking refuge?"

"No," said a voice.

In that one word, was a profound softness and a melodic lilt. They all turned to where they thought the voice emanated from. Nothing. Then they realised that the voice was everywhere, all around them when the voice said, "We are a caring people and have visited hundreds of planets, we helped where the residents were less advanced than us."

As the voice spoke, a shimmering shape appeared before them, dancing, which then to their awe and amazement morphed into Astra. Some audibly gasped, others stood with surprised eyes open wide.

Astra's form shimmered and pulsed with a soft, ethereal glow. She was human in shape, yet her features were finely sculpted, otherworldly. Her eyes, the colour of distant nebulae, seemed to hold the wisdom of countless ages.

"I am Astra," she said, her voice resonating with a gentle warmth that calmed their racing hearts. "An echo of my kind, left behind to guide and protect those who discover our legacy."

A stunned silence hung in the air as the team absorbed the revelation. They were not alone in deciphering the Astraea's secrets. They had an unexpected ally, a being of pure energy and ancient wisdom.

"You... you're real?" stammered Mia, her voice barely a whisper.

Astra smiled, the gesture radiating a comforting light. "As real as the stars above. And just as eager to share their secrets."

Ferris, ever the sceptic, stepped forward. "If you are who you claim to be, why have you remained hidden until now?"

"I have observed you, Astra replied. "Studied your intentions. And I believe you are worthy of the knowledge we possess."

Chris found his voice, a mixture of awe and curiosity. "You mentioned protecting those who discover your legacy. From what?"

Astra's expression turned grave. "The Shadow. The malevolent force that drove my people from our home world. It is a ravenous entity, a devourer of light and life. It seeks to extinguish all that shines bright in the universe. It is what you call a black hole."

A shiver ran down their spines as the full weight of Astra's words sank in. They were not just dealing with advanced technology; they were on the front lines of a cosmic struggle between light and darkness.

"And you believe this black hole is coming for Earth?" asked Dr Sharma, trying to hide her fear. "The scientific community on earth believe that black holes do not move around the cosmos."

"It is a possibility," Astra admitted. "The Shadow is drawn to energy, to life. And Earth, Earth is teeming with both. However, it will be millennium before the Shadow reaches the Milky Way."

Their sense of urgency dissipated when they heard that. But, they had to learn as much as they could, as quickly as possible. They had to prepare for a potential threat of unimaginable magnitude.

Astra offered a glimmer of hope. "The Astraea were not defeated. We fought back, found ways to resist the Shadow. And I am here to share those secrets with you."

The team exchanged determined glances. They were no longer just scientists or explorers. They were now defenders of Earth, entrusted with the knowledge and technology of an ancient civilization. And with Astra as their guide, they were ready to face whatever the cosmos threw their way.

Ferris's ears pricked up. Now was her chance to take control, for Omega to take control. She took a couple of steps towards Astra when suddenly she felt as though she was walking through treacle. She stopped, took a step back, the treacle had gone. She walked forward again. The treacle was back. She stared at Astra. "I'm not going to hurt you. I welcome you."

"You cannot hurt me," Astra said. "I needed to show you that I can manipulate anything around me to my advantage. Hence changing the molecular structure of the air in front of you, to a treacle like consistency."

Astra paused as she waited for a hologram to descend from the ceiling. "I'm going to take you on a short version of my journey from Euclid, my home planet to the planet you call earth."

As the hologram flickered to life, a vibrant tableau of Euclid unfolded before them. Verdant valleys stretched towards towering, crystalline mountains, shimmering under the light of three suns. Rivers of molten silver snaked through the landscape, reflecting the alien flora that pulsated with bioluminescent hues. It was a world teeming with life, yet strikingly different from Earth.

Astra's voice, soft and melodic, filled the chamber as she narrated their journey. "Euclid, our home world, resides in the Andromeda Galaxy, a vast spiral of billions of stars. We were a curious and adventurous species, driven by an insatiable thirst for knowledge and exploration."

The screen transitioned, showing a breathtaking panorama of Andromeda. Its spiral arms, adorned with glittering star clusters and swirling nebulae, stretched across the cosmos like a celestial masterpiece.

"Our first foray into interstellar travel took us to the Trigonikos Galaxy, a smaller spiral nestled near Andromeda," Astra continued. "Here, we encountered the enigmatic Cetus Nebula, a vast cloud of interstellar gas and dust, where new stars were being born in a fiery ballet of creation."

The screen displayed the Cetus Nebula in all its glory. Wispy tendrils of gas, illuminated by the intense radiation of young stars, danced and swirled in a mesmerizing spectacle of cosmic artistry.

"Our journey continued to the Strobillismos Galaxy, a grand design spiral known for its intricate structure and vibrant star-forming regions," Astra narrated. "Here, we witnessed the awe-inspiring power of supermassive black holes, warping space-time and devouring entire stars."

The screen displayed the Strobillismos Galaxy, its spiral arms intertwined in a cosmic embrace. At its heart, a supermassive black hole lurked, its immense gravity distorting the very fabric of reality.

"As we ventured further into the universe, we encountered the Kapela Galaxy, a majestic spiral with a prominent dust lane that obscured its central bulge," Astra explained. "This galaxy was a haven for globular clusters, ancient swarms of stars that held clues to the early universe."

The Kapela Galaxy appeared on the screen, its broad-brimmed silhouette resembling a cosmic hat. Thousands of globular clusters, like sparkling jewels, adorned its halo, a testament to the galaxy's age and complexity.

"Our path then led us to the Troxoskarphitsa Galaxy, a sprawling spiral with delicate, feathery arms," Astra continued. "This galaxy was home to a multitude of supernova remnants, the glowing debris of exploded stars that seeded the cosmos with new elements."

The Troxoskarphitsa Galaxy graced the screen, its spiral arms unfurling like the petals of a cosmic flower. The remnants of supernovae, glowing with the energy of a thousand suns, punctuated the galaxy's serene beauty.

"As our journey neared its end, we reached the Milky Way, your own galaxy," Astra said. "Here, we encountered the Orion Nebula, a stellar nursery where new stars were being born in a breathtaking display of cosmic fireworks."

The Orion Nebula filled the screen, its glowing clouds of gas and dust teeming with newborn stars. Pillars of creation, sculpted by intense stellar winds, rose majestically from the nebula's depths.

"Finally, after countless light-years and aeons of travel, we arrived at Earth," Astra concluded. "A small, blue planet orbiting an unremarkable star. Yet, to us, it was a treasure trove of life, a jewel in the vast expanse of the cosmos."

The massive hologram displayed the breathtaking view of Earth, a vibrant blue marble suspended in the vast expanse of space. Continents, oceans, and swirling clouds painted a portrait of a planet packed with biodiversity and natural beauty, shining like a jewel in the darkness.

Astra's voice echoed through the silent chamber, carrying a sense of wonder and curiosity. Her words seemed to reverberate off the ancient stone walls, filling the space with a palpable energy. "We come to you in peace," she said, her voice ringing with sincerity and hope. "With a deep desire to learn and share our knowledge." As she spoke, her eyes sparkled with an otherworldly intelligence.

Again, Ferris saw this as her opportunity to take control. She strode forward confidently, determined to impress upon Astra the importance of meeting with the President of the United States. Her heels clicked loudly against the stone floor, echoing Astra's words. The air was charged with tension and excitement as everyone in the chamber held their breath in anticipation.

"You must meet with our president," Ferris urged, before gesturing towards Chuck who stood by her side like a loyal guard. His eyes burned with determination and his jaw was set in a firm line. He spoke up in agreement, his voice strong and commanding. "President Rogers is the ideal leader to oversee your technology. And having access to it would solidify America's role as a global superpower."

As if responding to their words, Astra began morphing once again, shifting from her alien form into that of a human woman. The sight was mesmerizing and awe-inspiring, causing gasps and murmurs to erupt throughout the chamber. Standing before them now was the same Astra that Takis had met just the day before - but there was something different about her now. She exuded an air of power and confidence that was almost tangible.

"Secretary of State," Astra said calmly, addressing Ferris directly. "When I was narrating the Astraea's journey..." Her words trailed off, leaving an air of mystery and intrigue hanging over the room. She looked pointedly at Chuck who was holding his wrist to his mouth, as if communicating with someone.

"Do you have a wrist transmitter, Mr. Harris?" Astra asked, although she already knew the answer.

Ferris's mind raced as she realized that Astra must know about their plans. But she said in her calm, composed voice. "We have left a squad of marines - about twenty men - back on Milos. They were waiting for our signal to leave and join us here."

Chris and Mia exchanged worried glances as they realized the gravity of the situation. Ferris and Harris were intent on taking the technology and weaponry by force if necessary. Panic began to set in as they understood that their colleagues had put them all in danger.

"You can't do this," Chris protested, his voice filled with desperation. "The Astraea have come in peace to help us."

But Ferris just laughed, a cold, calculating sound that sent shivers down everyone's spines. "I was hoping you were going to join us, Chris," she said. "But it seems you are just as naive as the rest." Her eyes gleamed with a hunger for power and control as she spoke. "This is all smoke and mirrors. Astra may be powerful, but she is only one woman against thirty elite marines - not counting the ten we have here. You will all be arrested once the marines arrive. Including your girlfriend." Fear and ambition battled inside Ferris, but ultimately her desire for power won out as she plotted to secure the high-tech weapons for the United States – by any means necessary.

Astra's expression remained unreadable as she listened to Ferris's words, her eyes flickering with a mixture of sadness and resolve. She knew the danger that lay ahead, the consequences of a clash between humanity and the advanced technology aboard the spacecraft. But she also understood the depths of greed and ambition that drove certain individuals to seek power at any cost.

Without a word, Astra turned towards Chris and Mia, her gaze soft yet commanding. "We must act swiftly," she said, her voice cutting through the tension in the chamber. "There is a way to prevent this conflict from escalating further."

Chris nodded, his mind racing with possibilities. He looked at Mia, their silent communication speaking volumes as they shared a plan without uttering a single word. Together, they moved towards Astra who was by the control panel at the centre of the chamber, their movements deliberate and focused. To their surprise, Dr Sharma and the other scientists joined them, leaving Ferris, Harris and ten marines facing them some ten metres away.

As Ferris and Harris watched with growing unease, Astra's fingers danced across the panel in front of her. The room was filled with tense energy as if anticipating some great and terrible event. With a sudden shout from Ferris, the marines snapped into action.

"Raise your arms, shoot to kill!"

The sound of their M27's firing erupted in the confined space of the chamber, shattering the uneasy silence. The scientists scrambled to cover, but Chris and Mia were quicker due to their combat training. They hit the floor just as the bullets sprayed through the air like angry hornets. But instead of screams and cries of pain, there was only the deafening roar of gunfire and the sound of bullets embedding into an invisible wall in front of them.

It was then that they realized what Astra had done - activated a shield to protect herself and her allies. The marines' firing ceased as they came to this realization, dropping their weapons in disbelief. Astra calmly walked through the shimmering barrier towards them, as if it were nothing more than a curtain of mist. When she was only a few meters away, she extended her arms out towards them.

The marines, along with Ferris and Harris, clamped their hands over their ears as a loud buzzing sound filled their heads.

It was almost unbearable - like trying to think through a swarm of angry bees. Several seconds passed before one by one they collapsed onto the floor, completely still and unconscious.

"Are they dead?" asked Chris nervously.

"No," said Astra emphatically. "We do not take lives unless we are truly threatened. Their bullets could do me no harm at all as you saw. Once you leave here and go to join Alex in hanger three, I will have them transported back to Athens airport and on the next plane to the USA. They won't remember much of their encounters here.

Chapter 37

In the third hangar, Alex, Gitta, and the scientists huddled around a table in the crew library aboard *The Pegasus*, a name they'd gleaned from the tablets scattered throughout the spaceship.

"Fascinating," the linguist remarked, tapping a stylus against a screen. "The Astraea incorporate many Greek words into their vocabulary. All the galaxies, stars, even the planets in our solar system have Greek names."

Alex leaned forward, intrigued. "Earth is Yi, Mars is Ari. Just as they were named by the ancient Greeks."

"Exactly," the linguist nodded. "It raises an interesting question. Did the Astraea bestow these names upon the Greeks when they first arrived here two thousand five-hundred years ago? Or did they adopt the names from an existing Greek language, one far older than we ever imagined?"

A thoughtful silence settled over the group as they pondered the implications. Gitta, her brow furrowed, broke the quiet. "If the Greek language predates the Astraea's arrival, it would rewrite our entire understanding of human history."

"Not to mention the origins of language itself," added another scientist.

The linguist cleared her throat. "While the idea of a pre-existing Greek language is intriguing, the evidence suggests otherwise. The Astraea's advanced technology and their influence on early human civilizations point to them as the source of the Greek language."

Alex nodded in agreement. "It makes sense. The Astraea likely introduced their language as a way to communicate and educate early humans."

"But what about the Greek myths and legends?" Gitta countered. "Many of them depict interactions with beings from the stars. Could those stories be distorted accounts of encounters with the Astraea?"

"A possibility worth exploring," the linguist conceded. "Perhaps, the Astraea intentionally seeded those stories as a way to guide humanity's development."

"We…I mean they did," admitted Alex. "I remember now. I saw it being done in those images that Astra has put in my head. My head is so full of stuff that she has put in there that it will take time for me to sort it out. It must be the same for each of you?"

"Yes," Gitta conceded. "I think I can speak for everyone that we all seem to know how to get around this spaceship, understand the controls, and where everything on board is, without ever reading a user manual."

A murmur of agreement rippled around the table, the conversation deepening as the scientists delved further into the labyrinth of linguistic origins and cultural evolution. But Alex, lost in his own thoughts, remained silent.

His mind raced, replaying the moment Astra had unlocked hidden depths within him. A surge of power, a glimpse of untapped potential. The memory sent a shiver down his spine. If Astra could awaken such abilities, what else might she be capable of? Could he, too, one day wield the extraordinary powers of the Astraea? The thought was both exhilarating and terrifying.

He imagined soaring through the cosmos, bending the fabric of reality, manipulating matter and energy at will. But with such power came immense responsibility. Would he be worthy of it? Could he resist the temptation to use it for personal gain? Alex knew he had a long way to go before reaching that level of enlightenment. For now, he would focus on honing his newfound abilities, learning to control the energy that coursed through his veins. The path ahead was uncertain, but he was determined to walk it, guided by Astra's wisdom and his own unwavering resolve.

A sudden metallic clang jolted Alex back to the present. The sound echoed through the hangar, cutting through the hum of conversation. He turned to the others with a questioning look in his eyes. "Did you hear that?"

The scientists nodded, their curiosity piqued. "Sounds like it came from outside," Gitta remarked, rising from her chair.

"Let's go investigate," Alex suggested, already heading for the exit.

The group filed out of *The Pegasus*, their footsteps echoing in the cavernous hangar. As they emerged into the open air, a sight met their eyes that made them gasp.

One of the sleek, high-tech transports from hangar two hovered just above the ground, its main doors open like a welcoming maw. A ramp extended from the belly of the craft, touching down on the hangar floor. Descending the ramp were three figures: Chris, Mia, and Dr Sharma.

A wave of relief washed over Alex. "Chris!" he shouted, breaking into a run.

His best friend's face lit up at the sight of him. "Alex!" Chris exclaimed, rushing forward to meet him.

They collided in a fierce embrace, their relief and joy palpable. "I'm so glad you're safe," Chris choked out, his voice thick with emotion.

"Me too," Alex replied, returning the hug with equal fervour.

Mia and Dr Sharma joined the reunion, their faces etched with gratitude and relief. They exchanged warm greetings with the scientists, recounting their harrowing experience in the second hanger and their subsequent journey aboard the transport.

"Astra found us the transport in the hangar," Dr Sharma explained. "It was fully fuelled and operational."

"Astra taught us the controls and how to navigate our way back here, through a hidden tunnel linking the two hangers," Mia added, a hint of pride in her voice.

The group gathered around the transport, marvelling at its sleek design and advanced technology. The scientists peppered Chris, Mia, and Dr Sharma with questions, eager to learn more about their experiences and the secrets they had uncovered.

The group decided to wait for Astra in *The Pegasus* where Alex's team could show Chris's team around. They piled into the spaceship, eager to share stories and bask in the warmth of camaraderie.

The spaceship was filled with laughter and animated conversation, a stark contrast to the tension and uncertainty of the past few days. Alex sat beside Chris, a silent testament to their unbreakable bond. He knew their adventures were far from over, but for now, he was content to savour this moment of triumph with his friends.

"What happened to Kappa?" asked Alex.

"Arrested. He should be in a holding cell in an EKAM black site by now. Unfortunately, Yannis was forced to kill Takis."

"I saw your face when Yannis confirmed Takis was dead. You were hoping it was Kappa, weren't you?" said Mia, proffering a hand on Chris's arm.

Chris exhaled slowly, a weight settling on his shoulders. "I won't lie, Mia. A part of me hoped it was Kappa. The man deserves a slow, painful death for what he's done."

He glanced at Alex, the unspoken question hanging in the air. The Prime Minister, his friend, the man who always sought the best in people, would no doubt disapprove of such a sentiment. But Chris was no politician. He'd seen the darkness Kappa wrought, the lives shattered, the families torn apart. Justice, swift and brutal, felt like the only fitting end.

Alex regarded Chris with a mix of understanding and concern. "You've been through a lot, Chris. It's understandable to feel that way. But remember, vengeance is a hollow victory."

Gitta who had suffered from many bad men and women over the years when she was in the field as a CIA agent, leaned towards Chris. "I understand your emotion for vengeance, Chris. When I started out as a CIA field operative I wanted vengeance on everyone who hurt me or hurt my colleagues. But as time goes by, I became immune from such feelings because I realised they were eating me alive."

"Easy for you to say," Chris retorted, his voice laced with bitterness. "You haven't seen what I've seen. The bodies, the fear – the way Kappa relished in it all."

Astra stepped forward, one moment the space in the corner of the lounge was empty, next moment she was there, her ethereal presence casting a calming aura over the tense atmosphere. "Chris Horsman," she began, her voice a soothing melody, "Anger is a natural response to pain and injustice. But it can also consume you, twisting your noble intentions into something dark. The Astraea believe in balance, in seeking justice tempered with compassion."

Chris met Astra's gaze, her alien eyes shimmering with an ancient wisdom. He felt a pang of guilt, a realization that his thirst for revenge was clouding his judgment.

"I know, Astra," he said quietly. "But it's hard to let go of the anger when the wounds are still so fresh."

Mia squeezed his arm reassuringly. "We're here for you, darling. We understand."

Alex nodded in agreement. "We'll get through this together. Just remember, you're not alone now."

A flicker of warmth touched Chris's heart. He was surrounded by friends, people who cared for him, who shared his burdens. He took a deep breath, the tension in his shoulders easing slightly.

"You're right," he said, his voice steadier now. "We have a bigger problem to deal with. We must close Omega down and do it without bloodshed."

Gitta stepped forward, her gaze focused on Astra. "You mentioned Pericles and the Astraea's influence on ancient Greece. What about the technology? The weapons, the ship, what was their purpose?"

Astra regarded Gitta with a thoughtful expression. "The technology we planned to share with the Greeks. It was meant to uplift them, to expand their understanding of the universe. But, as with any tool, it can be used for good or for ill. The weapons were never intended for war, but for defence against potential threats on your beautiful planet and also from beyond your world."

"Threats? Like other aliens?" Alex asked, his eyes wide with curiosity.

Astra nodded. "The cosmos is vast, and not all civilizations are benevolent. The Astraea have faced many challenges in our long history. We wanted to ensure humanity had the means to protect itself should the need arise."

"But Omega..." Chris began, a sense of foreboding washing over him.

"Omega sought to misuse our technology for their own selfish ends," Astra confirmed. "They see it as a means to power, to control. But they do not understand the true nature of these weapons, the delicate balance of energies they harness. If they tamper with them recklessly, they could unleash a cataclysm that would destroy not only your world but countless others."

A heavy silence descended upon the group. The revelation of Omega's true intentions cast a dark shadow over their discovery. The stakes had just risen exponentially.

"We have to stop them," Mia said, her voice filled with determination. "We can't let them get their hands on this technology."

Alex nodded resolutely. "We'll find a way. We have to."

"I have shown you the way, Alex. You don't realise it yet but the Astraea have passed down to you through Pericles the wisdom and knowledge you need to lead your people, to police your planet, ensuring that the great democracies, republics and dictatorships, remain with heads bowed forever. When you have achieved that you will be able to build and replicate the high-tech weaponry you have witnessed in hanger two. Weaponry that will only be used against alien forces."

"Then how will we police the world without using the weaponry?" asked Alex, although something in his subconscious was already telling him how.

"The spaceship - it will be your home until peace is everywhere."

"But. I don't know how to pilot it," said Alex.

A gentle smile graced Astra's ethereal feature. "You possess within you the latent abilities of your ancestors. We have merely awakened what was already there. The ship will respond to you, as it would to any Astraea."

Alex glanced around the majestic vessel, its sleek curves and intricate details a testament to a technology far beyond human comprehension. The sheer audacity of Astra's claim both exhilarated and terrified him.

"What about my family?" Alex asked, his voice tinged with concern. "Gitta and my son?"

Astra's gaze softened. "Your family will be cared for, Alex. They will be with you living on this ship. You have seen how huge it is. It can easily accommodate five hundred people. They will understand your mission, and the sacrifices you are making for the greater good. All your friends will live on this vessel with you, as will Dr Sharma and the rest of the scientists."

"Sacrifices?" Chris interjected, his voice sharp with concern. "What kind of sacrifices are we talking about?"

Astra turned to Chris, her eyes filled with ancient wisdom. "The path to peace is rarely smooth, Chris. There will be challenges, trials, and maybe even losses. But in the end, the reward will be worth it."

Mia stepped forward, her gaze unwavering. "We're with you, Alex. Whatever it takes."

Yannis, who had been silently observing the exchange, nodded in agreement. "Greece stands with you, Prime Minister. Kaliope and I will support your mission, no matter the cost."

"Hello, you two," said Alex in astonishment. "How did you two get here?"

"To tell you the truth we don't know, it happened in a flash. I suspect Astra had something to do with it."

Alex felt a surge of gratitude for his friends, their unwavering loyalty a balm to his troubled heart. He turned back to Astra, a newfound resolve in his eyes.

"I accept your guidance, Astra," he declared, his voice firm. "I will lead my people towards a more peaceful future. But I will do it my way, upholding the values of democracy and freedom that Greece holds dear."

Astra nodded approvingly. "As it should be, Alex. You are not a puppet, but a partner. We offer our knowledge and guidance, but the decisions, ultimately, rest with you."

With that, Astra turned and asked them to follow her, her graceful movements belying the technological marvel she commanded. Alex and his team followed, their hearts pounding with a mixture of anticipation and trepidation.

As they moved through the vessel, a wave of warmth enveloped them as if the ship itself welcomed their presence. The interior was a symphony of light and form with sleek consoles and holographic displays illuminating the space.

They entered the expansive control area. Astra gestured towards a central command chair, its contours perfectly moulded to Alex's form. "Take your place, Alex. It is time to begin."

Alex hesitated for a moment, then slowly lowered himself into the chair. As he did, a surge of energy coursed through him, connecting him to the ship's systems. His senses expanded, his mind merging with the vast intelligence of the Astraea technology.

He saw the world with new eyes, a symphony of interconnected patterns and energies. He felt the pulse of the planet, the ebb and flow of human emotions, the undercurrents of political machinations.

"The ship is yours, Alex," Astra said. "It is a tool, a weapon, but also a sanctuary. Use it wisely, for the good of all." With that, she walked out of the control centre, down to the floor below. There she entered a room which she masked from prying eyes so she would never be disturbed, but she could still watch over them if and when the need arose.

Alex took a deep breath, his fingers dancing over the control panel.

"*Artimis,* take us up to the surface," commanded Alex to the onboard artificial intelligence computer.

The ship hummed in response, its engines coming to life with a gentle thrum. He felt a surge of power, a sense of unlimited possibility.

The hanger's ceiling began to slowly slide back letting in gallons of water into the space where the giant spacecraft hovered. Then it pushed upwards towards the surface and the blue sky beyond.

Once free of the sea, Alex was tempted to take the spaceship beyond the atmosphere, but he knew that games could come later now he had a mission.

"Oh no," exclaimed Chris who was watching the radar. "We have a squadron of F16s heading our way."

Alex immediately commanded *Artimis* to contact Tatoi, the headquarters of the Greek air-force command base. Alex watched in amazement as *Artimis* simply took over everything. It contacted the base, used the identification protocol that would identify Alex as the Prime Minister, and then contacted the air force planes requesting them to stand down.

Artimis didn't stop there. It contacted Athens air traffic control computers, instructing them to re-route the commercial planes away from the hovering spaceship.

The friends looked at each other, astonishment on their faces. "*Artimis* is artificial superintelligence," claimed Alex.

"Amazing," agreed Chris. The others simply grinned happily accepting the advanced technology surrounding them.

"I'm feeling tired and need a nap," admitted Alex. "I suggest we all retire to our quarters for a couple of hours, get some rest, then spruce ourselves up ready for a visit to Athens."

Ten minutes later, Alex and Gitta were admiring the luxury yet simplicity of their suite. It had everything they could possibly want. Access to food and drink by commanding *Artimis* to prepare it for them. Access to every news channel in the world. Board games, card games, a chess board and to their surprise in the bed side drawer sex toys.

"Take a look at these," said Gitta laughingly holding up a vibrator and dildo.

"Gosh," uttered Alex smiling, his tiredness vanishing at the thought of using them on Gitta.

Half an hour later, after showering together Alex and Gitta lay down on the bed. Both naked they cuddled up facing each other kissing passionately. Alex caressed Gitta's back. He loved to feel the curve of her back where it joined her buttocks. Gitta picked up the sex toys from the pillow and threw them across the room. "We don't need these," she said smiling seductively as she rolled on top of Alex cow-girl style. "You are my sex toy and don't you forget it!"

Half an hour later, they lay in each other's arms, totally spent but their skin glowing in the half-light. The steam from the hot shower they had been too busy to turn off, swirled around them, clinging to their skin like a lover's embrace. Alex reached out, his fingers tracing the curve of Gitta's cheekbone, marvelling at its delicate strength.

Her eyes, the colour of emerald skies, held a depth that he could lose himself in. Gitta, in turn, admired the gentle determination etched in Alex's brow, the warmth that radiated from his touch. In each other's gaze, they found a reflection of their own deepest desires, a promise of a love that transcended the boundaries of words.

Gitta gazed into Alex's eyes reflecting the love that she had for him. "I'm proud of you, darling, the Astraea made the right choice in you. The legacy of Pericles and the ancients will live on through you forever."

Alex became emotional at Gitta's words. Cupping her face in his hands, he saw the love she had for him and he hoped she saw the love he had for her.

"Σ" αγαπώ Alex," whispered Gitta, telling Alex that she adored him.

"Κι εγώ αγάπη μου, στο φεγγάρι και πίσω," replied Alex telling her that he too loved her, to the moon and back.

Later in the Command Centre, Alex outlined to the team, who had gathered to witness their first mission, his vision and the journey they would now take. Athens naturally would be their first stop. He offered anyone who wished not to take the journey with him a safe passage off the spaceship in Athens. Nobody took him up. He looked at his closest friends, Yannis and Kaliope, arms around each other nodded and smiled encouragement, Chris who was holding Mia's hand, gave him a salute, while Mia simply smiled.

Alex felt grateful for their support, especially his closest friends. "Okay, let's see if *The Pegasus* fits into Syntagma Square in Athens," said Alex. "*Artimis* - Syntagma Square Athens." The gigantic craft's bulbous nose turned slowly and majestically towards the horizon where Athens lay.

The future was uncertain, the path ahead fraught with danger. But Alex knew, deep down, that he was not alone. The Astraea, the spirit of his ancestors, and the unwavering support of his friends would guide him on his journey.

He looked upwards at the vastness of space, a universe teeming with life and mystery. And as the ship left its subterranean hangar far behind. Alex Kalfas, the unlikely leader of a new era, embraced his destiny with both trepidation and hope.

Chapter 38

Prime Minister Kalfas Addresses Nation from Syntagma Square After Mysterious Arrival

Athens, Greece, June 4th - In an unprecedented event that has stunned the world, Prime Minister Alexander Kalfas addressed the Greek nation from Syntagma Square today, following a dramatic and unexplained arrival in a massive, unidentified spacecraft.

Thousands of citizens gathered in the historic square, their faces etched with a mixture of awe, confusion, and anticipation. As the sun dipped below the horizon, the enigmatic craft descended silently from the sky, its black obsidian hull gleaming in the twilight.

Emerging from the vessel onto a platform high up on the prow of the *Pegasus,* Prime Minister Kalfas stood tall and resolute before the crowd, his voice echoing through the square from twenty-five holograms of himself, spaced around the vast area, as he began his address. "People of Greece," he declared, "Today marks a turning point in our history, a moment that will forever alter our understanding of our beloved earth and our place in the universe."

He recounted a tale that seemed ripped from the pages of science fiction – of an ancient alien civilization, the Astraea, who visited Earth millennia ago, imparting wisdom and knowledge that shaped the course of human civilization.

"I stand before you today," Kalfas continued, "Not just as your Prime Minister, but as a descendant of those ancient Greeks who were touched by the Astraea's wisdom. I have been chosen to lead our world into a new era, one of peace, prosperity, and unity."

The crowd listened in rapt silence as Kalfas outlined his vision for a world free from corruption and strife and a Greek nation that would serve as a beacon of hope for all the world. He spoke of advanced technologies, of a future where humanity would transcend its petty differences and work together towards a common goal.

Yet, he also warned of the dangers that lurked in the shadows – rogue nations that would stop at nothing to get hold of the Astraea's technology for their own nefarious purposes. "We must be vigilant," Kalfas urged, "For there are those who would seek to divide us, to sow chaos and discord. But we will not falter. We will stand united, as Greeks, as humanity, and we will overcome any challenge that comes our way."

As his speech concluded, the crowd erupted in cheers, their voices echoing through the ancient square. Whether they fully believed Kalfas's extraordinary tale or not, they were captivated by his charisma, his vision, and the promise of a brighter future.

But for us in the media, many questions remain.

What is the true nature of the Astraea? What are their intentions for humanity? And what role will Prime Minister Kalfas play in this unfolding saga?

Only time will tell, but for now, the world watches Greece with bated breath, as the morning of a new epoch in human history dawns.

The End

Printed in Great Britain
by Amazon